The Finder

The Finder

Margaret Buffie

Kids Can Press

KCP Fiction is an imprint of Kids Can Press

Kids Can Press acknowledges the financial support of the Government of Ontario, through the Ontario Media Development Corporation's Ontario Book Initiative; the Ontario Arts Council; the Canada Council for the Arts; and the Government of Canada, through the BPIDP, for our publishing activity.

Published in Canada by
Kids Can Press Ltd.
29 Birch Avenue
Toronto, ON M4V 1E2

Published in the U.S. by
Kids Can Press Ltd.
2250 Military Road
Tonawanda, NY 14150

www.kidscanpress.com

Edited by Charis Wahl
Designed by Marie Bartholomew
Dedication page and part-title art by Jim Macfarlane
Interior set by Carolyn Sebestyen

Printed and bound in Canada

CM 04 0 9 8 7 6 5 4 3 2 1
CM PA 04 0 9 8 7 6 5 4 3 2 1

National Library of Canada Cataloguing in Publication Data
Buffie, Margaret
    The finder / Margaret Buffie.

(The watcher's quest)

ISBN 1-55337-671-4 (bound).   ISBN 1-55337-672-2 (pbk.)

I. Title. II. Series: Buffie, Margaret. Watcher's quest.

PS8553.U453F55 2004   jC813'.54   C2003-906452-2

Kids Can Press is a *lorus*™ Entertainment company

For Emily – Welcome to Eorthe!

Aire breathes memories of
Waeter's sea nest and the birthing in
Erthe's chambered secrets of the
Fyre-winged Scion flying home.

Written by Moraan of Fadanys

1

As I fall, my first reaction is not a Watcher's but a human one — sheer *panic*. A heavy wind bears down on me like a huge hand. Histal, high on the top of the ravine, is controlling it.

My inner voice shouts, *Never mind him! Figure out what to do.*

I change into Watcher mode. I visualize a pair of wings sprouting from my back and feel the familiar tug between my shoulder blades. I've practiced in private, and although the pale green wings are small, they're stronger and less stunted than when I first Conjured them in the fight with Yegg at Moling Bridge, almost fifteen mooncrests ago. Those pathetic little wings almost got me killed.

Suddenly a gust tosses me violently in the air. It takes me a few seconds to right myself. Boy, Histal must be *really* mad at me.

I struggle through the wind, and finally rise above the edge of the cliff trying to remain dignified — but my legs thrash the air, and my wings and arms are all over the place. But — woomph! — at least I made it! I spot Histal across the chasm, smile uncertainly and fly toward him. When I get close enough to see the expression in his eyes, dread washes through me like black ink.

"Will you obey me now?" he calls.

"I can explain, Master Histal. Let me try to —"

"This is not about *you*, Watcher. It is about obedience, discipline, loyalty, *trust*."

Trust? *Loyalty*? Those words make me see red.

"How can I be obedient to rules I don't understand?" I cry. "How can I have discipline when I don't agree with most of the rules? How can I give you loyalty when I don't feel *yours*? How can I trust if I'm not trusted? How can I —?" Oh heck, how can I keep my big fat mouth shut?

Histal raises his hand.

"Oh — oh please, Histal. No! Wait! I'm sorry, I —"

Scorching heat sears my wings. A great weight falls on my head and once again I drop into the ravine. As I tumble head over heels, I open my arms and legs into a free-fall position. I try to make new wings but can't concentrate with all this wind and panic. I pull the strips that allow webs of fabric in my uniform to open up between my arms and body. They slow my descent considerably, making me look like the flying rodent they call a risrac in these worlds. I can't see a bottom to this ravine. If I don't stop soon, I'll be in deep trouble.

The ravine walls are layers of different-colored rock — dull grays and browns slashed with blue, green and red. If I can move closer to the wall, maybe I can grab a ledge. In a few seconds, a narrow projection appears just below me. My fingers scrabble at the rocky shelf, but I can't get a firm grip. I keep dropping. When another projection appears, I scrape my hands along the rock to slow down, and finally collapse onto cold stone.

My relief lasts only a few seconds. I've really gone too far this time. The frustrating thing is, I know Histal isn't doing this to be nasty. As he explained to me once, "Being cruel solves nothing — it neither encourages nor discourages a Watcher and is ultimately a waste of energy." He's showing me how unprepared I am for a big challenge. He's expecting me to withdraw my request and to beg his forgiveness for being argumentative and disobedient. Well, not this time.

Big words for someone sitting on a ledge over Black Nothingness, says my nitpicking inner voice. I chew my lip. Sheesh, all I did was ask him if I could go on a Quest of my own — well, two really, but I *began* with one. And I actually thought he'd say yes. How dumb was *that*?

"Absolutely not," he'd said. "It is not the time, Watcher Emma Sweeney. Free Action is not for Noviates. Once you become a Master, perhaps *then* you can choose your own Obligation." He'd flicked his hand at me in dismissal and added, "Return to your training."

I shouldn't have gone to him in the first place. I should have just left the Watchers Campan and done the Quests on my own, but I'd wanted to show him that I was disciplined enough to ask his permission. Dumb, *dumb* idea.

I said, "Master Histal. *Please*. It isn't just that I *want* to do this — er — Quest, I *have* to. To find what I'm actually *capable* of. I have to discover what ... *who* ... I really am. If you —"

He made a tsking sound and said, "More *human* nonsense. You *are* a Watcher, endowed with innate abilities that must be nurtured — *here* at the Campan. You don't need to know more than that."

Arguing is always a risk with Histal, but I went for it. "You said once that I have *unique* promise. But, most of the time, I just feel like a human girl from Earth. My mother, Leto, says I must discover what's inside of *me* — not just do everything I'm told by you and the Watcher Kinn."

"Your Earth *mother*, Leto Sweeney, is human. You are not. She has strange human ideas. You will train to be a Watcher and *in time* your strengths will develop. Only then will you come into your own."

I cleared my throat, organized my thoughts *again*, then bowed, using a submissive (read, grov-eling) tone. "Master ... my sister Summer — er ... Elen ... the Suzarain of Argadnel, has agreed to let

me go through the border cave that lies on
Argadnel's east shore. Remember, I discovered it
when my family arrived on the island?"

"How is one allowed to forget?" he answered
with a slight smirk.

I took a deep breath and added, "With *your* permission, I would like to see where that border cave
leads. I —"

Histal's eyes narrowed. "If I didn't know you
have extremely acute hearing, Noviate, I would
think you had not heard me. After what happened
the last time you disobeyed me, I'm surprised
you'd try again so soon."

My voice was tight and high. "But Master Histal,
didn't I prove I could handle myself during that
Seeker's Quest? After all, I saved both my parents
and their real child, Ailla."

This time his voice was so cold I should have
shape-changed into a Popsicle. "Yes, and you spent
almost two Earth months recovering from your
wounds and spending time with your Earth family —
especially with your *father*, Dennis Sweeney, and his
daughter Ailla. Now you have been back at the
Campan the same length of time, repeating your
Noviate training. Your reckless disregard for our rules
— by taking on a Seeker's Quest — is the reason
why you have *not* advanced with your peers. And by
arguing with a High Master, you prove — *once again*
— that you are not ready for real responsibility."

"But these Quests have been eating away at me the entire time and are now interfering with my training," I moaned.

"Eating *away* at you? Those are human words with no meaning. And why do you use the plural? Why *Quests?*"

I ignored him. "Master Histal, it isn't just for *me* I ask this. If I don't go to this world I found very soon, then Fergus of Cleave will strike a new Game and grab it for *himself.* He has a bit more than one Earth month left before he is allowed to once again interfere in my life! Who knows how many innocent beings he'll make his slaves if he goes through the portal! I — *we* have to *stop* him." I was not looking at him anymore, in case I lost my nerve under that intense green stare. Instead, I was looking at my toes curling inside the thin leather of my boots.

"Fergus of Cleave has no way of getting into this new world," he said. "You will not convince me with human unreason, Watcher. You don't seem to grasp the fact that your inexperience and ignorance endanger yourself and others. That's why Free Actions are carefully monitored and guided by the Watcher Kinn."

"But surely *you* know I wouldn't be doing this Quest for selfish reasons."

Histal raised his eyebrows. "Is this the truth, Watcher?"

I crossed my fingers behind my back and nodded. I had no convincing argument left. But even if I couldn't get him to agree to that Quest, maybe he'd let me try my second — more urgent — request.

"Actually," I said, "I was — um — also hoping, Master Histal ... I need to go back to Cymmarian Market to help Pictree Bragg free the young slaves of Mirour the mask maker and Wefta the rug merchant. If you allow me to do *that* Quest *first* — and if I prove I can handle myself — maybe *then* you'd allow me to go to the world behind Argadnel's border cave — to keep it safe from Fergus."

I kept my head down and waited. When Histal spoke again, his voice was low, almost gentle. "So. You wish to do *two* Quests, not one?"

I swallowed hard. "Yes. It's clear that neither you nor the Watcher Kinn is ever going to help free the youngers at Cymmarian Market. So why can't I try?"

"And how do you plan to release these youngers from two powerful merchants?"

"I have to talk to Pictree Bragg. I know he's anxiously waiting for my help. He'll know how best to handle it. Then I'll take it from there."

Histal snorted. "You are not without audacity, I'll give you that."

"Please may I go?"

He waited ten beats of my heart. "You have been told that the youngers of Wefta and Mirour will be helped *when the time is right*. It takes careful consideration before we decide on a mission of Free Action rather than hired Obligations. The Pathfinder must weigh all options."

He looked so smug and certain and *unbending*, it made me seethe. "But, Master, doesn't that make you and the other Watchers no different from the humans you despise? Humans who hire themselves out — *mercenaries*?"

But Histal didn't get angry. "I care nothing for what humans say or do. I've given you my answer. I've been more patient than you deserve."

I tried to hold my tongue. I *did*. But he was wrong. So my tongue burst out with "It's not fair! It's just not *fair*!" sounding like a whiny human teenager whose parents won't let her go to a movie on a school night.

Histal smiled at my outburst. Uh-oh — that was definitely *not* a good sign. Histal *never* smiles. Suddenly, my feet left the ground. Histal stepped toward me and I drifted back the same distance. We kept pace — right through the shifting wall of his sanctum. The air outside was cold and lit with a dark green light.

He twirled his hand. I pivoted and dropped to the ground, barely catching myself from falling over the edge of the steep cliff. My knees buckled, but I managed to keep my balance. The wind blew around us in icy whistling gusts. Histal, as a High Master, could Conjure any environment he wished. Maybe he'd created this deep crevasse just to make a *point* — maybe he wouldn't actually *throw* me into it.

Lost in an intense, silent introspection, he gazed straight ahead, his white hair standing straight up in the wind. After more than a *slightly* theatrical pause, he blinked twice and gazed at me, as if from a great distance.

"You think I am unfair. That I lie. That you can order *me* to obey *you*."

My heart shook in my chest. "I know you don't ... well ... actually *lie*, Master. If you'd allow me to do these Quests, my Watcher instincts would only get *better*. As you say, I've been back here for two Earth months — but it feels *much* longer. You sent Tom away on Obligations so I could concentrate on my training. But all I've done is hang around doing baby stuff when there are really, *really* important things to do! The Masters won't let me even *try* advanced shape-changing or anything interesting. I know I'm being punished, but it's so *boring*!"

"And it is ... *boredom* that drives you to save the youngers — to go through this cave portal you've discovered?"

"Oh no," I said firmly. "I didn't mean *that* ... exactly. I need to find out what *future* I have — here *and* Out There. To find out if I can make a *difference*. I'm not *like* the other Noviate Watchers. You've even said so yourself."

Histal snorted again. "*That* is clear. And it is your greatest flaw, Watcher, this thinking only about yourself and what *you* want."

"But this isn't just about *me*. Okay, refuse my request to explore the uncharted world, but if you aren't going to save the youngers at the Market, why can't I try to do it? They *need* me. They've waited long enough."

"Tell me, Watcher, what makes you think you can interfere in issues that a Noviate Watcher has *no* business even asking about?"

I frowned at him. "Kidnapping youngers to work like slaves, without food or love, is *wrong*. It's not *humane*. It's evil."

His voice was as impersonal as his gaze. "Evil? Humane? Perhaps you should be saying 'irrational' or ... 'illogical.' It would be *logical* for Wefta to feed his youngers well so they could work more efficiently, would it not? You don't hobble a drakon's wings to help it fly, do you? It's not logical."

Inside, I mutter, *You've missed the point, Mr. Spock. No being should ever be a slave.*

I'm groping for a way to say this, wondering if Histal would even understand, when he says, "If I allowed you to do independent Obligations, I would be going against the Pandict of the Watcher Kinn. As for your concerns, you can be sure I — we — have everything under control."

I know he's fibbing. "But you're the highest Master next to the Pathfinder. You could give me special permission and —"

"Perhaps I could," he said. "But I won't. You always press me too hard, Watcher. Your time on Eorthe was destructive to your instincts. You have no inner signal to warn you when you have over-reached."

"But —" I began.

"One final time — *no*."

What difference would it make to him if I wanted to risk my life? I couldn't let Pictree down — or the young slaves he watched over. And if I didn't go through the border cave, then Fergus, Supreme Player of all the Games in all the worlds, would find a way to beat me there. I *knew* Fergus — and I *knew* he was lusting after that world.

"All you and the Kinn do is sit around in *cloud-land* planning who will watch over stupid, greedy Game Players like Fergus, instead of Pictree's youngers, who are mistreated and starved!"

There, I'd said it. I'd *thought* it often enough.

Histal grew very tall and looked down at me, his long face tight. "You display your ignorance with inaccurate nonsense!"

But my tongue now had a life of its own. "Nonsense schmonsense! You *know* Fergus *will* find a way into my new world. His Druvid Mathus will help him break the code for it. He'll make slaves of the beings who live there, and you'll just stand by while he does it! You're indifferent, you're cold and you're *useless*!"

I planned to stomp away, head held high, but was suddenly swept into the wind above the gorge. "No!" I shrieked. "Don't do this, Master Histal. I — I just wanted —"

Histal cut me off with a low bellow. "You have always been naive, willful, disobedient and difficult. That is why you have not been made privy to the Grand Plan of the Watcher Kinn. When you learn to obey without question, finish your full training and take on enough Obligations to become a Master Watcher — only *then* will you know the Plan."

My legs pummeled the air, my face hot as a sunburn.

"Plan?" I shouted. "You mean *Game Plans*! It's *always* about some stupid Game in your stupid worlds! You're no better than Fergus, or Rhona of Fomorii. I won't be fooled anymore — because I choose *not* to be a Watcher! I *quit*!"

Histal's eyes looked straight into mine. In a horrible blink of stopped time, I knew what was about to happen. And it did. I fell into the gorge like a stone. And that's how I ended up crouched on this ledge with no means of going up — or down — to safety.

2

"Well," I sigh, "you handled yourself *very* well. And look where it got you. On a windy ledge hanging over a bottomless ravine. Well done, Emma Sweeney, Watcher of the Year."

I must figure out a way to escape this Conjure of Histal's. Then I'll sneak out of the Campan. I've done it before. Four months ago, I found out my mother, Leto, was dying of grief. I disobeyed the Kinn and went on my own Seeker's Quest — to find my father and my parents' lost child, so Mom could be well again. I unintentionally started a whole series of Games rolling at the same time, putting my friend Tom and me at great risk. But with his and some new friends' help, I blundered around and managed to finish the Quest.

When I returned to the Campan two months ago, after recovering from being clawed by the bakke, Yegg, I was ordered to appear before the Watcher Kinn — the Highest Masters. To my utter shock, Histal stood up for me, explaining how long

I'd lived with humans and how they'd contaminated my Watcher instincts. But the Kinn had to punish me for defying its rules, and that's when they decided I would have to go through my Watcher training all over again. Tom, who had been sent the year before to Earth to watch over me and my family on our bee farm, was knocked down from a Preliminary High Master to Third-Level Master — a vicious punishment for a proud Watcher of Tom's abilities.

He's been gone for most of the time I've been back, but when he's here, he acts weird — distant ... almost angry. I think he resents me for asking him to go on that Seeker's Quest — and angry at himself for agreeing to go. Still ... if I talk to him before I leave, maybe, just maybe, I can entice him to come with me. Maybe even convince him he doesn't need Histal and the others — that we don't *have* to be Watchers. That we can be *individual* beings, not slaves to the Campan rules.

My heart, as always, beats a little faster thinking about Tom. I love Tom. He's never had a family — never had anyone to *show* him what loving can be like. He grew up in the Campan, where having feelings is frowned upon — and *showing* them is never allowed. I wish I didn't love him, but it's part of *human* nature — and I was raised as a human, after all. You can't *help* loving someone, can you? And if the other person is only capable of ... well, loyalty, duty ... maybe friendship, you have to accept it, hard as it is.

I've decided — and I say it out loud. "No matter what Tom decides, *I will no longer be a Watcher*."

I wait a moment to see if Histal's going to send a flying gromand to eat my poor little no-more-Watcher self, but nothing happens. Whew! Now that I've announced out loud I'm not a Watcher anymore, do I lose my abilities? I change into Emma mode. Then I transmute invisible. My hands vanish first, as always, then the rest of me. Good, that still works. I become visible again and change back into Watcher mode. Then I concentrate hard and in a few seconds, there's a tug between my shoulder blades. I can still shape-change, even though my wings are kind of pathetic — small green stunted things. Looks like I'm a Watcher, no matter what. But I don't have to be a prisoner in the Campan. The other Noviates — like Tom — were raised there. They don't know any other way of living or thinking. I grew up on Earth, brought up to think for myself. No one can stop me from leaving the Campan if I want to go.

Oh yes they can, that little voice inside my head warns. *They can lock you in a dungeon confiner and throw away the key. Or Histal can just keep tossing you over this cliff until you agree to obey him.*

Knees tucked under my chin, I lean against the stone wall, close my eyes and try to think.

Suddenly, masklike faces float behind my eyelids —
silver, brown, orange and blue masks calling
out gibberish that sounds something like,
"Finerfinderfinterfindher!" They dissolve and one
white mask with straggling red hair appears shrieking, "Gettergethergether!"

I come to with a jolt, echoes of their images still
hanging in the air. Did I fall asleep and dream? No,
not a dream. Watchers don't dream. The only other
times I *thought* I was dreaming, I was "Watcher-
traveling," which I find hard to explain — except
that it's similar to what Earth people call astral-
travelling. But if it wasn't a dream — and I haven't
moved — then what were those masks saying? I
repeat the sounds very slowly, then quickly. Finally
it comes to me. The first set of masks was calling
out "Find her, find her, find her." And the white
mask was yelling "Get her. Get her. Get her!"

Who needs to find *me*? Histal knows where I am.
And no one could possibly enter one of Histal's
Conjures. Does this mean I've dreamed for the first
time ever? Do dreams have meanings? Mom might
know. Or my earth sister, Ailla, or Dad. They all
dream.

That annoying inner voice of mine pipes up,
*Yeah, but you won't be talking to anyone ever again
unless you can get out of here.*

I really have only one option. To give in. Or
maybe I could *appear* to give in. I give that some
thought. Yes, it might work.

I set off, wings churning. Before I rise above the ledge where Histal waits, I cross my fingers behind my back and call out my Big Lie. "I *will* obey you, Master Histal. I won't ask for the two Quests. I'll go back to my training. I'll do what I'm told."

To my relief, the wind dies down and as I rise above the edge of the cliff, Histal turns, and without a word, walks back to his sanctum. I dissolve my wings and follow. Inside that shifting blue space, he says, "Is this your *solemn* promise, Watcher?"

I nod vigorously, fingers still crossed.

"You know a Watcher's promise cannot be broken without dire consequences."

Inside I say, *I do know that. And I've made my choice. I'll take dire consequences. But later, I hope.*

Out loud I say, "Yes, Histal."

His eyes narrow, but to my relief he nods. "Report to your Obligation Master. He will give you a small Obligation — we will see how you perform. Your Noviate training will continue. Also …The Kinn will look closely at the situation of the youngers in Cymmarian Market — you need no longer concern yourself about it."

I thank him gravely, but inside I'm fuming. *"Look closely" doesn't promise anything — not to Pictree or the youngers. More words without action.*

As I turn to walk away, Histal adds, "You will go on this small Obligation on your own. Tamhas — Tom — will not go with you. He will no longer be your Tutor."

I gape at him. "You can't take Tom away. He's *my* Watcher, my mentor."

"It was Tamhas's choice. If he wishes to rise in rank again, he will do it more quickly on his own."

My voice trembles. "Tom would never leave me for good. You — you're *lying!*"

Histal stares at me.

"I — I'm sorry, Master Histal. You aren't lying, but … thank you, I'll just go now … straight to the Obligation Master."

I run through the Campan's blue wavering hallways, stopping every Noviate I see to ask if they've heard when Tom's latest Obligation is over. They all look at me with contempt before they shake their heads. I'm a freak of nature to these perfect little beings, with their smooth white skin, long floating white hair and indifferent, cool faces. I usually walk around in Emma form, short pale hair close to my head. I know it irritates them, though they try to hide it. One snotty Noviate told me once that they *all* believe I'm more *human* than Watcher. They say "human" like it's a dirty word.

I head for the Entry Ring of the Campan. The ring is the launching place for Obligations as well as an arrival pad for any Watcher returning to the Campan. The Master who runs it, Warder Whinge, is a fat, irritable little Watcher, but he's good at his job.

"What do you want?" he demands, holding up a pudgy hand to stop me as I rush in. "I am busy setting up a passage for someone to return."

"Is it for Tom — uh — Tamhas?" I ask, without much hope.

"Tamhas has just left on a new Obligation."

"Do you know where?"

"Of course I do, but I cannot tell you! Return to your quarters before I report you to Histal!"

I wander back to my small space in the Campan and fall on my pallet bed. So ... Tom was here and now he's gone again. Without even saying good-bye. Is he really so angry about being demoted? He *must* blame me. And yet, he never seemed angry when he visited me on my family's island while my wounds healed. I ignore the tears that slide down my face and force anger to push aside my despair. Well, if that's how he wants it, fine! See if I ever talk to *him* again!

I slap my belt with its pouch of necessities around my waist, then pace, trying to work out a plan for escape. I can't stay here one second longer. I've heard that Whinge will take a bribe. Maybe he'll take my gold ring for transport back to Argadnel.

I'm about to leave when Histal appears in my room. He looks strained. Uh-oh, does he know I've been asking about Tom?

But he surprises me by saying, "Tell me, did you hear anything when you were in the ravine?"

"Hear anything?"

"No one spoke to you?"

"Well ... I had a dream — some masklike faces spoke to me. But that's all."

"Watchers do not dream, Emma," he says in a clipped voice. "Something invaded *my* Conjure. I have never had such a thing happen before." The wariness is still on his face — as if he's expecting a drakon to leap out of a corner.

He lowers his voice. "After you left, I swept the test area, as I always do before removing a Conjure and the words were caught in the sweep. Do you know where these images came from?"

"No. Why?"

Histal ignores my question. "Rather than go on an Obligation, you will return to Argadnel for one mooncrest. You will *not* enter the border cave. You will stay close to your family."

The leap of joy at seeing my parents and sisters turns to a jab of fear. "Is my family at risk?"

He says stiffly, "Do as you are ordered."

Bewildered, I manage to say, "I will. Thank you, Histal."

"Give me your solemn promise, Emma, that you will not enter the border cave."

"I promise." No longer a Watcher, I don't bother to cross my fingers behind my back. I don't care about lying to him anymore.

After Histal fades away, I run to find Warder Whinge. Histal has unwittingly given me my escape. I stop in my tracks. Why? Why is he sending me to Argadnel — and the border cave? Why not send me far away to watch over some king's child?

As I stand in the amethyst light stream, ready to be transported to Argadnel, I'm still wondering, but the happiness at seeing my family again so soon dispels any worry. And I know that after one mooncrest, I won't be coming back to the Campan as Histal ordered. I will never return.

I am free of the Campan for good.

3

One minute I'm in the Entry Ring of the Campan and the next, home — if one can call this huge, drafty pile of black stone, lightcrests from Earth, a *home*. My family is on the island, but I miss our Earth bee farm with a constant dull ache.

Yet when I was on the farm, I was always home-sick for ... I didn't know where or what. I'm always in a muddle about where my true home lies. I know, from overhearing the Druvids Mathus and Huw, that my real parents — my *Source* — are beings called Aibell and Clust. Who are they? No one wants to tell me, so I've given up asking.

I land in one of the lower hallways of Argadnel Castel in the evening. My family will be at dinner — an Earth custom Mom insists on, for it's the only time everyone gets together during their busy day.

My Argadnelian sister, Summer, has her royal duties as Suzarain — Queen — of this island world. Our Earth sister, Ailla, helps Mom,

Branwen and the Druvid Huw run the huge greenhouses that hold thousands of Stygia Mantle plants — magnificent black orchidlike flowers. Thanks to Mom, they are now exported for medicinal purposes throughout the worlds.

Dad is one of Summer's principal court ministers. He was resented at first by the stiffly coiffed and formal Argadnelian courtiers, but his keen interest in learning about Argadnel has made him popular. Trust Dad to win them over simply by his sheer love of *life*.

My family will be surprised to see me, but I won't tell them I've left the Campan for good until just before my mooncrest is up. I wonder what Tom will say when he finds out I'm not going back.

That nagging inner voice of mine says, *Why should he care? He left without saying good-bye this time, didn't he? He's been on any number of Independent Obligations — trying to get his Master rank back — but he always said good-bye. Now you find out he returned to the Campan for a while and didn't even tell you. Why? Was he hiding from you because Histal told him he was no longer your mentor? Did he think you'd try to talk him out of it?*

Tom's a Watcher who follows orders. No doubt Histal didn't allow him to say good-bye this time, knowing Tom was bound to tell me.

If you were leaving him for good, you'd have found a way to tell him! He's betrayed you. Again!

I try to tell that voice inside that Tom didn't betray me during my Seeker's Quest. I just *thought* he had. That he had only been thinking of my safety. He explained it all afterward — and I believed him.

Aah, but did you? You still wonder why he contacted Fergus — why he got Fergus involved in the final battle at Moling Bridge without telling you — going behind your back.

Yeah, well, he fought for me, didn't he? Saved my life, but ... The battle scar just above my left ear throbs, and my chest feels as tight as my fists. What would I do if I saw Tom right now? Would I lose it completely? Smack him one? No, I'd probably just bawl and embarrass us both. I shake myself. What difference does it make? He's gone. And right now, I just need to see my family.

Mom likes me to wear my chiton robe when I'm at home, so I head to my tower room to change. As I hurry around a corner, I come upon two beings walking arm in arm away from me down the hall.

Branwen and Huw.

I'd transmute invisible, but Summer's council laid down a new rule that I can't be invisible in the castel unless I'm in life-threatening danger. Maybe if I hang back, they won't notice me.

Branwen is Fergus of Cleave's sister. Fergus "owns" the island, and although he allows my sister to rule it, with the help of her council, he still takes a healthy share of the profits from the island's expanding agricultural ventures. Branwen is his emissary here.

She wears a pale green chiton with sheer flowing arms and a long scarf of vibrant orange over her shoulders. Her hair is high and varnished, with two long pins toggled with orange gems like exotic antennae. She looks like an otherworldly luna moth. She posed as a man named Albert Maxim when she, Fergus and Tom went to Earth to take Summer, and since then she's been friends with my family. But I know her real loyalty is to her greedy Game-playing brother, so I've warned my family to be cautious.

Huw is of the Celtoi Clann, which originated in Earth's misty past. He was the fawning Druvid of my powerful enemy, Rhona — Sover-reign of the undersea world of Fomorii — and he has vast knowledge of the oceans of the worlds. His loyalty to Rhona lasted as long as he took part in the major decision making of her court. When she started keeping secrets from him during my Seeker's Quest, he joined our fight against her. He told me once, "I am a Celtoi. I follow my own way." He can be as ruthless and contrary as the worst human.

He's dressed in leggings of different-colored viper skins, with a tight tunic to his knees. His bare arms display the dense tattoos that cover his thin muscular body. Whenever Huw moves, a pale light, like a glowing green echo, flutters in the air behind him.

Huw and Branwen are talking, heads together. My Watcher instincts tell me they're up to something. I'm wondering if I should disobey Argadnel's rules and transmute invisible, but as I round another corner right behind them, they're waiting for me.

"Rats," I mutter. A double meaning there, believe me.

Branwen may or may not be my friend, but she hugs me, then holds me at arm's length and gives me the once-over. "Emma, dear *dear* Emma! You look terrible. Are you all right?"

The left side of her face is decorated with paintings of Stygia Mantle flowers, celebrating the abundance of the crop. Branwen paints plant images on everything — walls, doors, ceilings, staircases — even herself. It used to be the vines and trees of Cleave, but she's proud of her work in Mom's greenhouses. I admit, she *should* be proud. She's worked hard.

I smile at her. "I'm fine. Never better."

Huw gives me a fox grin. Exactly one half of his narrow face is covered in swirls of dull blue tattoos that continue, with the addition of dye, into his gray wedge-shaped beard. His hair is shaved clear in a single wide swath from ear to ear and is gathered at the back into a long white ponytail. Smooth bangs lie flat on his forehead. A cap of silver sweeps away from the crown of his head like a curling wave. Both ears are heavily decorated with snail shells and pearls.

He leans close. "But, little Watcher, more important is *why* are you back in Argadnel? You haven't been gone all that long."

I know he wants me to go through the border cave so he can follow me into the new world. They *all* covet my new world, especially Branwen's brother, Fergus. And Huw, who claims allegiance to Fergus, would still love to beat him there.

"Just a short visit," I say. "I'm — er — being sent on an Obligation by High Master Histal, so he allowed me to come home for a few days first."

Huw raises one eyebrow. "And will this Obligation take place near Argadnel?" His smile is knowing, his black eyes sly.

I refuse to play his little game and snarl, "Don't worry. I'm not going anywhere near the border cave."

He and Branwen share a glance that makes my hackles rise.

Huw sweeps his arm through the air, a slash of green light sliding after it. "Don't let us keep you. Enjoy your stay, little Watcher."

Branwen hugs me again. "Come to the greenhouse soon, so we can have a real visit — without nosy men around!" She smiles a dimpled smile so sincere that it makes me even more suspicious.

Huw takes Branwen's arm and they strut down the hall. I walk slowly, grinding my teeth at Branwen's giggles and Huw's sniggering snorts.

My family may be together, but it doesn't mean they're *safe*. Fergus is ultimately in control. And

Huw and Branwen represent Fergus's interests, including my border cave. I hate the way things are set up, but I can't change it. Summer would die in Earth's atmosphere and, besides, she's happy here. So is my father. Mom would go back to Earth in a second, but her heart is with her family, so she stays. As for Ailla, Argadnel is the first she's known of a happy home, and she revels in the attention and affection lavished on her. She wouldn't care where she was, as long as the family was with her.

After the Battle of Moling Bridge, Fergus promised Tom and me that he wouldn't interfere in the running of Argadnel — or our lives — for twenty mooncrests. It was Tom's reward for saving Fergus's life — four different times — during the battle. Fifteen crests have already passed; but the court gossip when I was home was that Fergus was getting impatient waiting for the final five mooncrests to pass. He wants full control back, and I know why — he wants the border cave. And Fergus always gets what he wants — usually by twisting things around to look like he's the one in the right. I know Huw and Branwen tell Fergus everything that goes on in Argadnel. He allowed Summer to return as the rightful Suzarain of Argadnel a little over a year ago, but she and my family will always be under his thumb — a hazardous place to be.

I run up the stairs to my turret room. *Worry, worry, worry.* Even though I've stopped being a Watcher, I can't turn off my instincts — to watch over my family's welfare and to protect the island's cave portal from Fergus.

Then there's Histal. The voices that invaded his Test Conjure clearly worried him. Why did he send me home, knowing how hard it'll be for me to stay away from the cave portal? Will I have time to help Pictree Bragg save the youngers *before* Fergus makes his move? Which should I do first?

As I reach a small alcove, a soft voice calls me from the shadows. "Emma!"

"Cill!" I cry. "What are you doing here?"

My dear friend wraps me in a leafy embrace that smells of earth and spices. "I come to see you, Emma."

I've hardly seen Cill since our Seeker's Quest. She's a leaf being of the ancient Barroch tribe, Fergus's slaves on Cleave. Cill's ancestors once ruled the forested land, but Fergus took it during a Game, renaming the world Cleave. After the Seeker's Quest, Cill returned to her duties as Fergus's primary servant. But Tom and I know it's because she's determined to free the Barrochs from Fergus's bondage. *Another* Quest for the future? There's so much to do.

I try to smile at the fan of gray-green leaves that make up my friend's strange and wonderful face. Her red eyes are bright, but worried.

"I be so happy to find you, Emma," she says. "I decide if you not here, I talk to Ailla. But here you be! I must go back very quick."

My chest instantly tightens. "What is it, Cill?"

"Fergus gone now from Cleave. He go with Druvid Mathus to Readers of Fymric to find out how to break code of Argadnel border cave. He come here soon, I think."

"But Fergus still has to stay away five *more* mooncrests — that's forty Earth days!"

Cill rustles closer and whispers, "Fergus now say he save *Tom* four times during battle, not other way round."

I grind out, "That filthy liar! It was recorded and everything."

Cill snorts. "Recorded by *Mathus*. He loyal to Fergus, not to truth."

I growl, "So now, of course, Mathus remembers things as Fergus does!"

Cill grabs my arm with gnarled fingers. "Fergus do *anything* ... even break Game rules to get to new world before you. You must warn Tom."

"I can't," I say bitterly. "I don't know where he is."

"You must find. He never leave you for long."

I sigh. "That's what you think." I tell her about Tom's new role at the Campan, which doesn't include me.

She looks at me intently. "Send out mind thought to him."

"I don't know if he'd hear me if I telepathed to him. But I'll try."

She nods and the tips of her leaves flush a dark red. "I be feared for you, Emma. Now I return Cleave. Find out when Fergus make move and tell you — so you be ready."

"Do you need an airship to take you back?"

"I come to Argadnel port in sloop. Gyro the Searcher gave Barroch tribe two of them. Gyro wait for me." She lowers her voice. "With *Badba*."

"They're both here?" I cry. "I'd love to see them."

Gyro, grand Searcher and inventor, who looks like a robotic tin man, and his new friend Badba, a wild half bird half humanoid, risked their lives many times for Tom, Cill and me during my Seeker's Quest. They are as unlikely a pair as you'd find anywhere. Gyro is inventive, creative, nervously precise and ordered (in a disorderly way). Badba, crazy as a loon, always ready for a fight, is as dependable and as brave as any being I've met. I love them both — even though Badba scares the wits out of me sometimes.

Cill says, "They want come to castel. I say too dangerous. Fergus not know about secret sloops. Gyro I trust. But Badba ... *big* mouth. Must go, Emma, before she come visit — create chaos."

I laugh. "Yes. *Go!* We don't want Branwen or Huw reporting you to Fergus."

Her leaves crackle up in a smile. "So right, Emma. Here, take this. If needs be, blow it. I hear, no matter where I be. It be protected from cunnings by charm wood."

She hands me a knot of wood with a gold bead buried deep in its center. At one end is a small opening. A whistle.

"Keep an eye out for Branwen and Huw. They're not far!" I whisper, slipping the wooden knot into my pouch.

Cill raises a gnarled little hand, runs down the stairs and is gone.

I listen hard. Her padding footsteps are followed by silence. I breathe a sigh of relief, certain she is away safely.

On the last curve of the turret stairs, I stop at a small window overlooking the ocean and the eastern edge of the island where the portal lies. What is it about the border cave that draws me so strongly? Why am I the only one who can trigger its visions? When I sit in front of it and touch a small section of its moonstone wall, scenes of amazing beauty come to me — a world that Fergus must never be allowed to enter. But the urge to go *into* this magical place grows stronger every time I visit the portal. And why is it connected to Argadnel, just one of many small worlds?

Earth is an ancient part of these worlds, but rarely visited now, even by Gamers. The Game is a never-ending plunder of weaker worlds by stronger ones. One or more powerful clanns will set up a Game — competing for a rich region, a hidden treasure or a strategically placed kingdom.

If necessary, the Players drop all allegiances and go head to head — even to the death.

Fergus is now the Supreme Player. He and Rhona were once equal, but in my Seeker's Quest, we beat her soundly. Now she's hiding out in her undersea kingdom of Fomorii, licking her wounds.

Once I asked Tom why no one seemed to know about this world I'd stumbled upon. He'd shrugged and said, "Our worlds are a lot like Eorthe. For centuries, humans existed in small pockets dotted around the globe. Many thought that their little kingdom, village or clann were the only beings. Most thought Earth was flat and if they went too far, they'd fall off. Then slowly they began to reach out and discover other beings. They'd steal the land, believing that those who lived there were of no consequence."

"And they're *still* at it," I said.

Tom continued, "Here, worlds are conquered for the sheer excitement of Game playing and the power it gives the winners. The youngers that your friend Pictree Bragg is so worried about were taken from their worlds by Players who won a Game and sold them to the likes of Wefta and Mirour. If the citizens of a losing world are taken as slaves, so be it."

"And, like Earth's explorers, the Gamers take over, treating the inhabitants like *non*-beings! Winning the Game is everything! How many will eventually fight over the new world *I've* found?" I asked.

"No one knew about it until you discovered its existence. You can't imagine how exciting this is for High Game Players like Fergus. He wants to get there before other Players hear about it. But he can't, because only *you* have the Way into it."

"But, Tom," I cried, "why am I the only one who has the ability to make this world appear?"

He looked at me intently. "I wish I knew, Creirwy."

I ground out, "I *hate* the Game."

"There are those who feel as you do."

"And you, Tom?"

"'Hate' is not a word Watchers use. 'Wasteful,' 'destructive' and 'illogical' are used instead."

"So what is the Watcher word for '*love*'?" I asked.

"They don't have one. I never knew it existed until I saw your family. I began to wonder about these ... *feelings* you had. I'm not sure why Histal allowed you to corrupt me for so long. But he's threatened to send me away." He laughed when I stared at him, then added, "Don't worry. You won't get rid of me that easily."

No. He just left on his own.

I gaze out over the silver ocean. A fine mist rises in wavering sheets around the island. If I could see a star through the haze, I'd make a wish on it — to take me to where he is. The loneliness I felt on the bee farm, despite my family's love, is still crushing me.

No. I have to be *tougher*. I have to do the Quests. But which first? Given Cill's warning, I have no choice — it must be the cave. Tonight. Without Tom. I must try not to think about the youngers and Pictree Bragg — despite my promise to return to Cymmarian Market to help them. Thanks to Fergus, I have to put them second. I *hate* Fergus of Cleave.

I run up the final few stairs and bang through the door into my room. Something's not right. The room is usually chilly when I've been away, but now a fire burns in the grate. Out of the corner of my eye, I see a shadow move across the floor toward me — *Tom?*

A surge of joy flushes through me, then quickly turns to anger. "What are you doing here? Shouldn't you be Watching some nasty king somewhere?"

Tom stares at me unblinkingly.

"Well? No point in showing up now. I don't need you." I hate the way my voice is shaking.

Feet apart, heavy arms crossed firmly across his broad chest, Tom is wearing the calf-length hooded chiton of a working Master Watcher, with soft leggings and boots. His hair is short and black, his face the ugly lovely face that ... *used* to make my heart ... I *must* stop.

"You're angry with me again, Emma." He's trying not to smile.

"I — I don't know what you mean," I say brightly. "I'm perfectly upset-free. Just going to see my family for dinner."

"You and Histal had quite a run-in, I hear."

"You know? How?"

"Histal called me back and gave me the gist of it. I've been sent to Watch over you until you return to the Campan. Then I will take up my Obligation once more."

"*Watch* over me?" I sneer. "You mean Histal sent you here to guard me — to make sure I don't go to the border cave. Well, go on your Obligation. I don't need you." That I've left the Campan for good is none of his business.

Tom says, "I must do my duty."

My laugh is harsh and tight. "Histal is sure I'll go into the new world, isn't he? Your *duty*. Ha!"

Tom sighs. "I am not your guard, Creirwy. I am your Watcher and Tutor — for a bit longer anyway. And your friend. *Always*. If I take on new Obligations, it doesn't mean I've left you forever. In fact —"

"Don't call me Creirwy anymore! I'm not your 'dear little one.' I don't care if you leave. You were getting on my nerves anyway. Bossing me when you were around — that's when you weren't ignoring me. Playing Master Watcher — third class, of course."

As soon as I say it, I regret it but, as always, my mouth runs ahead of my brain.

"I thought we were friends, Emma."

"You're the one who decided *you* didn't want to be *my* friend anymore. I just happen to agree."

Tom leans his head back and looks down at me, assessing. I hate it when he does that.

Only polite fellowship is allowed between Watchers unless the Watcher Kinn has "ordained" it otherwise. I mean, baby Watchers *do* come from *somewhere*. But Histal has made it clear that Tom and I are too close — and *unsuitable* mates. Obviously, Tom thinks so, too. Besides, even if he didn't, he'd obey Histal anyway — just to regain his rank. I glare at him to cover the ache in my chest.

"I can't let you go there, Emma," he says.

"Huh?" I say, feigning confusion. "Go where?"

He sighs. "You know where."

"Oh, don't worry your tiny, obedient Watcher head about it. I'll keep my promise. You can go back to your little Obligation — the one you no doubt *specially* asked for."

I want to *hurt* him, but he just looks at me with that unwavering gaze. Is that another hint of laughter in his dark eyes?

"Did you have your fingers crossed when you gave Histal your word to be a good and obedient Watcher?" Tom asks, and this time he grins.

"I should never have told you about that human trick!"

"A trick that is used in order to *lie* ..." he says, one eyebrow up. "But it holds no power here. Your word has been given, crossed fingers or not."

"Don't preach to me!" I say. "And besides, since when does Histal or anyone at the Campan keep *their* word! Oh yes, they do their Obligations. They're reliable *that* way! But Histal promised *me* he'd look after Pictree's poor youngers when I got back to the Campan. He hasn't kept *his* word! So why should I keep mine?"

Tom shakes his head. "You are so *exhausting*, Emma. I may have grown up at the Campan, but I started out like you, questioning, challenging the Ways. I was told I would have to earn the answers. I didn't want to go to Earth and serve Fergus. But I was told it would further the Watcher Kinn's Plan. I had no choice. I *had* to trust them. I had to do my duty."

"But you broke your Obligation to Fergus," I say.

"Yes. I broke my Obligation to Fergus. And to Histal. *For you*. And I was punished for it. And then I let you persuade me to go on your Seeker's Quest. And got demoted. If I ever disobey again, I won't be allowed —"

"Oh, don't bother!" I march to the door. I'll tell Mom I arrived too late to change for dinner.

"Where are you going?"

"To see my family. Go away, Tom!"

I'm reaching for the latch when a warm hand grasps my shoulder. Gently, Tom turns me to face him.

"I know what you're up to, Creirwy."

I say through my teeth, "I told you. Don't call me that ... *ever*."

"Don't be angry, Emma."

"I'm not angry."

"You might want to tell your face that."

"Ha, ha," I say. But my throat hurts from holding back tears.

"You cannot go to this new world, Emma. Not yet. You're not ready — and you gave your word."

I scowl at his chest. "Histal doesn't understand. I don't just want to poke around. You know I feel a strong bond with this place — that must mean *something*, even if I don't know what. All I know is I have to get there before Fergus."

Should I tell Tom what Cill said? Should I tell him I've left the Campan for good? No, I can't trust him. Not anymore. I turn away, unable to be so close to him.

He turns me back and cups my chin with his fingers, forcing me to look up into his eyes. "You *will* go to your new world one day, Emma. You're just *not ready* yet."

I push his hand away roughly.

"Fergus and Mathus won't find a way into the border cave on their own," he says. "The lock is solid. I tested it."

"Without telling me?"

"That doesn't matter! Emma, you're using Fergus and Mathus — and the Game — as an *excuse*. To justify going without permission."

"*Permission*? You may be a slave of the Watcher Clann, but *I'm* not. I've *quit*. Histal just doesn't know yet."

Tom laughs. "You've quit? You can't *quit* being a Watcher, Emma. It's *what you are.*"

Tears of anger prick my eyes. "Don't laugh at me! I don't have to be *your* kind of Watcher, groveling before some never-to-be-seen Pathfinder and some puffed-up board of directors called a Watcher Kinn who make its Watchers do Obligations that are *wrong!*"

His neck and cheeks turn pink. "You know *nothing* about the Pathfinder or the Kinn or its —"

"Yeah, yeah, the *Grand Plan*. You're *so* full of yourself tonight, aren't you?" I try to sneer but my quivering chin ruins the image.

Tom shakes his head. "Emma, seriously, aren't you afraid to go to this strange world all alone?"

Our eyes always say more than our words. But I look away. "I have no choice, Tom. Please don't tell Histal."

He grabs my arm. "You're not *ready*, Emma. If you fall, who will catch you —"

Suddenly, words rush out of my mouth before I can stop them. "You — if you'd come with me ... we could explore this world together. This is an *amazing* chance to —"

"No, Emma. You know I can't do that."

He might as well have slapped my face.

"Then I'll do it on my own. And if I fall, I'll just have to catch myself."

Tom puts both hands on my shoulders and tightens his grip. I glare at the soft moleskin ties of his chiton. "I have never asked you for anything, Creirwy ... Emma. But I'm asking you now — promise me you won't go, not yet. With no crossed fingers. Will you promise?"

I blink back tears. "I won't promise you anything, Tom. You don't belong with me anymore."

"Emma, please." His voice is low, urgent.

"It's too hard, Tom," I say, my words tight and small.

"What is?"

"This. You. Me. Being a Watcher. All of it."

I turn away, open the door and walk down the stairs, hardly able to see for the tears I finally let fall.

4

I stumble down a serpentine corridor, bump into someone near the dining hall, mutter "Sorry" and keep going.

"Emma! I was told to wait here for an audience with Suzarain Elen. I wanted to ask her how to get hold of *you*. And now here you are!"

The boy is my height, wearing the glue-spattered shirt, knee-length pants and bare feet of Mirour's slaves. His shock of tawny hair, golden skin, snub features and yellow eyes give him the look of a lion cub.

"Pictree Bragg! Where did you come from? What are you doing away from the Cymmarian Market? Mirour will kill you!"

A towering Argadnel guard standing nearby watches us closely. I have no official power in my sister's castel. Only Summer or Mom could tell him to get lost.

"Mirour is my smallest problem," Pictree says urgently. "Emma, something terrible has happened!" He looks at the guard and whispers, "My youngers. They've *vanished*!"

I gasp. "W-what?"

He grasps my arm. "And Wefta's slaves are gone, too."

"How? When?"

He stares. "So it wasn't you who arranged this?"

"No! Tell me what happened."

"I was trying to get my youngers to finish a batch of masks for a Triumph in the world of Merkle. A Game was won there against a set of Upstart Players. Mirour just wouldn't *shut up* about how slow we were. I told him to go check the inventory — to prove we *were* getting the job done. Then I turned to reassure my workers and — and — they were *gone!*"

Is this Histal's doing? Is he *that* powerful?

"They're all gone?" I whisper. "*All?*"

Pictree suddenly dissolves into choked laughter. "You should have seen Mirour when he saw the empty shop. He screeched so hard his mask cracked. He ran into his little sanctum to get a new one, then whipped me like a crazed baboon."

He lifts his sleeve. The red welts make my stomach tighten with anger.

"How did you get away?"

"He finally yelled at me to find out if Wefta had taken them. But Wefta was running around the market demanding to know who took *his* workers.

I ran back to Mirour's. He was face down on the floor, crying his eyes out, threatening revenge on the whole market. I knew it was only a matter of time before I got blamed, so I rifled through his strong box, took a pile of coins, hired myself an air sloop and came here."

"And they let you in?" I ask, glancing over his shoulder at the looming guard.

"I told them I was a friend of yours and needed to talk to you on a matter of great importance. They checked with your mother, the Belldam, and she gave her permission. The sentries brought me here and said the Belldam or Suzarain Elen would speak to me after dinner."

"Mom and my sister Summer, who's called Elen by her people, know you saved my life at the market. They'd want to meet you."

"But who could have worked this magick on Wefta and Mirour?"

"I don't know. Tom is here — maybe he knows something."

"Knows what?" a deep voice says behind us.

Pictree looks past my shoulder. "That voice — I recognize it."

I say stiffly, "Tom was my owl — the one you met at the market. My Watcher. Remember?"

Pictree looks at Tom with curiosity. Tom looks cool and indifferent, but I can tell by his eyes I've hurt him.

I tell him what's happened. "Do you think Histal could have done this?"

He frowns. "I suppose, but —"

"If it was him, he moved awfully fast. Wouldn't he have to go through the Kinn and the Pathfinder first? You just saw him. Did he say anything about it?"

Tom smiles wryly. "Histal confides in no one."

I clutch his arm. "You don't think it was Fergus, do you? To blackmail me into taking him into the new world? He must know how worried Ailla and I have been about the youngers."

Tom's eyes narrow. "Fergus has no idea of your interest in the youngers, I'm sure of it."

How can he be so sure what Fergus does or doesn't know? His certainty worries me. To Pictree, I say, "Tom and I don't know how this happened, Pictree."

"I only hope it was someone who will care for them," he says, echoing my thoughts. His face sags, crestfallen and tired.

"Are you hungry?" I ask him.

Pictree shrugs. "I'm always hungry. Mirour is a miser. Porray and water once a day are all we get."

"Come with me. There's always plenty at my family's table."

"I'm hungry, too," Tom interjects.

I say snidely, "I thought you were about to leave."

He rolls his eyes. "Emma, I don't understand your anger. I —"

"You must be the stupidest Watcher ever," I whisper, then raise my voice, "You may as well eat before you leave."

I push the dining room door open. My family is sitting on cushions around a low black table. Thank goodness neither Branwen nor Huw is allowed at family meals. They'd be too curious about Pictree.

Argadnel attendants hover, pouring mead. The table is dotted with bowls of delicious-smelling food. In the middle is a huge vase filled with Stygia Mantle blooms.

Mom's simple robe is the dark, rich purple of the flowers' stamens. Her pile of salt-and-pepper hair is held off her neck by a clasp edged with moonstones. Her health has greatly improved since I found Dad and Ailla, but making sure everything stays on an even keel on Argadnel is hard — especially with Fergus's presence always there in the shape of Branwen and Huw. The lines in her face and the dark hollows under her eyes show the strain she's under.

Summer is covered in bangles and strings of jewels, her snug red garment edged in gold, its wide overskirt a vibrant orange satin. Her varnished ear-length hair is sprinkled with tiny yellow and pink pearls, moonstones and other precious stones native to the rocky island.

Mom's human daughter, Ailla, is in pale yellow, her unruly mop of black hair held under control by a net dotted in snowy moonstones.

Dad, lounging on his pillows, wears the fitted garment of black that high-ranking Argadnelians wear, his thinning reddish hair cut shoulder length. In one ear is a large blue moonstone. Only royalty is allowed to wear this most perfect gem of the island. With his dark auburn beard, he looks like a knight from King Arthur's Round Table. He's taken to Argadnel life like a fish to water. Life for Dad is to be enjoyed without reservation — something I wish I could learn from him. I wish Mom could, too.

Everyone cries out when they see me. Mom grabs my hand and I kiss her thin cheek. Dad gives me a huge hug. Ailla is right behind him squealing with delight. Summer remains seated, the perfect Suzarain, but her eyes are bright with pleasure.

She peers around me, then blushes a warm pink. "Tom! You're here, too!"

The young queen of Argadnel has a crush on Tom. But she's never seen him in Watcher form — the *real* Tamhas. She might not be so in love with the white skin, thistledown hair, long face and large slanted eyes. He always takes on the human form of Tom on Argadnel. It's the Way of the Watcher Clann — to change to the shape of the beings you mingle with. It's always seemed to me that Tom, like me, is most comfortable in human form. I even thought it might be because he knew how attracted I was to him as Tom, but now I know different.

Ailla suddenly spots Pictree. Almost as tall as Mom, she gives the poor little guy a bear hug, lifting his feet off the floor. Back on solid ground, Pictree laughs and holds her at arm's length, exclaiming, "This can't be the tiny waif of Mirour and Wefta's labor shops?"

Ailla grins at him. "Yes. Haven't I grown since I came home to my family?"

Summer rises regally and interrupts in an imperious tone. "*Who* is this?"

Ailla takes Pictree's hand. "This is my friend, Pictree Bragg. Next to Emma and Tom, Pictree is the bravest being I have ever met. Without him, I would never have survived the long years of slaving for Mirour and Wefta, or the ..." Ailla's voice falters and Summer, turning into the sister we both love, leaves the table and hugs her.

"Pictree Bragg," Summer says warmly, "you are welcome in Argadnel any time. Please, join our table." She smiles up at Tom. "Tom, you may sit next to me."

Tom suddenly looks as if he has too many arms and legs. As he shuffles toward the table, I can't resist a dig. "Play your cards right and you could become Suzar of Argadnel. What an Obligation *that* would be."

He glares at me.

"Oh, don't look like a bear with a sore paw. I know you're already married to Histal and the Watcher Clann!"

5

I perch between Pictree and Tom, who sits as far from Summer as he can without insulting her. Her adoration makes him nervous. He turns a stony face away from my evil cat's grin. Fine. I eat some of my favorite dish, pale orange rice studded with roasted nuts and a honey sauce edged with a vinegary tang. Then, as I see Ailla and Pictree chatting, I remember the youngers and my appetite vanishes. The blood drains from my head. My upper lip is moist. I feel like I'm going to be sick.

"You okay?" Tom asks.

"Of course I am." I tear off a piece of wafer-thin herb bread and eat it, but it turns sour in my mouth. Out of the corner of my eye, I watch Pictree. The food disappears as fast as it hits his plate. He's lived with constant hunger and knows that he must eat when he can.

Tom nudges my arm. Under his breath he says, "I've been thinking. I doubt it was Histal who took the youngers — considering how slow the Kinn is to make decisions. But it is pretty *bizarre*, to use one of your favorite words. We must consider Fergus."

He's actually willing to think of Fergus as the culprit! I look to see if anyone's listening, but my family's attention is on Ailla's bright face.

I mutter, "If it *was* Fergus, I'll kill him. I swear it!"

Tom growls softly, "Until we find them, you have *no choice* but to stay away from that border cave."

Rats! He's right. If Fergus has them, he'll soon let us know — demanding a way into the world behind the moonstone wall in exchange for them. But ... what if it *is* Histal?

"I don't suppose you'd consider helping me find out who has them?" I ask. "Or would that interfere with guard duty?"

"Give it a rest, Emma. I'll go to the Campan and consult with Histal. If it *was* the Kinn who took the youngers, he'll have to tell me. If not, I'll ask permission to find out what happened to them. Okay? That satisfy you?"

I mutter, "Okay — but meanwhile, Pictree and I will go back to Cymmarian Market and look around."

"Oh no you won't!" Tom says. "Fumbling around the market will only make things worse! You will come with me and talk to Histal."

"No way!"

"If it *wasn't* Histal who took the youngers, he may think *you're* somehow responsible. You have to come."

I say loudly, "No! I *won't*. That's blackmail, Tom!"

My family gapes at us. Pictree looks worried. Tom's face is thunderous.

I say, with my best false laugh, "I have to go on a training Obligation soon and Tom says if I don't stop shoveling in the food, I'll be too big to get off the ground."

Dad hoots. "That'll never happen, Tom. She eats like a baby elephant and never gains an ounce. Takes after me."

Mom smiles at Dad before giving Tom her Feminist Frown.

I love it when my parents talk about me as if I'm really their child. The best thing is, neither of them seems to notice they're doing it. Guilt nudges at me. Tom would never say anything as cheesy as that about my weight. But I don't defend him.

"Hey, Pictree, want me to show you around the gardens?" I ask, trying to divert attention from Tom's stiff face.

"I'll come, too," Ailla says, but Mom shakes her head.

"We have to do those Stygia cuttings tonight by the new moons, remember?"

Ailla pouts, but Mom says to Pictree, "You'll stay on the island through star span, won't you? You can see that Ailla is anxious to spend time with you."

Pictree nods. "Isn't Argadnel raised on a silver pedestal at night? Maybe after it's lowered in morn-light, you can show me your beaches, Ailla?"

That seems to satisfy her. He and I walk quickly to the castel's main doors. The night is fragrant and cool, the low mist trailing through the grasses and along the paths. The twin moons look like circles of rice paper against the black sky. I try to relax, but my stomach is tight. Where *are* the youngers? And where is Fergus?

I still haven't told Tom about Cill's news. I should, now that Tom thinks Fergus might be behind the disappearance of the youngers.

As Pictree examines one of the star-shaped gray flowers that bloom only at night, I realize he's someone I trust completely. I decide to tell him about my secret world — and how Histal is keeping me from going into it. He listens carefully. I also tell him Cill's news.

He says, "Fergus is an obvious danger. And now you must worry about my news as well. I feel the weight of your burden. I'm sorry."

"It can't be helped," I say. "We should think about where to start looking for the youngers — set up a plan tonight."

"Are you not going through the border cave first? To get there before Fergus?"

"How can I when it might put the youngers in danger?"

Pictree's yellow eyes gleam in the dark. "Thank you, Emma. When the time is right for you to go to this new world, I will gladly go with you."

"Would you really?" I ask. "*Tom* wouldn't!"

"I think Tom would follow you to the ends of all the worlds," Pictree replies.

I snort. "You don't know him like I do. Anyway, he says he *has* to talk to Histal about the youngers. Meanwhile, would you like to *see* an image from my new world?"

"I'd love to see any part of it."

"As long as that is all you do, Emma," says Tom, appearing behind us.

I roll my eyes. "I thought you'd left for the Campan! Don't worry, I'm not going anywhere until you talk to Histal. Which will be *soon*, I hope? Like *now*?"

Tom looks at me hard. I know he's torn between leaving me so near the cave entrance and going to see Histal. I make a face at him before leading Pictree along the path to a trail behind a barrier of prickly gorse. After a few minutes' climb through the shadowy darkness, we reach the curved wall of moonstone that holds the border cave.

Not long after we first arrived on the island, I wandered up here exploring and leaned against the moonstone wall to rest. Suddenly, a majestic castel appeared in the air in front of me — whirls and swirling peaks like flowing water. I've visited this spot many times since, and each time I see something different.

Sometimes it feels like I'm hovering above a wide forest or floating over a beautiful garden, lush with dark blue foliage and dotted with ornate pools of water. Sometimes the scene is endless winding mazes and once I saw a space of palest blue filled with gray fluttering wings. Not long before I left on my Seeker's Quest, a rolling yellow sea appeared that frightened me. And the last time I was here, I saw dim points of light that seemed to be roaming through darkness looking for something. Yet I've never seen any beings in this baffling place.

I told no one else what I had seen. I searched through the island's binnacles in the castel's library to see if anything had been recorded on the island. I found nothing — not even a hint of a border cave's existence. But, unknown to me, on more than one night, I was followed by a spy for Rhona and Huw — a young female servant — who told them she had seen bits of the images in the air. Since then, Rhona and Huw and Fergus and Mathus have tried to break into this new world. So far, none of them has managed to crack the code.

"Is this the place?" Pictree asks eagerly.

"Yes," Tom says, behind us. "Emma can show you its strange beauty, as she has shown me, but that is *all*."

"Are you going to creep around after us all night?" I demand. "I'm just going to show Pictree a quick view of what's on the other side."

"Do you promise that's all you'll do, Emma?"

"Of course I promise! I'm as worried about the youngers as you are!"

He nods curtly and walks away. I smile apologetically at Pictree and lay my hand against the moonstone that triggers the images. But instead of a beautiful scene, a heavy fog drops over us like a huge gray blanket, blotting out the ocean, the moons, even the cave wall.

6

Tom looms out of the fog. "What in Ochain's name have you done, Emma?"

"I didn't do anything," I shout. "It just happened!"

"Something is always just happening with you!"

Before I can shout at him again, he shape-changes into owl form and flies into the mist, his voice trailing behind. "Stay here! I'll see how far this fog goes."

The island is always shrouded in a light silvery mist at night. Summer's people have developed blue lights that cut right through it. But there's no light visible now.

"Tom!" I shout. "Come back!" But only silence thrums through the night.

"Don't move," I say to Pictree. I run, letting my feet take their own course through the grayness. "Guards!" I shout. "Mom! Dad! Suuuummmmer!" I stop, heart pounding. Tom transforms in front of me. "Tom! What is it! *Tell* me!"

"I don't know. I can't get through this fog — can't even locate the castel."

I try to run past him, but he grabs my arm.

"Someone's put a massive cunning over Argadnel. We're caught in an impenetrable vapor web. I don't think Druvid Mathus has the power to block out the castel. I have to try and contact Histal. Where's Pictree?"

"Right here. I followed Emma's voice."

I say, "My family will worry and come find us."

"I don't think so, Emma," Tom says. "They probably don't know we're gone."

I stare at him, unable to think.

He tries to smile. "We'll figure it out, Emma. Just don't panic, okay?"

I swallow hard and nod. In a twist of air, he's gone.

Pictree smacks his fist into his other hand. "Why can't I *sense* anything more than this ... nothingness?" A Sensitive, he can usually pick up on the essences of living things. Not this time, though. Neither can I.

"My Homing Circle is in my pouch," I say. "I use it to get to and from the Watchers Campan. Why didn't I think of it before!" I dig around until I find it.

"Why didn't Tom use his?" Pictree asks.

I point at the circle of dull useless metal in my hand. "He probably did. Ruined somehow."

Pictree shakes his head. "Let's try and find the border cave. We're closest to that, right? All things have energy — stone has a deep throbbing essence. Maybe ... wait ... who's that?"

We hear the pat pat of footsteps running past, just out of sight. Then silence.

"Hello!" I shout. "Who's there?"

Pictree murmurs, "Two beings —"

Again, the patter of bare feet, a hiss of whispers and a tiny figure, gray cloak streaming behind, appears ... and disappears.

"Wait!" I cry. "Who are you?"

"Not Argadnelians," Pictree says. "Come on! I bet they came from the cave!"

I change into Watcher mode. We run through the fog following the footsteps. I open my senses and pick up a scent that's strangely familiar. But who — what? At that moment, heavier feet tromp past us going in the same direction. We follow these new sounds. Suddenly, in the distance, a door slams with a loud bang, followed by two loud shouts. Once again, a wash of silence.

"What's going on?" I whisper as we run to where the noise came from.

Pictree puffs, "Those feet were wearing boots. Four beings now."

"But *who*? If it was my family or their guards, they'd have answered me —"

"I coded the essences of your family at dinner, Emma. It wasn't them. Wait. I feel a tremor of stone — over here — look!"

A wall of moonstone flutters out of the dark haze, no more solid than a painting on silk, and behind it, a cave. A curious prickling starts in my head and travels straight to the soles of my feet.

"The Way into the cave is open. Will you come with me?" I ask.

"Shouldn't we wait for Tom?"

"If I wait, maybe I'll lose the chance. Something's wrong. I feel it."

"Emma. Wait!"

"Pictree, I feel … I'm being told to enter — no, not told, *summoned*."

"Just wait for Tom, please."

"We don't know how long he'll be!" I look at the dim cave opening. "This portal will disappear soon. But portals always have an exit, Pictree. We won't stay long."

"The fog may lift soon and —"

"Stay or come. It's up to you. I have to go." Holding my breath, I walk through the thin wall.

Behind me, Pictree's arm emerges, then his body slides through.

We're no sooner through than Tom appears on the other side of the shifting curtain. "Emma! Come out! It's too dangerous!"

I shout back, "Did you find Histal?"

"I can't find any way through this fog, but —"

"Come with us! It may help us find a way to make the fog vanish."

"Listen to me, Emma!" His voice is harsh, commanding. "Come back before it's too late."

"You should hear him out, Emma," Pictree says.

"I don't know *what* to do," I say, pressing my hands to my cheeks.

"Emma!"

"Okay, okay," I call. "We're coming. But not for long." As I walk toward the translucent wall, it begins to solidify.

Tom's hands push through and chunks of opal moonstone crumble to the floor.

"Hold hands and each of you grab one of mine!" he shouts.

We try, but a strong slap of wind knocks Pictree and me down. The wall is now solid moonstone. I struggle to my feet, shouting for Tom. But there's no answer.

I know that the first layer of a stone wall is always the easiest to go through, but I can't even get a tip of a finger through this one. I prowl along the wall. There has to be an exit hole — there's one in every border cave. But not here. Why? I slap the moonstone and shout Tom's name again and again, but there's no response.

"Tom can go through any stone wall — why can't he get through?" I cry. "Why is there no way out?"

"We should have waited, Emma," Pictree says. "Tom might be hurt."

"Do you think so? Can't you feel his essence?"

"No. Nothing. But at least I don't feel any pain from him, either."

Just then, a small twist of moonstone dust swirls around Pictree, tangling his hair. He coughs and flails his arms. "Cack! Where did this wind come from?"

"There must be an opening!" My stomach is tight with dread. Is Tom stuck halfway through the wall? I bang my fists against it. "Tom. Tom!"

"Can you hear anything?" Pictree asks, his ear against the stone.

"Nothing! If he — he's hurt, it's all my fault."

And all because you ran headlong into something you knew nothing about, my inner voice chides.

"Oh shut up," I growl.

"What?"

I shake my head. "Not you, Pictree." Blistering tears sting my cheeks and chin. At the same time I can almost hear Tom telling me to stop being so *human* — to stop crying and *think*. As I look down at the stone floor, my tears drop into the dust. It takes me a second to become aware of a light breeze around my ankles.

"Emma, the breeze. It's coming from over there. Look, an opening in the floor." Pictree runs to a dark corner. "Stairs! Should we go down?"

I look back at the silent wall of stone. "I — I can't leave Tom."

Pictree says firmly, "We have no choice but to move forward, Emma. It's the only way to find out what's going on — and to help Tom."

He's right of course. I walk over to the opening in the cave floor and look down at the narrow stone steps. "Okay, let's see what's down there."

7

We have no light, but the pale moonstone walls glow softly as we spiral down. The stairs are covered in dust scuffled by footprints.

"Bare feet. And look, boots. Who are they? Will they be waiting for us?" I wonder aloud, but when we reach the bottom step, no one's there.

Across a small landing are two grillwork doors of silver, each divided into two sections. Holding them shut is a mechanism of two half-moons with a tiny sword through them. I peer through the grill. Nothing but more fog.

"One of them had the key for this," I say, rattling the mechanism.

Pictree says, "This section shows a fire in a forge with sparks flying off it — and each spark is a winged being."

I point to the top of the other door. "This one has curled waves all over it. And look, there's a ..." I peer at it. "... one of those Muirgens I've read about."

The half-fish, half-humanoid beings called Muirgens once lived in all the seas of the worlds, but many spancrests ago they vanished, except in one body of water — the Sea of Fomorii. Then, when misery-guts Rhona took over the kingdom of Fomorii, she destroyed what few remained. The now-extinct Muirgens live only in the myths of the worlds they left behind.

Pictree examines the lower sections of both doors. "This has zigzag lines across it with moons, suns and stars — and a sword. The other has a rounded hill ringed by trees. Look, there's a giant figure crafted into the hill."

I don't care what's on the doors. "How do we get through this stupid thing?" I jiggle the metal contraption again.

"Hey!" I shout. "Anyone there?" No answer — but my left wrist is starting to burn.

I glance down at the tattoo on my wrist — two crescent moons, their rounded backs facing each other — a small arrow running through both. It's usually flat and a pale pinkish blue. But now the crescent moons swell and lift, turning dark blue with red edges. The arrow is almost black. I run the tip of my finger over their soft ridged surfaces and a sharp pain takes my breath away.

"Look!" breathes Pictree. "That locking mechanism is the same design except the moons are backward. You *must* have a connection to this place!"

I pull on the device's sword, but it doesn't move.

"Oh well," I puff, "I didn't think it would be easy."

"Maybe if we could flip the moons somehow," Pictree suggests.

I grab one and it shifts slightly, but doesn't give. I'm about to use my knife to pry it open when I spot three tiny gold balls in an arc over each moon. I pull on one of them and it comes away in my hand.

"Hey!" I say. "It's a *peg!*"

"There are holes dotted all over the pictures," Pictree says. "I bet you have to move those six pegs to their proper places in the door."

"Where?"

Pictree points to three holes in each panel.

"But there are six moons and — one, two, three, four ... twelve holes in all," I say.

"Obviously there's a correct number for each panel. Some holes will stay empty."

"This'll take hours ... days! Think of the number of combinations!" I moan.

"Then we'd better get started." He grins at me, his yellow eyes bright.

I gather up the six little gold pegs and we try to work out a pattern — three moons in one, two in another, one here, one there — on and on. But nothing works. There are thousands of possibilities. I wish there was a computer nearby.

"My brain is hurting. This is hopeless!" I poke the moons back in their original places and fling myself on the stairs. I lay my pounding head back on one of the treads and stare blindly at the landing ceiling. When my eyes focus, I surprise Pictree by laughing out loud. Across the ceiling is a faint painting of this very door. The one with fire has three moons marked in gold dots, the one with the waves has one, the zigzag one has none and the one with the hill and trees has two. I point up at it and Pictree gives a shout of glee.

I dash over and put the pegs in their right places. As the last one is pushed in, the crescent moons spin, turning the same way as my tattoo's moons, and the sword slides out and lands with a clatter. I try to pick it up, but it's fused into the floor.

The doors swing open.

8

On the other side of the gate, the fog hides everything but a small area of flat stone. As I edge out onto it, the haze opens for a few feet, exposing a deep chasm. My stomach turns to water.

"L-let's go back inside. Maybe there's another way." But the door clangs shut behind us and the grating sound of the sword being sheathed between the moons tells us it's locked again. There's no device on this side to open it. I try to go through it, but it's as solid as steel.

A distant burble of laughter sounds through the mist. In alarm, I pull my knife out of my belt, but the laughter drifts away to silence once again. I lean against the door, shaking. I've got to stop this. I'm acting just like a human kid — scared to death and wanting to go home. But there's no way out. My family will be worried sick. And what about Tom? I was so angry at him for deserting me, but now I'd *give* him his freedom from me just to know he's okay.

Pictree begins a soft chant. I try not to cry. I dreamed about entering this world, and I've managed to louse it up. Why didn't I *listen* to Tom — stay on the other side of the cave until we'd figured out how to approach it properly? Why, why, *why*?

Pictree looks at me with a worried frown. "There is great confusion, turmoil and fear in this place, Emma. But there's also a calm — not peaceful, more like silence before a storm. And there's something … deep … malignant … guarding everything like a gromand pacing at his victim's door."

Hearing him, I tip over from fear to numb acceptance. I say through gritted teeth, "We have to follow those beings. But how?"

Pictree nods. "I sense two of them across the gorge."

Thin high-pitched giggles echo back to us.

"Now, they're taunting us. Clearly there *is* a way to get off this platform."

Pictree grins. "Let's find it."

That grin does it. I kneel and run my hands over the stone platform. Nothing in front. To the left of the door is only foggy air.

On the other side of the door, where the mist is very thick, I feel a ledge a few inches higher than the platform and quite wide. I creep along it on hands and knees. As my fingers explore, I come upon a ring of bumps around a raised dome. Faint lights glow through the mist.

"Pictree! I found a … gadget of some kind."

"See how it works." Pictree is close behind me. "The worst thing that can happen is the ledge vanishes and we drop like stones."

"Great. Thanks. That's really encouraging."

"You can fly. I can't. Just grab me on the way down, okay?"

"You're not helping, Pictree."

He laughs. "Well, it's either try or sit here until we turn to dust."

I push the dome. Nothing happens. What would Histal say? *Look. Touch. Smell. Hear.* I put my ear against it and pick up a soft shushing sound. I run my fingertips over the dome's smooth surface and feel a sharp edge. I give it a tug. A thin lever slides up at a slight angle. I push and pull it but nothing happens.

Pictree, leaning over me, says, "Could it be a winch?"

"A winch?"

"See if you can turn it — in a circle."

I give the lever a twist and it turns on its own. The shushing grows as it whirls faster, then stops with a loud whoosh.

"Well, it's done something!" Pictree says as we back off the ledge.

A bridge of light has cut through the mist between our platform and the other side of the ravine.

"Now we can cross. But ... what do they want?" I whisper. "Why don't they just talk to us?"

"One thing is sure," Pictree murmurs. "They had lots of time to harm us on Argadnel and they didn't. Look, this light bridge might not stay long, Emma. We should cross it."

I tentatively put one foot on it and press down. "Feels solid. Take my hand. If we fall, we'll fall together."

9

As we step onto firm ground on the other side, a gust of wind roars past us tearing away the fog and the light bridge. Two tiny figures, cloaks flying, run giggling down a long dim hall and through a door at the far end.

"They're goading us to follow," I say.

The hall is vaulted like a cathedral. Pools of green light from arched openings lie across the floor. Are they windows — or doors leading down more corridors?

"Emma, something upsetting is here."

"Like what?" I ask.

"I don't *know* ... I'm not much help. I'm sorry, Emma."

"Don't be. My dad says life should be one big adventure. Well, this sure qualifies."

"Even without me, Emma," Pictree asks, "you will continue, won't you?"

I give him a little push. "We'll finish this together." I don't add that I wish that he was Tom. "Come on, let's see what's down this hall."

The first lighted archway isn't a doorway but a kind of display case covered by thick green glass. At first I don't understand what I'm seeing.

Pictree says urgently, as my eyes widen with horror, "It's not really her, Emma."

The figure is wearing the yellow chiton she had on at dinner. The net of moonstones in her hair is slightly askew, her skin pale, almost translucent. She's looking straight ahead, frowning slightly.

"Ailla?" I cry, slapping my hands on the glass. But she doesn't move.

I run from alcove to alcove. They're all here! Ailla, Mom, Dad, Summer. And other Argadnel citizens. Dad looks surprised. Mom eyes are cast down, as if she knows I'm looking at her and doesn't want me to see the pain in her eyes. Summer's right hand is up, palm forward. She looks surprised and regally offended. No, it can't be! Not my family. Surely they're still in Argadnel Castel. The room spins. Pictree pushes me to the floor and puts my head between my knees. He's talking to me, but my head is full of terrible sounds.

Once the room stops turning, I lurch to my feet and run back to Mom's window, throw my shoulder against it and knock myself onto the floor. I transmute invisible and try to slide through the green glass, but it's impenetrable.

Pictree drags me away. "Emma. It's not really them!"

"We have to get them *out!*"

"Emma," Pictree shouts, shaking me by the shoulders, "listen to me. Now!"

I stare at him.

"Listen carefully. *It's not really them.* These images are light pictures."

"Like ... like holograms?" I gasp, feeling a sliver of hope.

He nods. "No life essences off them at all. Your family is probably still in Argadnel."

"Maybe," I say, "or jailed in confiners where I'll *never* find them."

I stumble down the corridor, looking into each window again. Some beings I recognize, not others. Then, out of the corner of my eye, I see her. Like Ailla, her eyes look straight ahead, but not at me.

"Oh, Cill," I whisper. "You didn't make it off the island after all."

I don't want to look anymore but I can't stop myself. In one window — two beings float side by side. Dear, goofy, brilliant Gyro the Searcher — wearing his riveted helmet with the miniature tele-scope over one eye and his lacy metal armor that makes him look part space alien and part old-fash-ioned knight.

I swallow hard. "Look at him, Pictree. That armor is even *more* rusty than the last time I saw him. No wonder he squeaks like a broken gate when he walks." I swallow down a sob.

Pictree whispers, "He's with Badba — the scariest Ravan that ever came to Cymmarian Market."

I smile. "Yeah. She's crazy all right. And Gyro's best friend."

Badba — more than seven feet tall — is dressed in her black leathers. Her unclad feet are covered in fine feathers, the green toes long and bony, the nails yellow talons. She's ready for travel in her leather helmet with its knot of sharp black feathers. Over her shoulder is her bag of weapons. A dark blue hand is frozen in the act of pulling off her helmet, revealing the beautiful dark face with its yellow beaky nose and piercing blue eyes.

"Oh why didn't they get away before all this happened!" I say. "Now they're captives, too."

"But Emma, it's not really —" Pictree begins, but I glower at him and he stops.

With a deadened heart, I continue toward the final two windows. Huw's long thin body is clad in the same leggings of viper skins and sleeveless tight tunic I last saw him wearing. The blue tattoos on his bare arms seem pale — almost colorless. He's looking through narrowed eyes toward Branwen across the hall. Her arms are stretched out, level with her shoulders, the long sleeves of her chiton hanging to the hem of her skirt. She looks like an elegant moth caught in green amber.

Pictree gently leads me to the door at the end of the hall. It's as black as ebony, and its carved images

mirror those on the doors across the ravine —
except for a large smooth moonstone in the middle. Pictree pushes the stone, but nothing happens.

I stammer, "This *place*. I always thought it was *cut
off* from the other worlds, you know? I wasn't even
sure it was *inhabited*. Who is doing this? And *why?*"

"Maybe they felt threatened."

"How?" I cry. "I never once tried to go through
their border cave."

"We won't find answers unless we look," he says.
"Try to open this door. I can't."

I put my hand against the moonstone. My tattoo
burns and I grit my teeth against the pain. The door
swings open a crack.

"There! That *proves* you're connected to this
place."

"But *how?*"

"I guess the only way to find out is ..." Pictree
points at the door.

I push it open. Straight ahead is a wall of finely
woven branches. Everything else is shrouded in
darkness. Under our feet are gold tiles, many broken. Thousands of tiny dry leaves are strewn over
them, and thousands more are thickly gathered
under a small table in front of the hedge wall.

A gust of wind lifts my hair, drops and swirls
across the tabletop, lifting a pile of dust into a small
volcano. As it scatters, a flat piece of crystal with a
Celtic knot of inlaid silver is revealed. The silver

line winds around and around, intersecting again and again, forming four knots — each with a symbol in the middle. The center of the design is a circle with small gold lines like roots joining at a black indentation. The design reminds me of one of the mazes I saw when this new world showed itself to me. Is this tangled wall of dead branches part of a maze? The hedge runs to the left and to the right. Maybe the crystal is an overview. I try to lift it to take it with me as a guide, but it's stuck fast.

"Which way do you want to go?" The words are no sooner out of Pictree's mouth than two gray hoods pop out from behind the prickly hedge to our right. Pale hands beckon, then vanish. We take off after them at a run.

10

We race around the corner of the hedge, but there's no one in sight. Two prickly walls with a shadowy walkway between continue straight ahead.

"Be careful," I whisper to Pictree as we creep down it.

Two small cloaked heads poke out of a gap farther down, then pull back tittering.

When we reach the opening, we hear a spurt of whispered giggling, then the splash of water. My heart is pounding so hard I'm sure my throat will burst. Suddenly, a hard thrust of wind hits me between the shoulder blades and shoves me through the opening. On the other side of the gap lies a sandy path between two more hedges. As we walk down it, the path widens into a sandy clearing dotted with rocks. A narrow black waterway laps against the shore. Beyond it is another wall of hedge.

I say, "It *is* a maze! With a water path!"

From behind a pile of rocks we hear high screechy voices arguing. Pictree taps me on the shoulder and points to a rock with a flat top. We peer over it. On the other side, the hooded figures are wrestling with a small boat made of smoky green glass. One end is a rearing fish head with bulging gold eyes, the other end a large tail, inset with gold scales. One of the figures pushes against the fish head, the other figure pushes against the tail.

I stifle my own giggle.

A few angry yips from one triggers the other to run around the boat and repeatedly slap her partner. More slaps and a couple of yips and snarls, then more pulling and pushing. They'll go nowhere at this rate.

"Hey!" I shout. "Going our way?"

A flash of two startled gray faces, and they suddenly burst into coordinated wrestling that finally drags the tiny boat to the shore and into the water. They run clumsily back to the rock, grab two long poles, then climb into the boat and sit side by side in the stern, poles trailing in the water. They turn their hoods expectantly toward us.

"Once we get in that boat, Pictree, there's no going back."

"We have no choice. I only hope they'll let me come, too."

I stare at him. "Well, I'm not going alone!"

I step into the boat, followed by Pictree. We sit facing the figures. The hoods consult in thin whispers, then one makes a twirling motion with a stubby blue hand before pointing ahead.

"Come on," Pictree says. "They want us facing forward."

I put one leg over the smooth glass seat — so I can watch both them *and* the waterway ahead. The little figures argue, all the while twirling their hands at me. I shake my head and cross my arms. They mutter, then stand up and pole away from shore.

The little boat slides through the black water. The web of brown branches joins overhead in places. Soon, we come to a crossroads. The twins, as I've decided to call them, point at me, then at the two channels. I shrug and point right.

"I used to play computer games," I whisper to Pictree. "I've learned that it's always best to stay to the right through a maze unless you're given no other choice."

"What's a computer game?"

It would take too long to explain, so I say, "It's like Fidchell inside an electric box."

"Electric? Sounds interesting. Can we play it sometime?"

I laugh and say, "It'd be boring after this!"

After what seems like a hundred right turns and corners, we veer sharply and slide directly into a tiny inlet. Just ahead, the waterway stops at a curved shoreline, where I can see another sandy path.

I point at it and ask, "Do we walk from here?"

The twins shake their heads, talk at me in high-pitched squeals and point down at the black water. I let my Watcher brain translate, calling on the dialect training I've been given. Watchers must learn many different languages. It's difficult, but I soon get the hang of theirs.

"You want me ... *us* to get into the water?"

They nod and squeal in garbled unison. Then I realize what they want me to do.

"Wait — you want me to dive under the water and find an entrance? To *what?*"

They nod frantically. Then they're over the side of the boat with barely a splash, their discarded cloaks floating like small gray islands. Shiny black tails thrash the water, before webbed hands grab the edge of the boat and tip us in. I flounder for a second and yelp when two gray faces with eyes as white as opals pop up in front of me. Green hair floats on the water like waves of sea grass.

I wipe the water from my face and gasp. "You're Muirgens!"

In high, thin voices they say in unison, "Go now. She's waiting for you."

I'm about to ask again what entrance I'm looking for when loud gurgling and frenzied splashing starts up behind me. "Emma!" Pictree gasps. "I — I don't *float!*"

"Try to swim! Use your hands like this." I do a dog paddle to show him.

"I — just — sink!" As if to prove it, his head vanishes, only to bob up again with wild spluttering. The Muirgens laugh with screeching hoots.

"Please!" I call to them. "Help me get him back into the boat! He'll drown!"

Together they say, "We must go now. We are in danger. And you must go quickly, too. They will be here soon."

"Help me first!" I shout. "You must!"

I thrash toward Pictree, grab him and drag him toward the little boat which is now banging against the hedge. A shower of brown leaves drops from above. Pictree grasps the gunnel with one hand. A deep surge of bubbles swirls up beside us, and suddenly Pictree rises into the air and flops into the boat. Two dark tails slide down into the black waters.

"Something helped me. Under the water," Pictree gasps, spitting up water.

"It was the Muirgens. Can you pole the boat to the pathway?"

He pokes one of the poles into the water up to his elbow. "It doesn't touch the bottom. See? How did they move the boat? I can paddle with my hands, though."

The Muirgens' heads pop above water again, chanting, "Beware of Eefa. Beware of the Kuls, her servants of the Waeter. Help our Sover-reign return to her full glory."

"Help who? Who's Eefa? What are Kuls?" I cry.

"We must return to the water caves or they will extinguish us for our treachery." With a slap of their long tails, the Muirgen twins are gone.

I lower my face into the water and look down, hoping this Eefa and her Kuls aren't under there, but don't see anything. And now I'm supposed to dive and find an entrance — to *what*? Why not just use the pathway?

"Stay here!" I call to Pictree. I swim over to the path, but when I try to climb up onto it, I smack into a hard clear surface.

I swim back to Pictree. "There's an invisible wall in front of it. I hate being in unknown water. Who knows what's down there! I guess I have to find this entrance — maybe there's a lever or button in it that opens the walkway."

"I'll — come with you," Pictree says, shivering blue.

I say, "No. I'll find a way out of here without drowning you, I promise! Just sit tight for now."

"I c-can't let you go b-b-by yourself, Emma." Pictree stands up, rocks the boat and falls back on the seat with a wet slap.

"I can't teach you how to swim right now, Pictree. Stay here as my lookout. Hit the water with one of the poles as a warning if you see any-

thing weird. With luck, I'll hear it. Did you understand what the twins said about this Eefa being and
her Kuls?"

"I heard th-them screeching, that's all."

"Do you know someone called Eefa?"

"No, I d-don't," Pictree answers, his snub face
crumpled with worry. "I knew I'd have to l-leave
you alone, but n-not this soon."

I try to smile brightly. "You're not leaving me.
I'll explore underwater and get back as fast as I
can, okay?"

He offers me a shivery smile. "Well, I g-guess
the sooner you go, the sooner you're b-b-back,
right?"

"Right!" I say it cheerfully, even though my
heart's beating like a hummingbird's wings. I take a
deep breath and dive straight in.

11

The maze's spiky wall goes very deep and the water is dark. I can't see an opening anywhere. I rise quickly, wave reassuringly at a blue-faced, shivering Pictree, take a huge gulp of air and dive again.

This time, I change my vision, and the black water becomes a dull green. I swim straight down. Before long, my lungs are aching. I concentrate on opening them and I can feel the change immediately. If only I was a Muirgen. Can I shape-change underwater? I close my eyes and concentrate on making my legs into a mermaid's tail. When I open them again, my legs are still ... legs. Darn! I try again. Nothing. Why didn't they teach anything useful at the Campan? I kept being told, "All things in their time, Watcher." Well, it's time! I try again. Again nothing.

I give up and kick farther down, suddenly catching a glimpse of an irregular opening in the hedge. I poke my head inside. It's dark but I can make out a narrow tunnel ahead. I go into Watcher mode —

best to stay as small as I can. I slide inside with just enough room to flutter my feet and propel myself forward, my arms tight to my sides. There is a deep, slow pounding wash in my ears.

The tunnel seems endless, winding like a water snake, but curving slightly upward. The pounding reverberates through the tunnel, making my ears ache and spurring me on. My lungs are overfilled balloons, pressing against my ribs. I'll drown in this narrow space if I don't find the end of it soon. Just when I'm sure I'll explode, the tunnel takes a sharp upward turn. A light ahead!

The tunnel widens and the light grows brighter. I kick hard. It's an exit, covered by a frosted opaque circle. In the center is a tiny design of two fish chasing each other's tail fins, creating an inner circle. Small hard bubbles forced from my swollen lungs escape my lips. I push my left hand against the design, then yank it back as an icy jolt goes straight up my arm. On the fleshy part of my palm, below my thumb, the fish have been seared into my skin. I hiss in through my teeth, almost blinded by the pain, as the small round gate opens above my head. I aim for the opening.

As soon as I'm through it, a mass of icy water pushes down on me like an enormous hand. I sink rapidly, the vast clear blue light above receding farther and farther. Just when I'm sure my lungs will burst through my ribs, my feet hit bottom. I bend my knees, brace my feet and push hard with my legs. With arms above my head, I begin a fast ascent to the surface. I need to breathe, but I must *not* panic.

Suddenly, to my horror, something grabs one of my legs. Frantically, I look down. My right leg is held by what looks like a piece of black seaweed. I try to untangle it, but the seaweed tightens and with sudden jerks, I'm yanked back toward the bottom.

I grab my small knife from my belt and slash at the twist of stuff holding me. A low bellow sounds below, throwing up frothy spume. A lumpy fish as big as a whale surges out of the bubbles. It's this monster's fin that's wrapped around my ankle. He slides rapidly toward me, his tiny eyes in the thick crusted head full of greedy intent.

As the giant's head looms close, I jab him as hard as I can right in the eye. With a deep echoing screech and a swipe of a giant tail that just misses me, the beast releases me and disappears into the gloom. As I stare at the churning bubbles, icy water suddenly pours into my lungs.

I don't feel any pain, but I can't move. Images of our farm on Earth roll through my mind — the bees bumbling through the puffs of purple clover on a bright sunny day; the wind in my hair as I ride my bicycle along the old highway; my mother collecting honey from the hives; Summer reading on the veranda; Dad, artist of the century, high on a ladder building his ridiculous installation he called the Brute Energy of Bruide — the portal that brought the beings from the other worlds to Earth and changed our lives forever.

Something scrapes my arm. I glance at it listlessly. I'm now caught by one shoulder and one leg under a shelf of rock. An overwhelming sadness engulfs me. I won't see my family again. Or Tom. There was so much I had to do …

Millions of tiny bubbles surround me. They touch my skin, push into my nose, my open mouth, my ears. A dark shadow engulfs me. My heart has stopped. All is quiet now. I'll be free of all my worries soon. I smile at the blue surface above. And I drown.

12

I wake with a jerk. My right arm is floating out beside me, my knife still clasped in my hand, the other arm caught under something. When I remember where I am, the shock of it makes me suck in some water. But I don't choke. I can breathe right through it!

Am I dead? I'm still underwater ... but I'm *breathing*. Something flutters along my neck. A sizzle of alarm streaks through me when I feel soft fluttery skin covering a deep ridge of gills.

I'm lying half under the ledge. Something flashes beside me. What is it? I work my left arm loose, push away from the rock, twist slightly and look down. That's when I get a real jolt. A fish is swimming right below me! Using my arms and legs I try to flail away, but I can't escape — it follows me wherever I go. Suddenly, it dawns on me. My legs are now a green tail with a long, wide fan of salmon-colored tail fins! Scales of translucent green cover my body from my chest down to my wrists. I wiggle my legs and shoot backward about ten feet in a split second.

I laugh, and bubbles pour out of my mouth. I'm not only alive — I've shape-changed! I flick my tail and fly forward. I'm *alive* and I'm — a *mermaid*! I put my knife in my belt and practice swimming — dip and dive, swift and free.

As I do a neat little flip, something silvery zips past me. I see a flash of humanoid features. I swim rapidly away from it, but there it is again moving past in a wink. A Muirgen? Could this be the Eefa they warned me about? Is Eefa a Muirgen? The thing swims toward me through the bubbles. It *is* a Muirgen ... made of ... I focus on it ... of water? Outlined in light? I can see right through it. It flashes away, then swoops close. I stare at the translucent face. It can't be.

Tom?

I put my hands out and yes! I *can* feel his face! But how can this be, when he's transparent? Before I think about what I'm doing, I pull him toward me and kiss him right on the mouth — or at least the side of his mouth. Am I dreaming? No, I feel his hands on my back. I feel them spread across my shoulder blades as he pulls me closer. I'm sure he's going to kiss me back — but he just gives me a lop-sided grin.

I put my hands on his chest and stare at him. It's Tom. It *is*!

He grins at me, swirls in circles, dashes behind me and pushes me gently between the shoulders — giving me a chance to pretend I didn't kiss him.

Have you been here all along? I telepath. *Are you the one who changed me into a Muirgen?*

His clear eyes never leave my face. Then his voice is in my head. *You ... halfway there. I ... helped ... bit.*

I've been so worried. And why is your voice all garbled? You sound like Cill!

He laughs. *Was caught in wall. Work my way through and I ... something changed. Can't control shape. Hard ... me to telepath ... you.*

You've changed, all right! You look like water!

In ... air... invisible. Under water ... different. More myself ... and yet ... He takes my hand. I can feel his cool skin, but it looks as if I'm holding on to a glass hand. He squeezes mine. *... not really me.*

I grip his hand harder. *Did you see my family? Pictree says they're light images, not real. But someone must be holding them somewhere.*

Must find Histal. Didn't expect this. Too dangerous here ... back with me. Not too late. Emma. Tom's telepathing may be fragmented, but his determination is clear.

But there's no going back, Tom! The door is locked. Maybe you can pass through it. I can't. I tried. I have no choice. I have to keep going.

Emma, you must not ... go farther. Too risky!

He swims closer and we float in the heavy water, face to face. My heart aches with the longing to *touch* him again. But I can't — anymore than I can turn around and leave this place. Besides, now the excitement at seeing each other is over, he's remembered who he is. My *Watcher*, my guard — not a man. I can see it in his smooth, expressionless face.

I say, *I can't ... I won't go back, Tom. I mean it.*

He frowns. *Then ... must stay, too.*

Must *stay?* I ask sadly.

Want to.

Even though this could mean another demotion?

I don't think Kinn will judge us too harshly. We didn't ask for ... cunning fog.

You could have stayed on the other side of the cave portal, I say. *You followed me instead of finding Histal.*

He smiles. *Now, in that ... no choice. I'm your Watcher whether ... fired me or not! And ... friend, I hope?*

Tom has known for a long time how I feel. It embarrasses him at times. Maybe he's worried I'll kiss him again. So I return his smile. *Look at you! An owl for months on end and now you're water, wind and air? Hey, hot air — now* that *makes sense!*

He surges around me, throwing a ring of bubbles so thick I can't see. They tickle me and make me laugh.

He breaks through the froth, his head ringed in bubbles. He grins and points up. *Let's see what ... to find here. Sooner this is over ... sooner become Tom ... you'll be sorry!*

I clap my hands around his head and burst the bubbles. *Okay, let's explore. But what about Pictree? He can't swim.*

... safe for now. Let's go.

As we swim up, we come to a layer of clear blue water with shafts of opal light streaming through it. Every few feet, the water becomes colder. Whoever is up there, I'm ready for them — now that Tom is with me again.

WAETER

13

I burst through the surface with a crackling sound. Thin sheets of ice ping and tinkle around my head. The air is dark blue and frigid. My breath bursts out in white billows. I'm in an ice cave. At the far end, a huge structure of ice crystals rises out of the freezing water. It looks as if it was dropped from a great height and the collision caused a circle of water to rise up and freeze in position like a medieval crown. In the center of the icy circle is a long pointed spout of water with a misted ice bubble on top. Something is swimming around inside it.

I look for Tom, my teeth chattering. I'm growing numb, my webbed hands as blue as a Muirgen's. Tom tugs on my arm. I drop down so I can talk to him.

Can you change into something else if we finally get out of this water?

Tried. No luck. I — *keep trying. Trust me ... with you all the time. I haven't ... able telepath in open air ... under water ... easier.*

You're sounding better all the time.

Tom nods and grins. *You're cold and blue as ... Bruide winter sky. Inner thermostat ... Didn't Histal teach ... You must warm up.*

Yes, Histal did teach me, I say defensively. *I just haven't had much practice yet.*

I go inside myself the way Histal taught me. Warmth slides to the tips of my fins and along my arms to my fingers.

I grin at Tom. *Wouldn't Histal be pleased? Bet if he knew where I was, he'd change my inner thermostat to dead!*

Tom laughs. *We'll make sure he understands ... everything.*

If we ever make it back, I add.

Meanwhile ... we're avoiding ... frozen castel over there, aren't we?

Keeping just my eyes and the top of my head above water, I look at the castel again. Who is swimming around and around in that bubble? I drop underwater and say, *The Muirgen twins warned me about some being called Eefa and her minions called Kuls.*

He says, *I wonder who this Eefa is?*

The Muirgens were very afraid of her. I show him the smoky white burn on my palm. *I got it when I opened the portal into here. A symbol of some kind. But of what?*

Could this Eefa have put the light images of your family there? To pull you farther into this world? If so ... why?

Do you think Pictree's missing youngers and my missing family are connected?

I can't see how, but —

A shadow slips past above our heads, and two or three smaller creatures dart around us. I grab my knife from my belt. There's something else — in the distance. I can't make out what it is — just a large, dim shape — that seems to be waiting for us. As I stare at it, the smaller shadows dip and dart and I see the flash of a long black tail with a blood-red fin. Muirgens, but not the twins.

Suddenly a huge bubble breaks away from the shape and rolls toward us. I dodge out of its way. As it passes, the faces of my family turn on its surface.

When I look back, the dark shape is gone. I bob to the surface, determine the location of the ice castel, dive and swim as fast as I can toward it.

14

Tom moves around me on active alert. I keep swimming hard. The water is as clear as a pane of glass. No fish. No red-finned creatures dodging around. So far, so good. Just ahead, four long twisted pillars of ice form an entrance to the structure. The columns are encrusted with feathery ice designs, and each has a statue of a Muirgen sitting on its base looking straight ahead through frosted eyes.

Tom gives me a thumbs-up sign. I swim toward the entrance, the knife heavy in my hand. We enter a circular space glaring with opalescent whiteness.

Tom points. *Look, a vertical water tunnel. Going up?*

Here goes nothing, I mutter.

You won't see me if you have to climb out of the water, but I'll be there.

I nod and rise in the tunnel slowly then pick up the pace. I know where we're headed. To the center of the frozen crown — to the bubble at the top of the ice tower.

The passage narrows as we reach the summit, and suddenly my head pops out of the water. The air smells strongly of fish. Beside me, a set of stairs leads to the bubble overhead. I pull myself onto the bottom step and shape-change to Emma. A splash tells me where Tom is. His wet footprints run up the stairs. I follow, knife in hand.

In the bubble, a shadowy form slides close to the clouded surface, making the same high-pitched noises the twins made. I translate.

"… and here you are, Ena," a little voice squeaks.

"Who are you? Why can't I see you?" And why is she calling me Ena?

"Use your hand," the voice calls.

I run my left hand back and forth on the globe as if washing a window. The mark on my palm heats the frost, and a clear patch forms.

A Muirgen holds a stubby hand close to the window. On her palm is the same fish symbol I have on mine. Her long hair, floating around her head, is pale green, her eyes like moonstones, her skin the faintest blue. The scales that cover her long sinewy body rise in a swirling pattern of prismatic white over small breasts and hips, down to the end of her frost-white tail. On her head is a high row of bubbles, like huge pearls. In each bubble a small sea creature darts. She is strangely beautiful — despite flattened features and a thin mouth.

"Who are you?" I ask, putting my knife back in my belt.

"I am Mennow. It greatly pleases me to see you, Ena."

"My name is Emma."

"It is *you*, that's what matters. We knew you'd come, Ena."

I swallow hard. What does she mean? "How did you know?"

"Because you are *Ena*."

"My parents named me Winter, but *I* changed it to Emma. Not Ena … Emma."

She does a flip and brings her face close to the window. "You were named Ena by the great Druvid Moraan. He said that you would come. My heart is full of hope, oh yes it is!" She claps her hands, and dozens of small colored fish burst out from between them.

"Who … where is this Moraan?"

"Moraan is gone. He chose dissolution — death — rather than risk *her* finding his secrets." Tears bubble from Mennow's eyes, encircling her head. "Oh, how I still grieve for him!"

"What secrets?"

"Why, the hiding places of the four Wands."

"What Wands?" I sound like a parrot, but I can't help myself.

"I am the Regent of Waeter. The Wand I was born to protect was taken from me by Moraan and hidden. *You* must find it — and three more."

"Why me?"

"Because you are Ena."

I sigh. "If Moraan took four Wands, and one was yours — who owned the others?"

"Lilith, Gernac and Pillan. We are the Albion Tetrad — the four Elemental Regents who created the world of Fadanys. We need our Wands back to bring balance and harmony once more."

"What are they?"

"They are the receptacles of our powers. Mine contains the energies of the Waeters." Her voice grows higher, tighter. "The Waeters hold the hidden secrets, the emotions, the temperament — the deep impulses ... the *spirit* of Fadanys. You must use your emotions and impulses to find my Wand."

Mennow puts her palms together and twirls in a circle. "Oh, such happiness ... and such apprehension! I pray to Llyr that you do not fail in this Finder's Quest."

"Finder's Quest? But why me?"

She glares at me. "I've just *told* you!"

Wishing she'd stay in one mood for more than a few seconds, I grind out, "I know ... because I'm Ena. But why did Moraan hide the Wands?"

This time her voice is a hissing whisper. "To protect Fadanys. To protect the Albion Tetrad from the Druvid Eefa. To *help* us, he put us into Dormancy."

"Why don't all of you go and find your own Wands? If you're so powerful, surely you can break out of your confiners."

Mennow shakes her head, and red bubbles fly around her like angry bees. "No, no! We *must* stay confined. Otherwise, our unconstrained forces would destroy our world faster than Eefa could! We need the Wands to *channel* — to control — our powers."

"So you have to send someone to collect your Wands? Do you *know* where they're hidden?"

"Of course not, you silly being!" Then she looks contrite and whines, "But it is so hard to be a captive, Ena, unable to move from this gentle prison Moraan has created, even though it is my — and Fadanys's — protection from Eefa."

"What does Eefa want?"

She spits out a circle of dark blue bubbles. "Eefa? The Wands, of course! She is a powerful Druvid who duped us into believing that she came here to help turn Fadanys into the most perfect of worlds. She used our raw, untouched elements to develop her immense knowledge of magick. She wants to rule Fadanys. She Conjured Kuls, dangerous sea beings as her warriors. Be careful, Ena."

"I saw red Muirgen tails. Was that the Kuls? They —"

Eyes bulging, she screeches, "Kuls are NOT Muirgens!"

I hold up my hands. "Okay, okay! Take it easy."

"Since our imprisonment, Eefa has searched for the Wands, but Moraan has hidden them well. She will follow you, and she will try to trick them away from you. Then she can create her own Tetrad. We will be *destroyed*."

"If a powerful Druvid like Eefa can't find the Wands, what makes you think I can?"

"We don't, of course. But Moraan said that if all went well, you would finish the Quest successfully." She states it matter-of-factly, arms folded.

"If all went well? You mean, if I don't get killed?"

She smiles with great benevolence. "Exactly."

I'm so shocked I can only stare.

"You must try your hardest, Ena. Rely on your strengths, your intellect, your emotions and your creativity. We depend on you."

I think my eyes are bulging out of my head. My brain is whirling with questions. Who is Moraan, anyway? How does he know me? Where did he find me in the first place? Did he hide me on Earth all those years ago? I thought Fergus did. And if Moraan did hide me, why? And what do I do now?

I blurt out, "Why doesn't Eefa just kill you and the others?"

Mennow displays sharp teeth in a wide grin of triumph. "We're safeguarded by Moraan's final protective cunning. As long as the Wands remain hidden, we live — and we'll be safe forever after you find them." Her face falls. "But time is running out, Ena. Once you begin the Quest, a time limit is set. If you don't find the Wands in that time, Fadanys will perish."

"H-how long would I have?"

"It's already begun — the moment you first spoke to me. You have half a mooncrest." Her features loom close, dark with worry.

"H-half a mooncrest? But that's only four Earth days!"

Even though Watchers rely a lot on instinct, I was allowed to have a Mooncrest Timer. During my Seeker's Quest, it was up to my friend Cill to keep time for me. I didn't want to have to rely on someone else if I found myself in a tight spot again, so Histal gave in. But he warned me to use it only in emergencies or he'd take it back. He said I had to develop my own inner clock or I would never become a Master Watcher. But if this isn't a tight spot I don't know what is. The time keeper is in my pouch. I have to set it. I take it out, only to find to my horror, that like my Homing Circle, it's not working.

"My Mooncrest Timer is broken! How am I supposed to know how much time is passing?" I demand.

"You may ask the Regent in each Element and they will tell you — only once, mind you — how much time you have left to complete the Quest. We are able to communicate with each other — but not in much detail, so they can only tell you general times — not exact. You must be swift, Ena. Don't rely on us."

I look around, frantically searching for Tom.

I need *help*.

15

A breeze swirls around my body like a hug. I know it's Tom trying to give me comfort. He knows I have no choice but to take on the Quest. I sigh with relief. I'm not alone.

I change to Watcher mode.

"Aaaah, so you can shape to a Watcher." Mennow smiles her ghastly smile.

I stand as tall as my small body will allow. "I *am* a Watcher. If I'm to find the Wands, I need to ask you questions."

She nods. "Quickly. We have so little time, oh my yes, so little time."

"No *kidding*. You say your Wand holds the power of all the Waeters of Fadanys, including its ... emotions. What powers do the others hold?"

Mennow stretches open her hands. Between each finger is a thin clear membrane. "Gernac's Wand contains the powers of the soil, plants, animals and all that is solid in Fadanys — and, with it, Fadanys's strengths and weaknesses ... its *Physical*

Essences. Pillan's Wand holds the great might of heat and fyre and, with it, the passions, energies — the flashes of *Destruction* and *Creativity* that make Fadanys an ever-evolving world; finally, Lilith's Wand holds the aire, wind, mists, fogs, clouds ... the very breath of Fadanys — its *Logic* and *Intellect*."

"How did Eefa become so powerful, if the Albion Tetrad controlled these things?"

Mennow replies solemnly, "Many spancrests ago, Lilith, Pillan, Gernac and I were part of the Astral Domain — the ancient Elements that created most all the worlds over the ages. The Astral Domain is made up of *many* like us."

She looks at me with a haughty tilt of her chin. "We four got weary of trying to keep so many worlds *balanced*. It is discouraging work. Too many clanns and tribes involved in the Game — *so* destructive! So we decided to make our own world, where the Game would be forbidden. But we should have known our happiness could not last. The Game is an insidious force." Those words are followed by hundreds of black bubbles.

"For a while, it was perfection here," she continues. "No noisy, messy sets of battling Players. However, in time, we realized for it to be a *true* world, we would *have* to select intelligent beings to inhabit it."

"Why didn't you just leave things perfect — as you'd made them?"

"We became ..." Mennow hesitates, then grimaces, "... *bored*. We had no independent beings to guide — or to entertain us. So we sent out Lilith with instructions to choose an intelligent male and female with no strong ties to any particular world or *Game* — lively beings with a purity of *spirit*. She found them — or so she *thought*. A male named Clust and a female called Aibell who had followed the Taithchuant — the wanderlust — for many spancrests. Both were tired of traveling. And they had no connection with any Game. We made them the Sover-reigns of Fadanys."

I gape at her. Clust? Aibell? That's who Huw and Fergus's Druvid Mathus said were the beings that gave me life — my Source.

Was I born to the two Sover-reigns of Fadanys? Is *that* my connection to this world?

16

Mennow is still talking. "— and Clust and Aibell *said* they wanted the same things we did — peace and beauty. And they agreed to populate Fadanys with youngers."

"And did they?"

"Soon after they arrived, they said Aibell was to bear a younger. Before the birthing, they wanted to bring carefully selected beings to Fadanys. After all, their younger would one day need a mate. But to our surprise, they chose two Druvids. Like all Sover-reigns, they said they needed magickal advisers. Moraan came as Aibell's Druvid and Eefa as Clust's."

"And you allowed the Druvids in?"

"Foolishly, yes." This time she spits out dark green bubbles. "We were *not* on our guard."

I say carefully, "And Aibell gave birth to her child?"

"Oh yes! Eefa foresaw it would be a male. But it was a *female*. Then immediately afterward, the male that Eefa predicted was born. A Doubling. It is known that in a Doubling, one younger is open to corrupt forces, while the other to noble virtues. No one knows which until they are almost grown."

Twins. *Was I the girl? If so, how did I become a Watcher?*

I try to concentrate on Mennow's story.

"They called the female Sima, which means 'listener' — and the day after the births, Fadanys welcomed her, as the eldest child, as its new heir. We, the Tetrad, pledged our loyalty to the future Suzarain, endowing her with many gifts. Eefa was *furious* that Sima would rule Fadanys, for a female is bound to the mother. Therefore, Eefa had no control over either mother or daughter."

"Eefa was the boy's Druvid?"

"Yes. Still is. Eefa insisted that the male, Arawn, be heir. His father, Clust, didn't care either way. But Eefa relentlessly pushed Aibell to allow her son to rule. Tired of Eefa's constant complaining and conniving, Aibell gave in to her old wanderlust and vanished. Moraan announced the next day that she had taken Sima with her, as she was rather sickly and needed her mother's care. No one saw them leave. Moraan said Aibell had left him in charge so that if she returned, Sima would rule."

"What about Clust and the boy?"

Mennow lifts her shoulders. "As time went by, Clust grew unhappy without his beloved Aibell.

One night he went away, leaving the boy, Arawn, in the care of *both* Druvids. He said he would return one day with Aibell and Sima. Eefa was *not* to intefere with the way things were set." She cries, "We should *never* have given our fragile world to those who live by the Taithchuant. When Aibell and Clust left, we should have told the rest of them to go as well!"

"Why didn't you?"

Her face grows fierce. "By that time, Eefa was so powerful, we couldn't get rid of her!"

"And she wanted Arawn to rule the kingdom?"

Mennow spews more fiery red bubbles. "We were forced to ask Moraan to stay to keep Eefa under control. She had *secretly* used the elements of this world and her knowledge of alchemy to Conjure magickal beings — to counter the Tetrad."

"The Kuls."

"Yes. As Aibell had not returned, Eefa announced she *would* crown Arawn as Sover-reign of Fadanys on his seventeenth spancrest. Once in power, she would use Fadanys as a home world to set up her ugly Games. But first she would need to gain control of the Four Wands. Moraan was determined to stop her."

"Is that when Moraan hid your Wands and put you in confiners?"

"Yes. And he said *you* would come — when the time was right. If you gather the Wands, Eefa's plans will be defeated."

"But Eefa found out what he had done?"

"And was wild with fury."

I swallow hard. "But she could just kill me, couldn't she? And take any Wands I might have found?"

Mennow swoops to the window. "Killing you would not be in her best interests."

"Why?"

"Moraan set the Quest so that Eefa can't just *take* a Wand from you — if she or any of her servants kill you. But she *can* trick you out of one. And she can take one if you die at another being's hand. You also may *give* her a Wand, of course, which you *won't* do. No doubt she will try to fool you into doing just that. She is clever."

"So she *could* get some other being to kill me."

Mennow looks stricken. "Yes. But Moraan has given you the advantage by carefully hiding the Wands so that only *you* can find them. That is the *theory*, at least."

"Doesn't sound like much of an advantage," I grumble.

"Also," she continues, "guides will show you the portals to each world where a Wand is hidden, but it's up to you to get through the portals. Find the Wands, Ena. Half a mooncrest — or we are doomed. You have no *choice*, Ena."

"If I do it, will my family and friends be returned to Argadnel?"

"I know nothing of *that*." She slides back, her hair covering her face like a green cloud.

"But I —"

She lunges at the window, pressing against it, eyes wide. "*You must listen to Mennow*. Eefa *will* follow you. But you must outwit her. Never let her trick you."

My chest feels as if a giant's hand is squeezing it. "Only if you promise that my family will be safe if I find your Wands!"

"I do not know where the beings of your world were taken."

"Do you know who took them?"

She shrugs. "How can I know more than I *know*, locked away like this?"

I shout, "If you can't guarantee they'll be returned, then forget it!"

I can see she's thinking. Then she nods. "If you find the Wands, we will see that the beings of Argadnel are freed. That is a promise."

I narrow my eyes. "Are you simply a Player in some Game set up by this Moraan? How do I know you aren't in it with Eefa?"

She laughs and a burst of blue minnows spins out of her mouth. "I am Mennow, the Regent of all the Waeters — the great ocean of Fadanys, its rivers, streams, wells, waeterfalls. I *abhor* the Game. I would never give up my regency to Eefa! *My* fear is that you will not find the Wands in time. You are so inexperienced. What was Moraan thinking! Are we doomed ... *are we?*"

I sneer at her, "I *will* do it, not to save the likes of *you* but to save my family! I'll find those Wands — and then decide what *I* want to do with them."

Mennow stares at me with surprised admiration. "You sound like Moraan! Perhaps you *can* give Eefa a good run, after all. Now you must begin your Quest, Ena."

"Mennow ... who *am* I?" I ask, not sure I want to know the answer. "Why was I chosen by Moraan?"

"Moraan told us only that he chose a newly birthed Watcher of good stock and imbued it with special powers and an inner homing device, so it would have to return here. Then he hid it — you — until the time was right."

Does this mean that my life has been laid out since the moment I was born? *Am* I the daughter of Aibell and Clust? If no one saw Aibell take Sima, she — I — might have been left with Moraan. Does that make sense?

"Where ... how do I begin to look for the Wands?" I say through dry lips.

"I can show you the way out of here. The rest you must do on your own. You can choose one being to help you find each Wand. Shout its name and it will come. A Calling is important. Whom you choose may determine where the Wand will lie. For Waeter it should be someone who knows the seas."

"You — you mean I could choose my mother or father?"

She shrugs again. "If you think these beings will help you."

Neither of my parents can swim. Should I choose Tom? Will he come as he is now? But he's already here — and she doesn't know. I'll keep him a secret. Who in my life knows all the seas and oceans of the worlds? Suddenly, a face pops into my head. *No*. Not *him*.

But who else is there?

I look at Mennow. "I don't like the being I've chosen, but —"

"On the other side of the first portal, Call his name and he will come. And remember, your way through the portal depends on your emotions ... your inner spirit."

Mennow raises the hand with the strange brand on it and holds it close to the glass, and I'm thrown forward into waters colder than ice.

17

I thrash around, trying to breathe, then quickly shape-change into Muirgen form.

"Here!" Mennow touches a spot near the bottom of the bubble and an opening appears, dark water swirling in the other side. She pushes a round gold disk into my hand. "To guide you. *Go* now!"

I shove the disk into my pouch. Where is Tom? I look around frantically, but can't see him. Is he on the other side of this bubble? I try to swim toward the glass again, but she grabs me.

"Go!" she says. "Why are you waiting?"

The water outside the dome is rising. There's a flicker of movement in it.

Tom? I telepath. *Can you hear me?*

Faintly, the words *Emma. Go ahead! I'll find you.*

No! I shout. *Hurry up!*

Emma! Go now!

The waters meet over the top of the sphere with a thundering roar. I almost choke on an intake of water when three red tail fins flash on the other side. The Kuls.

"Eefa's here!" Mennow cries. "Once through, Call a name! Get far ahead of her. *Go!*"

I slide into the hole. Behind me comes the loud grating crack of the hatch closing, then the pounding of heavy water in my ears.

I shout the name of the one I've chosen. "Huw!"

A tattooed face appears in front of me, eyes wide, mouth tightly closed. I put my face close to his. His eyes bulge with shock. I nod my head to tell him he's okay, then grab his hand and pull him down the tunnel with me. The maze hedge is all around us. I swim with hard thrusts of my fins, Huw trying to help by kicking his legs. The green light around him is faint now — is he losing air? I look around for Tom. Nothing. Why did I Call Huw's name? What have I *done*?

Ahead, long shafts of light break the watery gloom. I flap my fins and we swoop toward it. Huw's grip is holding — still alive. I head for the light — the maze vanishes as we break through the surface. I pull us up onto a stone floor, Huw choking and dragging in painful gulps of air.

"You — should — have — waited. I could — have transfigured gills ..." he gasps.

"We didn't have time."

I change into Emma and try to stand, but my legs are rubbery, and I fall on my knees.

The black walls of the cave drip with moisture. Lighted torches dot the walls.

"Where the devil are we?" Huw croaks, looking around with bloodshot eyes.

"Where have *you* been since the fog fell over Argadnel? Did you see my family?"

He shakes his head, water spraying off it with bursts of green light. "One minute I was in the Stygia greenhouses, then I was plunged into water, staring into your face! What have you done now, you stupid girl?"

"I did nothing. A thick fog fell at the border cave on Argadnel. I got inside it and after some traveling around, I talked to someone called Mennow. She told me I had to Call on one person to help me. And I Called you."

"But you *hate* me, as you so eloquently put it once. And who is Mennow?"

I tell him as much of the story as I think he needs to know. I lie and say I have only one Wand to find. "I chose you because this is a water challenge and I need someone who knows the waters of the worlds."

He raises one eyebrow. "Is that the only reason?"

"You're a Player and a fighter. You're good at Game strategy, even though this isn't a Game."

"How do you know it isn't?"

I shake my head. "I must trust Mennow when she says it isn't."

"And so you Called me. But you know you can't trust *me*, Emma."

"I also know that in a Game, if you're Called by a Lead Player, you're committed to that Player," I say, haughtily.

He laughs loudly. "But if it isn't a Game, then a Calling means nothing, Watcher."

Huw's right, but I'm hoping that he'll feel a commitment of some kind.

"I've heard of Eefa," he drawls. "A Druvid of huge ambitions. If her Kuls are like those I've met in other waters, you *are* in trouble."

"You mean *we're* in trouble. What do you know about Kuls?"

He gives a dry, you-*must*-be-kidding snicker. "Vicious — half fish, half humanoid. And some can change into water horses."

"Water horses? Like seahorses?"

"I mean like *Eorthe* horses — four legs galloping over the surface of water at enormous speed. Hard to outrun above or below the sea."

I turn away, hardly able to breathe. I telepath to Tom but get no response. I should have chosen him, not Huw. What was I thinking? I glance away from Huw's smirking face before he sees the guilt and fear in my eyes.

"What made you think I'd help you, little Emma of Eorthe?" he asks.

"You've helped me before."

"Only because it suited *me*."

"Maybe you can be of some use to *both* of us again." I point to the water lapping at the sides of the round opening where we emerged. "Can you tell where we are?"

"I doubt it. If this is a new world, I'll be no use to you in identifying the waters." Then he adds, "By the way, what makes you think I'll give you the Wand if I find it?"

"I'm the one who'll find it. You're only here to help me."

He snorts and walks over to the watery opening. At the same time, I reach into my pouch and read the disk Mennow gave me.

Waeter Pneuma
Submissive, weak, pliant
yet fit to attack the strong and powerful.
At the Seilisdear
Come close to Varra and take the deur
Then Call the name, and allow the sorrow
to slip through your grasp to fall
Upon the Muir Moon

I can understand most of the words, but I have no idea what they *mean*. Still, Mennow gave it to me for a reason. She said I'd have to use emotions to find the Wand. But what does *sorrow* refer to? I slip the disk inside my Watcher's pouch again, then go to where Huw is crouched, staring down into the dark water.

In a tight voice he says, "This water smells familiar. It better not be what I think."

"And what is *that* supposed to mean?" I say. I watch as he dips a blue-tattooed hand into the pool. When he pulls it out, the tattoos are a deep maroon. He shakes his head as if in disbelief.

I laugh and say, "Your hand is like litmus paper, isn't it?"

A dark glower.

"Well?" I ask. "Where are we?"

He doesn't answer. He walks around the cave smacking his hand against the walls. At the ninth slap comes the deep sound of stone scraping against stone and a narrow entrance opens up.

"Where *are* we?" I repeat, but Huw is already striding down the passage. I follow quickly before the entry closes.

"Hey!" I shout. "I'm in charge here. I decide — what's *that*?"

We're in a small room. The walls are black stone. Set into the far wall is a round windowlike aquarium filled with light and clear green water. I peer into it, but it's empty, except for a trail of bubbles circling the glass. On either side of the little aquarium are two identical stone faces with unseeing eyes, flattened features and thin lips, like the twin Muirgens.

Huw slaps his hand on the glass. Nothing happens. I hold my breath and lay my hand on it. The trail of bubbles circles faster and faster, multiplying, splitting apart and finally forming four images: Mom, Dad, Ailla and Summer.

"Wh-what does this mean?" I whisper.

"How should I know?" Huw snaps.

I hear faint whispering coming from the stone faces.

"They're repeating the same thing over and over again," Huw says.

"But what?" I wail.

"Listen, girl!"

I listen hard. The whispering is hushed and fast, but suddenly I understand. I press my knuckles to my teeth to keep from crying out.

Huw says, "You understand?"

I nod.

"One must be chosen," they hiss. "If you fail in your task, the one will die. One must be chosen. If you fail in your task, the one will die" — on and on again and again until I want to scream.

"I can't," I say, backing away. "This is too horrible … too awful." I turn to leave the room, but the door's gone.

Huw says gruffly, "You should choose the one who would *ask* to be chosen."

"But why isn't my face there, too? I could pick myself then! I won't choose any of my family!" The room spins, and I feel Huw's arm around my shoulder.

"If you succeed in your task, then whoever you choose won't die," he says. "You must choose the strongest, then find Mennow's Wand in order to save that life."

I look at the four dear faces. How can I choose one to die?

Huw smiles. "The Watcher Kinn hasn't done a very good job making you an independent Watcher, has it? Your ties to this Eorthe family are still too strong. Whoever set this Quest obviously wants to see if you can handle your emotions. Make a decision. Prove you can do it, Watcher."

The whispering Muirgens, the glowing faces of my family, the smell of the water dripping down the walls, Huw's watchful eyes, all fuse until I feel I'm going to blow up. Huw shakes me. I take three deep breaths. There's no way out. I must *make* a choice.

I walk up to the glass. "I know you'd want it this way, Dad." I press my hand against his gentle face.

The whispering stops, the images fade, except for Dad's, and the wall opens. Huw walks through. I can't move. I can't even cry. Does this pain in my stomach have anything to do with sorrow? Is this what the disk meant? It doesn't feel like sorrow. It feels like I want to crush anyone in my way with my bare hands.

Suddenly, in my head, I hear my dad's voice, telling me to keep going, never give up. That life is an adventure and worth all the risks. He's said it many times before — now's my chance to believe.

I won't let him down. I run through the opening in the wall and it slides closed with a grating crash.

18

I come out into a small cove surrounded by high walls of ebony shale. A slow wash of green waves slides up and down a curving span of black sand. The far end of the cove is thick with fog.

"Damn and blast," Huw says, then, "What will you give me if I find this Wand?"

I shout. "I'll find it! You're here to help *me*!"

He sighs. "Okay ... we'll find it *together*. You certainly won't find it *without* me, Watcher." His face twists into a tight humorless grin. "So what *will* you give me?"

"How about your *life?*" I say.

"Don't play games with a Game Player." His sly face comes closer. "Not with your *father's* life in the balance."

"Druvid, if we don't find Mennow's Wand, all of us will die." I hold out my hand. "So, why don't we call a truce?"

He grins his fox grin, takes my hand and puts his other over it. "Yes, why not? Truce ... *for now*. Let's see what I can Conjure for you."

He goes to the shore and shouts a word over and over. It sounds like, "Fin, fin, fin!"

"So you *do* know this place. Where are we?"

He ignores me, paces, then shouts again. A few moments later we hear a slow bell-like chime and the rhythmic sound of paddles slapping the water. Through the mist emerges a little vessel made of water reeds. At the bow, five small bells dangle from five leathery leaves.

There are two beings in the boat, one rowing, the other standing, his arms crossed over his chest. He has the head of a seal, with enormous liquid eyes and a narrow human nose covered in soft brown hair. The lower part of his face has human lips the color of dark chocolate and a narrow chin. Around his long furry neck hangs a Celtic knot of gold. His arms are furred, the hands long, the fingers webbed with inky skin, ending in thick black nails. His round head is smooth with flattened fur, his ears tiny and black. A garment of green and yellow sea grasses is wrapped around his lower body, tucked through his legs and into his waistband to create knee-length pantaloons.

"Greetings, Finn," Huw calls.

The rower neatly docks the boat. He's smaller than the one Huw called Finn, but both have sloped narrow shoulders, long flat muscles and large webbed feet.

Huw glances at me, then talks rapidly to Finn in grunts and squawks. I try to translate, but he's talking too fast. Finn answers in the same rapid way, looking over at me now and again. Then, with a courteous bow toward me, he slows his speech and I can understand.

He lays a cold hand on the top of my head. "I am Finn, of the Selkie Clann of this world. You have come on a Finder's Quest, Watcher." I nod my head under the weight of his hand. His liquid eyes are kind, but there's a sharp glint there, too. "Huw tells me you are under the threat of a great loss. I am sorry for that."

"Will you help me?"

He nods. "If you were human I would not. Our ancestors once lived on Eorthe. The humans made the lives of the Selkies intolerable — we were forced to leave and find a world of our own along with Eorthe's Muirgen Clann."

"How do you know Huw?"

He gives Huw a long hard look. "Huw and I go back a long way — but we have not always been on the same side. Still, I owe him a favor. Is that not so, Druvid of Celtoi? And when it is done, I owe you nothing more."

Huw nods sharply and growls, "Nor will I help you fight your old Game, Finn. Let's get on with this one."

"This isn't a Game — it's a Quest," I say. "What Game is Finn involved in?"

They both look at me, then Huw smacks Finn's shoulder and laughs. Clearly I'm not going to get an answer. Finn directs us toward the little boat. As Huw walks to the shore where it rests, Finn takes my arm and murmurs, "Do you know anything about your destination, Watcher?"

I whisper back, "I only know I have to go near something called the *Seilisdear* and the *Muir Moon*."

"Aah! Well, I suppose I shouldn't be surprised."

"Do you know this Seilisdear place?"

"Yes. What is it you wish to find there?"

"I can't tell you that," I say as politely as I can. "Did Huw tell you about the Druvid Eefa and her Kuls? They're chasing us."

Finn frowns, but doesn't answer me. We walk to the small vessel and he growls at Huw, "So ... you have brought my clann *more* danger, Huw. Eefa and her Kuls. When I have taken the Watcher to her destination, you will no longer Call me. I will not answer."

To my amazement, Huw looks hurt. That's a first.

"It's the Watcher they're after, not me," he says, but Finn turns his back on him and helps me into the boat.

"I hope you succeed in your Quest, Watcher," he says to me. "But after I leave you at your destination, do not expect any more help from me. Climb aboard."

Huw calls out, "Where will you take us? This is a dangerous place for me, too."

"You'll know soon enough," Finn says, then directs his oarsman seaward, and we push off into the mist.

19

I'm sitting on a straw seat in the middle of the little boat, facing the stern. The echo of the stone walls is gone and there are choppy green waves on all sides. The boat leaves behind a long open passage in the thick mist, but only more rough water is visible. I wonder where we are and how long it will be before I can find the Wand. If Huw knows this place, then it can't be Fadanys. The portal has led us to a known world. But which one? And how long will it take to find this first Wand? Time is ticking by, but I can't tell how fast. I wish my Mooncrest Timer was working. I can only hope Mennow was right, and the other Regents will give me some idea of how much time is left as I continue my search for the Wands. I swallow down panic and look around to distract myself.

Huw is sitting in the bow, which is good — I don't have to look at his smug tattooed face. I bet he'll try to steal Mennow's Wand when we find it — probably to sell it to Fergus of Cleave. I wouldn't put it past him to peddle it to Eefa herself. He's nothing as grand as Fergus's Druvid Mathus — or as powerful as this Eefa, who I hope I never meet — but still a shrewd and artful Druvid.

Will the aquarium portal stop Eefa from getting through?

I sit up and stare far down the watery passage behind us. What was that? Something flashed in the distance. No! Surely that wasn't the flicker of a red tail! I focus hard. A red fin surfaces, slaps the water and dives again. Oh, jeez, there's another one. And a third — no four, five — six, too many!

One pops its head above water and I let my Watcher eyes zoom in on it. It's hideous, with squashed heavy features the color of wet concrete. Right beside it, another head surfaces for a split second, and my stomach shrinks into an icy fist. The face is frog-belly white with bulging eyes surrounded by green-spotted goggles. Across its mouth is a silver rectangle from which a green tube rises up on either side of the head, ending in a cluster of clear balls like air bubbles. Over its head is an orange skullcap with sharp green spines.

It *has* to be Eefa.

"They're here!" I shout, pointing at the creatures relentlessly churning behind us.

"Who's here?" calls Huw.

"Eefa and the Kuls. How did they get past the portal?"

Finn snarls, "Looks like we made it just in time. Rower, come alongside quickly."

The rower gives one final strong pull on the

oars, lifts them high out of the water and we drift.

"Keep rowing. Don't stop!" I shout, but he ignores me.

I'm about to shout again when the boat thumps a rounded wall so high I almost tip out of the boat trying to see its top. It's made of the same reeds as the boat. Dozens of brown heads peer down at us. It's a huge ship!

Finn bellows, "Down creels! All hands — enemy to stern. SWARM!"

The air is suddenly filled with brown bodies as hundreds of Selkies dive over the side. They hit the water with barely a splash, then like a school of brown herring they slide past and under us, toward the Kuls. Silver weapons glint on their backs.

A basket bobs in front of me. Finn orders me to get in. Huw is already in another creel. Finn leaps onto the rope holding mine, his feet creating a dark lid overhead.

"Lift!" he shouts. "Rowers in place!"

As our creel moves quickly through the air, hundreds of curved oars appear out of the belly of the enormous boat like the ribs of a fish. We no sooner reach the deck than Finn jumps off my creel and cries, "Pull for Rodach Burlam!"

With the creak and slap of oars, the boat slides forward. In seconds we're flying over the water. The deck is narrow and the reeds are the color of the water. At a distance, the ship may seem to disappear — if we're lucky.

Finn turns to his rower, who came up on Huw's creel. "Take the Druvid to my cabin and post a guard."

As Rower leads him away, Huw calls out, "Don't forget to release me when we arrive! Remember, Emma, if it wasn't for me, Finn wouldn't be here!"

But Finn is more interested in what's going on over the side of the ship. "Blasted Kuls!" he growls. "They're harder to outrun than a bull-nosed shark."

I follow his gaze and my stomach lurches. The Selkies swarm Eefa and her Kuls, slowing them down, but in the distant churning spume, Eefa suddenly lifts out of the water — higher, higher — mounted on a blue horse. Ten more horses rise, each one carrying a rider. Tails and manes flying, the horses quickly gain on us.

Finn bellows, "SLEW!"

The boat tacks back and forth, seeming to flip right around and aim for the horses. Suddenly, the horses are gone. Finn stands in the middle of the deck shouting orders to the rowers.

Soon he calls to me, "Relax, Watcher. We've outrun them."

I'm dizzy from the jerky movements of the boat and have to sit next to a gunnel and close my eyes. In a few minutes the nausea subsides. I slide to the deck and fall asleep.

When I open my eyes again, the ship has slowed. *Why?*

20

The boat is drenched in a faint purple light. The unhurried slap and creak of the paddles tell me we're not in danger. I walk to the bow and watch as we ease into a lagoon, its walls covered in vines and palmlike trees. A waterfall foams into dark green water clogged thick with plants. Above is a dark mauve sky.

Finn stands beside me. "We call this tarn Rodach Burlam. One of our secret coves. As close as we can get to what you seek."

"Have we outrun the Kuls?"

"For now. But you must leave my boat, for my clann's safety is threatened."

"I'm truly sorry, Finn."

He bows slightly, but his face remains grim.

"Is the Seilisdear in this cove?" I ask as the boat slides to a stop alongside a flat stone. The thundering waterfall sprays us with warm mist. I can see a dim opening behind it. A plank slides from the ship and claps down on the rock.

Huw arrives, led by Rower. "I'm not familiar with this spot."

"I bet we have to go behind that waterfall," I say.

"It is so," Finn says.

"But where does it lead?" I ask.

"Your Druvid knows," Finn snaps, his eyes alert, angry.

"Why *did* you answer Huw's Call if you dislike him so much?" I ask.

"My clann roams these seas. We hide in covered inlets, dodge and weave when danger comes near. We can hear distress from any corner of this kingdom ... and we know which are real and which aren't." Huw looks uncomfortable as Finn continues. "It's curious how hard it is to ignore alliances of one's youth. Act in haste and later regret it."

"You know I had no choice," Huw says. "And I never betrayed you."

Finn smiles grimly. "That is so. You only deserted us. But that is in the past. And I will not regret this voyage, for your young Watcher needed a guide, and I am glad I could help her."

Huw steps forward as if to say something more, but Finn says to him, "The young Watcher has a fair heart. You are a knight of the Celtoi. Do not let that heart down." He turns to me. "I wish you success in your Quest, Watcher. We must go. Rower!"

Rower leads us smartly off the ship. When he returns, the plank vanishes, the oars appear, and the ship slides away from the pier and is gone.

"You used your old friendship with Finn knowing you'd endanger his clann. Even though you
deserted him once," I say.

Huw growls, "You know nothing, Watcher."

"Well, I know who I'd chose if I had to pick one
of you as a friend!" He doesn't answer, except for a
small snort.

I look up at the purple sky. The sea, the lagoon,
the falling water — they're all green. I choke out,
"Oh no! It can't be. Fomorii? Mennow didn't
say —" But then I remember her words: *Whom you
choose may determine where the Wand will lie.*

I repeat it out loud in disgust.

"So that's why we're here?" Huw says. "Because
you chose me. Clever Moraan. A movable Wand!
If you'd called on Tamhas, the Wand might be in
the Watchers Campan, a much friendlier place.
We're about to enter the castel of a Queen who
wants both our heads for beating her at the Battle
of Moling Bridge. If she catches us, she'll boil us
in seawater and feed us to her fish!" He laughs
loudly.

"I hate you."

He grins. "You never do things the easy way, do
you, Watcher?"

He's right. I chose him over Tom and look where
it's got me. Talk about a twisted sort of justice! But
curiously, I feel a tiny surge of hope. Huw knows
this place well. He lived in the castel as Rhona's

Druvid. And if he doesn't desert *me*, I stand a fair chance of finding the Wand and saving Dad.

Just as quickly, the hope sinks. Tom should have found his way to me by now. Where is he? He can't be dead. I'd *know* if he was dead. And what about Pictree? I abandoned him and now I'm stuck with a being I can't trust as far as I can throw him. I *deserve* to be boiled in seawater and fed to Rhona's fish. My father will die because I loused it all up. A huge sob breaks through.

Huw says jovially, "All isn't lost, Watcher. You still have *me*."

"We'll get caught as soon as we enter her castel," I growl. "It's hopeless."

"I didn't know Watchers gave up so easily. It's like you don't want to save your Earth father —"

I draw my knife and lunge at him. He leaps out of the way and crows, "If I die, you'll also die and so will Sweeney."

That snaps me out of it. I push my knife back into my belt and take a deep breath.

"Tell me exactly what you know about the location of this Wand, Emma. I'm not going in there without knowing where to look!"

"I have to find something called the Seilisdear … and a Muir Moon."

"The Seilisdear? *Interesting.* A rare jewel. The Muir Moon is very near it. They are Rhona's prized possessions."

"Then you know where we're to go?"

Huw barks out a dry laugh. "Oh yes, Rhona's private sanctuary. No one is allowed in but her — and one chosen servant." He shrugs. "It *used* to be me."

"Let's go then!" I run toward the waterfall.

"We'll have a tough time getting in. The Bluemen of Mirch patrol the castel. They're all over it, like barnacles on a ship's hull."

I turn around to say something, but stare at the heavy water plants that crisscross the surface of the pond.

"Aaah no. Now what!" he moans.

I gasp, "Something ... swimming through those lily pads. I saw ... red fins."

He pushes me through the waterfall and into a dark passage.

"Can't we block the waterfall entrance?" I'm wringing my hands.

"I was just thinking the same thing."

"You're a Druvid. *Do* something!" I command. "I have yet to see you use magick of any power."

He sneers, "*Really?* Well, it's *your* Quest. I can only help, remember? But first you'll have to make the water stand still."

"I'm not a Druvid, I'm a Watcher."

"If you can't do a simple thing like this, then —"

"Okay!" I shout. "But it won't work!" Furiously, I imitate every Master Watcher and Druvid I've ever seen, my hands sweeping over the entrance, my voice commanding the water to stop.

And it does.

While my mouth hangs open, Huw laughs, walks over to the wall of water and starts to jab at it with his fingers. With each jab, a huge-headed fish with a double row of enormous pointed teeth appears. Soon dozens of slate-gray muscular bodies swim back and forth, teeth exposed, waiting for prey.

"Wow!" I say. "You *can* do magick."

Huw slaps my back. "Not a bad team, eh? Eefa will have great difficulty getting through this double cunning, but she'll do it eventually, so let's get going."

With that, he runs down the corridor, me hard on his heels, still amazed at what we've just done. Soon, we come to a break in the wall smeared with a spider's web, a tumble of rocks beneath it. I poke my head through the web and we step into a narrower passage. Huw flicks one hand and the rubble fills the hole again.

"Well, I'll be a purple bakke," Huw whispers, creeping to the end of the passage. "Here's another breach, behind this wall hanging. This has to be Finn's doing." He chuckles. "A secret way into the castel. And I bet he's put his own cunning on it, so the Bluemen haven't picked up on it."

"Is Finn a Druvid?"

"Finn is an Ollav — a Sover-reign to the Selkie Clann, but also a Druvid. Ollavs are rare beings. Rhona would give the Muir Moon to get rid of him. He is a threat to her kingdom every day he remains alive. Many believe he is the true Sover-reign of Fomorii. He —?" He stops and holds a finger to his lips.

A tramp of feet comes toward us.

Huw whispers, "Bluemen."

He pulls back the edge of the tapestry just in time to see four tall, muscular beings with scaly arms and legs and thick spine fins marching away from us. They're wearing garments like Finn's, of a rich blue. Their heads shine with dark blue scales.

"They'll be back," Huw says. "With luck we can slide along the halls without them picking up our scent. I can't transmute invisible, but you can, for both of us."

"I can maintain invisibility for only short periods of time."

"That'll do. Let's go."

Hand in hand, we step out of our hiding place. I gaze around at the network of gilded water plants that snake over every inch of the rounded walls and ceiling. At regular intervals are gorgeous tapes-tries, glowing with undersea life, and doors of translucent black, filled with more water flowers, twisted grasses and the large flat fish with spiky teeth that Huw created in the waterfall — only these are suspended forever in their dark shadows. The floor is thick green glass under which water bubbles and slides. The deeply chilled air smells of sea salt and fish.

Huw suddenly growls, "What is this? I said invisible — not *half* invisible."

Uh-oh, he's a blur of green light.

"Sorry." I go inside myself and concentrate hard, but when I open my eyes I can still see him — and the faint outline of my own feet. "I — I don't know what's wrong."

He lets out a snort of disgust. "Well, this is a mess of dead fish, isn't it?"

I'm not listening. I'm looking at a ghostly figure right behind Huw.

"Tom! You're here!" I want to hug him, but Huw's grip holds me in place. "And I — I can *see* you."

Tom looks down at himself and lets out a small bark of surprise.

Huw hustles us back behind the wall hanging. "Great purple bakkes!" he exclaims. "*Now* what?"

"Where have you been?" I ask Tom, grinning from ear to ear, but wanting to burst into tears.

He says, "I've never left you. Being invisible has its advantages. It let me Watch over you — and make sure Huw or his friends didn't do something underhanded."

"But your powers are weakened," I say. "You could have been seriously hurt."

He frowns. "Don't you worry — I would have *found* a way to help you."

I nod. "I know you would."

"Enough talking!" Huw says. "What do we do now?"

"Clearly, Rhona has put a cunning on the castel to keep an invisible Watcher from invading," Tom replies. "But it doesn't work as well as she thought it would, it seems. Curiously, it's made me *more* visible."

"Must be her new Druvid. Not as good as I was!" Huw, says, smiling with satisfaction.

"Can you undo the cunning, Huw?" Tom asks.

Huw runs his hand in the air around Tom, checking the power of the cunning. "It would take too much time."

"Can you turn me into something else?"

"It would have to be something your body is used to." Huw smiles wickedly. "An owl, for instance?"

"Do it!" I say.

"Not an owl. Please, not an owl!" Tom moans.

"You'd have a better chance of getting away if we get caught," I say. "*One* of us has to be free to rescue the others."

"All right! Owl it is. I'll be able to scout things out."

Huw sends a crackling swish of green light over Tom. When it fades, a beautiful barn owl remains.

Tom flies to my shoulder. I lean my head against him and telepath, *I'm sorry, Tom, I should have Called you.*

You did the right thing, Creirwy. And I was there when you had to make your terrible decision about your father. I know it doesn't help to hear it, but these things will make you stronger — and more determined to succeed.

It doesn't feel like that now.

Huw sneers, "If you two are through gazing into each other's eyes, can we organize this invasion?"

"We'll hide here, wait for the guards to go by, then make our move," I say. "As long as you know exactly where to go."

Huw nods. "We're in the far north corridor. We'll follow the guards at a distance, turn right, cut across the sea garden and go straight to Rhona's sanctuary. Easy."

"Right," I say. "Tom will fly above us and telepath to me what he sees."

"Fine," Huw says. "But we'll all have to move quickly and cautiously, so they don't see us. Here they come."

The tramp of feet echoes in the distance. My pulse hammers in my ears as the four guards pass by. When they turn the corner, Huw pulls me into the corridor and we follow them. Tom's wings beat above us. Finally, we stop at an open doorway. Huw peers around it. With a sharp tug on my arm, he leads me into an enclosed courtyard filled with the rush and splash of waterfalls. Each is a different

color but all drop into a huge pond frothing with
fish and toadlike creatures that dart and croak and
plop from one water plant to another. Throughout
the pond are shell-strewn bridges. How can someone as cruel as Rhona create such beautiful things?

We skirt the waterfalls, getting soaked, but suddenly, with a thrashing of water, Bluemen rise out
of the pond, dragging plants behind them.

"The yellow waterfall!" Huw calls. He gallops
toward it, almost yanking my arm out of its socket.
Instantly I feel the weight of Tom on my shoulder.

"Get this door open!" he growls.

Huw touches a group of silver sea urchins on the
door and repeats three words that sound like "Cull,
cule, crete." The sea urchins squeak and scatter as
if they've been given a jolt of electricity. The door
swings open, we lunge through, and it slams shut
on the guards' shouts. Huw and I slide our hands
through the air. A blue glaze, like steel, hardens
over the entrance. The banging of fists and weapons
grows distant.

Huw cries, "Good work, Emma!"

We're in a wide grotto, the floor as shiny as an
emerald sea, the roof supported by black pillars.
The floor has been cut away to form a simple Celtic
knot, the open sections foaming water. Flickers of
shadows and flashes of watery light undulate over
the walls, making my head spin. In the center of the
knot, a tiny bridge leads to a chair in the shape of a

seated Muirgen, her long tail trailing down to form a footrest. On her head is a crown with a big yellow pearl in the middle.

Has Huw led me into a trap? How can I find a Wand in Rhona's private sanctuary?

Huw says, "When Rhona won this world in a Game, she called it Fomorii, in honor of the undersea world her ancestors inhabited on Eorthe. She set a Game to eliminate all remaining competition — those who had lived in harmony for thousands of spancrests. She hunted down the Selkies and Muirgens, including the Muirgens' queen, Varra. She sits on Varra's image, to show who's in power. But Rhona hasn't captured Finn yet."

"What a *monster* Rhona is!" I snarl.

Huw laughs. "Be careful or Rhona will turn *you* into a chair." He strides to the center of the knot. I follow. The face of the Muirgen statue, Varra, is similar to Mennow's, with slanted eyes and a flat nose, but her lips are full.

Huw points to the yellow pearl on her crown. "That, my dear little Watcher, is the Muir Moon."

I suck in a sharp breath. "And the Seilisdear?"

He points to a dark alcove. Inside, a flower stands on a silver stem. It looks like one of the blue irises my mother used to pick by the stream near our bee farm. But this flower is clear yellow, its throat encrusted with tiny orange pearls. Water drips off its petals onto a black stone.

"But I don't see a *Wand*," I say. "That's what I'm supposed to find. A *Wand*."

"And what do you think a Wand should look like?" Huw asks.

"I don't know! A stick of some kind. Not a big glass flower on a silver stem."

"The Seilisdear grows along the edges of the sea. And they are extremely rare. But there is only one Seilisdear made of the purest topaz."

"I need a *Wand*," I insist. "Moraan wrote directions on the gold disk Mennow gave me, but I don't know what they *mean*!"

"A gold disk? What does it say? Tell me!" Huw demands.

Tom says, "Whisper it to me and we'll work it out together."

Huw leans close. "Whisper it to *me* and I'll *know* what to do." Suddenly his face loses its smirk and softens to something that definitely isn't *Huw*. "I won't let you down, young Watcher. Tell both of us. We'll do it together. Three is the most fortunate of numbers in battle."

I hesitate.

"What have you got to lose?" Huw asks impatiently. "Rhona will be here in moments. Think! I am her enemy. You know that. I am as much at risk as you."

"Do it, Emma." Tom's voice is wary, but firm.

I repeat the words:

> *Waeter Pneuma*
> *Submissive, weak, pliant*
> *yet fit to attack the strong and powerful.*
> *At the Seilisdear*
> *Come close to Varra and take the deur*
> *Then Call the name, and allow the sorrow*
> *to slip through your grasp to fall*
> *Upon the Muir Moon*

"Deur means 'a tear,'" Huw says. "Varra's tears? Yours?"

Tom says, "Mennow said you should rely on your emotions to find the Wand. You've already opened the portal to this world using them. Maybe *that's* the key to this message as well."

I walk across the small bridge. I touch Varra's smooth face and a single drop of moisture forms in one of her eyes, drops and solidifies on my finger-tip. Sadness and despair flood me as I gaze at the teardrop in my hand. I hold it against the Muir Moon. The silver setting melts away and the heavy pearl falls into my hands.

Now what? I look at Varra's face. It is still and immobile, but I sense that she is aware of every-thing I'm doing. I go to the Seilisdear flower. Below the cluster of pearls is a shallow cup in a petal, water from the flower spilling over it. In my head the last words on the disk repeat them-selves.

Come close to Varra and take the deur
Then Call the name, and allow the sorrow
to slip through your grasp to fall
Upon the Muir Moon.

I walk close to the flower and place the pearl in its shallow cup. It fits perfectly. The message says to Call a name. But whose? I put my fingertips on the Muir Moon pearl.

I see bodies of Muirgens lying broken all along the shoreline around Fomorii Castel as Rhona stands triumphant on a balcony high on the castel wall. Hanging beside her in a creel, like the one that loaded us onto Finn's boat, is a Muirgen. Her jet black tail, twice as long as Mennow's, hangs limp in the air. Her dark gray hands grip the bars of the basket. She is very beautiful, her face dark blue, her eyes as pale as sea pearls, her hair rusty fronds lying wet down her slender back. She wears a strange black skullcap that rises above her forehead into two clear black spheres with a yellow pearl in the center. I'm standing somewhere in the crowd below. The sadness and defeat on the Muirgen's face hurt my heart. For this is the past and I know I can't help her.

My tears splash over my hands and mingle with the water flowing over the great pearl. Suddenly it pushes against my fingers and rises into the air. It hovers above the yellow sea flower. Whose name am I to Call? If I don't Call the right one will everything be lost? Will Mennow die? And my father? Why did Moraan do this to me? I can't *think*.

"Moraan, *why?*" I call out.

Suddenly the pearl shatters, spraying its light around the little alcove and arcing over my head. The Seilisdear flower bursts and in its place stands a rod of water with two comma-shaped curlicues swirling across its top. The Wand! My dad is safe!

There's a loud pounding at the grotto door.

Huw whispers, "Take the Wand. I'll try to hold them off."

I grab at the rod of water, expecting my hand to go right through it, but it's as solid as the pearl had been. To my amazement, it suddenly forms a small blue sphere. Immediately, I'm filled with an electric surge that makes my body hot from the pumping of my own blood. Frightened, I drop the sphere into my pouch just as Rhona and a pile of Bluemen charge into the room. I back away from the alcove, searching for a way out.

Rhona sweeps across the floor, her cape with its puffed hood spiked like a sea urchin flowing behind, her eyes taking in everything at once. Two hounds lope beside her, their nasty yellow eyes focused on me. In her high tinny voice, she cries, "The Muir Moon is gone! They're stealing my treasures!"

The Bluemen move with a swiftness and ease that is terrifying. Tom flies at them, talons outstretched, but is flung away like a feather duster.

"H-huw!" I cry, pulling out my knife. "Wh-what do we do?"

Huw calls out one word — "*Dive!*" — then flings a green light over Tom before drawing a triple-edged sword out of the air along with a wide shield.

"I'll fight, too. You must come with us," I cry.

Tom appears beside me in ghost form. He grabs my arm. "Let's go! Now!"

Huw shouts, "Emma! Save your family. Dive!"

He's surrounded by Bluemen and two slavering hounds. To one side of the fray, two ghostly figures stand watching. Who are *they*? One turns and its gray form leaps toward me. At the same moment, a figure separates from the throne and dives into the water.

I'm right behind her.

21

I change into Muirgen form and swim as hard as I can between the narrow walls of the water maze, searching for an opening. Varra's long black tail thrashes ahead.

I telepath to Tom. *There has to be a way out! They had to fill this water maze, and there must be pipes that lead to the open ocean. Maybe from there we can Call Finn.*

Tom's silvery form slides beside me. *Up there — just ahead — Varra!*

The dark Muirgen waits for us, pointing at a small hole in the wall. I look into her strange blue face. I don't know what I'm looking for — recognition? But her features give nothing away. She pushes me toward the hole, turns and swims away with swift flicks of her tail.

She's shown us the way, Emma! Rhona's guards are behind us! Go! Go!

The Bluemen are as fiercely quick underwater as above. I aim straight at the opening expecting to hit my shoulders on it, but I slide right through. Behind us comes a roar of fury from the Bluemen.

They're too big to go into the pipe, Tom calls in my head. *But they'll know where the other end comes out in the ocean. Move, Emma! Or they'll be there waiting for us!*

Where did Varra go? I cry. *They'll kill her — and Huw! We should have fought.*

No. Rhona would have killed you. We can't do anything for Huw and Varra.

The pipe is long and twisting. The end comes as a shock. One second we're in darkness, the next we're skimming through green-lit open water.

Dive lower, Tom orders, *and travel along the sea floor. They'll assume we'll head to the surface. Hurry!*

All he's done is yell at me to hurry and now he's ordering me to dive. He's right, though, darn it. The ocean floor is purple sand with clumps of waving plants and flashing schools of fish. I skim lower. After swimming for ages, Tom nagging me the whole way, I slide behind a large rock to rest.

We shouldn't stop, he says.

Tom, I'm tired. Go on ahead if you want. Besides, I have to think about where we're supposed to be headed. We could end up going in circles.

He frowns, then nods reluctantly.

Is there any way we can go back and help Varra or Huw? I ask.

No, Emma. Don't even think it. We must save the Wand for your family's sake. Those Bluemen are too dangerous to face on our own.

I know you're right, but I hope Varra is okay — and I never thought Huw would — I choke up. *I didn't like him much, but he came through in the end.*

Tom is in his patronizing mentor mode. *He was committed to you by the Call. The important thing now is getting back to Fadanys — assuming that's our goal.*

I think hard, then it comes to me. *Maybe the Wand will lead us!*

I take the sphere of Waeter from my pouch. It instantly turns into Mennow's Wand. *Yikes!* I shout in surprise, as it suddenly pulls me rapidly through the water. Tom races after me and grabs my waist. For a moment, we're in sync again, laughing at the speed and excitement of the ride.

Let's hope it knows where we're going! But be alert and tell me if you see or hear anything, Emma.

Again his command makes sense, but it bugs me anyway. I keep my eyes peeled and my ears wide — for any unusual movement or sound. Now and again there are faint high-pitched squeals followed by throbbing sighs. I tell Tom to keep checking over his shoulder.

Why?

Because I asked you to! I have this odd feeling some-one — or something — is following us.

No need to snap. I don't see anything. You're just nervous, Emma.

And you're a pain, I want to say, but don't. The Wand pulls us to a wall of blue rock and down through an entrance near its base. Here, the water is more yellow than green.

We must be getting closer to something, Tom says.

But look! We're in a rock maze. I hate mazes!

The Wand drags us along a series of curving passageways of blue rock. Then, it suddenly turns back into a sphere and we stop.

Has it lost its power? Tom asks. *Is this as far as it needs to take us?*

I guess so. I drop the sphere in my pouch.

Tom puts his hand on my shoulder. *Shhh. Listen. What's that?*

All I can hear is the swish of darting fish, the faint glug and burble of sea life, and the wash of heavy water all around us.

Now who's getting nervous?

Maybe for a reason, Emma. I'm sure I heard voices. We've got to find a way out before they catch up.

I swim along the left side of the rocky passage checking for an opening. Tom follows the right. I almost go past a small natural opening in the wall. Using my arms as scoops, I backpaddle to it. A sound is coming from inside, a low murmur — of voices? Suddenly, bubbles stream through the opening, like a long string of small glass beads. As they burst one by one, they send out little cries. Another line of bubbles follows and bursts. My skin prickles to the tips of my tail fins. I can hear *words*. Actual words. Tom floats up beside me.

Did you hear that? I ask.

Another string of dancing bubbles floats past. They all burst at once and yes! — the same words vibrate through the water: "Finderfinderfinderfinderfinder." Goosebumps run down my arms.

I've heard these voices before, I say. *In Histal's Test Conjure in the ravine.*

But who are they? Tom asks.

I'll have to go in and find out.

No. I'll do it, he says. *You stay here. It's too dangerous.*

No, Tom, I'll go. He frowns and I add, *Okay, okay — let's both go.*

Just then a ball of tiny bubbles floats out of the opening and stops right in front of me as if to say, "Wait."

I touch it and hear different words. "Geter GeterGETERGETERdangerDanger!" louder and louder, until all the bubbles explode and the voices stop.

I don't think we should go in there, Tom says.

We have to. We can't go back or we'll end up in Fomorii again. Come with me, or get out of the way.

I'm about to dive into the opening when a thunderous roar rips through the ocean. To my left, the water churns with Bluemen led by Rhona, her brightly colored tail and fins thrashing the water — and surging toward us on the other side are two black Kuls, carrying along the creature with the breathing apparatus. Twenty or more Kuls swim silently behind them.

Tom and I dive through the small opening into a cave, its walls glistening with black bubbles. I can't see another way out. We're caught. With sucking pops, the bubbles break away from the walls and come at us with high-pitched squeals. I try to swim straight up, but I'm stopped by solid rock. Rhona and her henchmen are trying to get in but are being pushed back by the black bubbles. Rhona slashes at them with a long knife but they dodge away. Behind her, a high-pitched voice gives orders. Rhona and the Bluemen turn with growls of rage. In seconds we hear the clash of a fight begin.

I call to Tom. *Whoever wins will grab us!*

The rolling black bubbles suddenly close in, surrounding me tightly.

Tom! I can't see you!

Hold up the Wand! Tom calls.

I can't get at it! I pull one arm free and try to punch one of the black orbs, but my fist is instantly caught by a scaly webbed hand. More hands grab my arms, my hair, my fins and hold me fast.

I can't see a thing, try to pull away but can't. The screeching is breaking my eardrums. I'm pulled through the water at great speed, down a dark passage that must have been hidden by the mass of bubbles. Now and again, the side of a dark gray-blue face emerges, or a pale eye, sometimes a thick wash of greenish hair.

Suddenly we change direction and go straight up through the foaming water. My head bursts through the surface, the hands lift high before tossing me onto sandy ground. I land with a thump. I sit up, rubbing my elbow. Where am I? It looks like — wait — I'm back in the maze at Fadanys — right where I left Pictree. But where's Tom? And where's Pictree and the little boat?

I change into Emma mode and shout their names. Gray-black tails thrash the water and nine Muirgen heads pop out, their green hair lying on the surface like silk lily pads. They look me over with great intensity, their white eyes full of curiosity.

One of them wears a black skullcap with two black spheres and a large yellow pearl. "Varra?" I gasp. "It's you? Thank heaven you're safe!"

She opens her mouth and an ear-piercing squeal comes out of it. It's the same language as the twins. "You have saved us, Ena. Some of my clann live. They heard my Call. They took me to the cave. We waited for you. The Wand brought you to us."

A slim white figure slides just below the water, then rises beside her, her face bright with excitement.

"Mennow!" I breathe. "You're free."

"I am released from the confiner, but have none of my powers back. You've done well, Ena. Soon, I will take Varra and the remnants of her clann back to my sanctum. There we will wait until you find all four Wands."

"Don't you want yours back now?"

She shakes her head and tears fall. "Alas, I cannot accept it yet. Rest now, Ena. We will warn you if

Eefa comes near. But remember, she will never be far behind."

"What about Rhona?"

"Eefa drove her away."

I have to smile. "Well, at least *half* of that is good news."

"We wish you success in your Quest, Ena." Varra's pale eyes are filled with hope and sadness. "Take care. Be strong. If we do not meet again —?"

"Now, now, Varra," says Mennow. "One must send a princeling off to battle with a cheer and a rousing farewell. Good hunting, Ena!"

With ear-shattering slaps of all their tails, they're gone.

22

Another figure moves quickly under the water toward me. I leap back as something hisses out of the water, shakes itself off and flies straight at me.

I cry out loud, "Tom! Huw's owl cunning is holding even *after* being in the water so long."

He lands on my shoulder. "Yeah — just what I wanted — my good old owl shape back! I was hoping I could stay invisible as Tom. The Muirgens are guarding the entrance. Maybe they'll hold Eefa off for a while."

"At least Dad's alive — as long as that wasn't just some sick game of Eefa's. And Varra's alive and safe with Mennow and the Muirgens. But ..."

"What?"

"But what about Huw? I feel so horrible about what's happened to him. The thing is, I hated him most of the time and he —"

"Huw did what any loyal Player would do for his Lead Player, Emma."

"But this isn't a *Game*!"

"Huw's life *was* the Game," Tom says. "One of the rules he lived by was to protect his leader. Don't feel sad for him. It would dishonor his memory. This Quest will test your Watcher's inner strengths, Emma. You always feel too much emotion. You must learn to control yourself."

"If you want me to have no feelings, you'll have to wait a long time," I say.

Yet, in a way he's right. I *must* control the fear and the anger. I *must* make my emotions work for me, not against me, or they'll just slow me down. I try to block out what happened to Huw, and suddenly I remember something else that happened in the grotto.

"I saw two ghostly figures in Rhona's sanctuary when the fight started," I say. "One of them started to run at me, but before I could make out who it was, Varra leaped into the water and I followed. Did you see them?"

Tom looks wary. "No. Uh — I was looking for a way out."

"Do you think one of them might have been Moraan?"

Before he can answer, a voice shouts, "Emma! Where have you been! I've been so worried!"

A small boat rocks toward us, the steerer using his long pole to dig into the hedge below water. "Look. I figured out how these poles work!"

"Pictree! You're safe!" I cry. "We found Mennow's Wand! We're going after the second one — I just don't know which one yet."

The little boat rides up on the sandy shore. Pictree leaps out and hugs me. "I couldn't sense you anywhere. My abilities are weakened here. What Wand? Who's Mennow? How many Wands do you have to find? How —?"

I hold both his hands, laughing. "Later. Too many questions! I'm so tired I could sleep for ten years."

Tom says, "Yes, a short rest is necessary."

"Ten years? Is that a short time? Wait! Tom! You got through the cave wall!"

"Doesn't this younger ever stop talking?" Tom grumbles.

I gape at Tom, then cry, "Talking! I just realized, you're speaking out loud again!"

His eyes in the heart-shaped face grow wider. "So I am. I didn't even notice it in all the excitement. Well, that's something to be thankful for."

"If *you* say so!" I laugh as he wraps one wing over my mouth.

Tom turns to a grinning Pictree. "Pull the boat up higher on shore and flip it over. We'll rest under it. Come on, Emma, you look ready to drop."

"For at *least* ten years," Pictree calls.

Tom and I laugh. We crawl under the glass boat. It smells of sea salt and sand.

In the silence, Pictree whispers, "I don't feel a threat of any kind nearby right now, more of a distant … er … gathering of something nasty. Can't you tell me a little of what has happened — so I can prepare myself?"

I say, "Okay. I'm too hyper to sleep now, any-way."

As Tom and I relate our adventure, it sounds too fantastic to my "human" ears. Could it really have happened? Is any of this happening? Pictree listens, his yellow eyes wide with interest. Finally we are quiet, each lost in our own thoughts.

I close my eyes, but all I see is Eefa and her Kuls racing toward us through black waters. I hope Mennow is still guarding the opening to this part of the maze.

"Tom?" I ask. "Why do you think Moraan made this hedge maze to confine the Tetrad?"

"Druvids use mazes for various reasons. Remember Fidchell, the board games you played with Fergus? Mathus created mazes in both of them."

"Right. But *why?*"

"There are many levels of ... physical existence for Druvids. Imagine these levels as colored ribbons that loop around one another. Let's say that the ribbon of *human* reality is a red one. Most humans believe that the red ribbon is the *only* ribbon of life.

"If one admits he sometimes sees a *blue* ribbon or a purple ribbon — something strange and magickal — the others say it's all in his imagination. A few *may* be a bit more open and decide it is something *super* natural — a mystery beyond logic."

I nod. "Yeah. Most people only believe in the Real World."

"But Druvids *know* that the *ribbons* move through one another and often join together — because they are part of the same reality. A maze represents all those ribbons of existence coming together."

"Kind of like how a border cave works — a regular cave to some beings, but for others it leads to a different world," Pictree says.

"Yes, like that," Tom agrees.

"So, why aren't Watchers Druvids?"

Tom's large eyes blink slowly. "They just *aren't*. But they can, at times, go *beyond* some Druvids. I know Histal can."

"Really?" I say, yawning. "Mighty powerful and *scary* beings, Druvids. Mind you, so is Histal, but ..." My brain can't think anymore. In an instant I'm asleep.

I have no idea how long I've slept when I hear Tom call, "Emma. Wake up. We have to go."

"*You've* started already, huh?"

"Started what?"

"Never mind, *boss*."

When I crawl out bleary-eyed from under the boat, a sapphire moon is draping everything in a blue light. Tom is sitting on the upturned boat like a pale ghostly owl. I say sleepily, "Wow. I didn't think this place had a night time."

Pictree sitting on the ground, legs crossed, says, "I can feel that gathering force coming closer. We must go, Emma. *Now*."

"Okay, okay. Jeez, give me time to think!" I wipe the sleep from my eyes and try to get my brain into gear.

I walk to the water's edge. The solid wall once again separates us from the little cove. No return to the hologram gallery. No way back at all.

"Well, I guess we'd better go through the stupid maze," I say, then add, "I wish I wasn't so darn hungry."

"Why didn't you say so?" Pictree runs toward me, his outstretched hand holding a cloth bundle.

He says sheepishly, "I took food from your family's table. I'm sorry. But I never know when my next meal might be."

Inside the package is a mishmash of food and slices of crisp bread, softened now into floppy pancakes. I drop some food onto a slice, roll it up and hand it to Pictree. Then I make Tom and myself one each and give the bundle back to Pictree. Tears sting my eyes when I taste the flavors of my last meal with my family.

"We'd better go," I say, swallowing my final bite and hoping they didn't see my weakness. "Pictree, I'd hoped you could take the boat back to the bridge of light. But with the invisible wall up, maybe you should wait here for us."

Pictree looks bewildered and hurt. "If you don't want me ..."

"It's not that."

"Then I'd like to stay with you — if it's okay with you and Tom."

Tom says sternly, "You'll have to take care of yourself and follow my orders."

"No," I say, through my teeth, "follow *my* orders."

Tom gives a feathery shrug.

Pictree answers, "Believe me, I've learned to take orders. *And* I can look after myself. I'm a survivor if nothing else."

I pat Pictree on the shoulder. "As long as you're sure."

"Oh yes, Emma, I'm sure. I —"

"Talk, talk, talk," Tom says. "Let's get going or Eefa will shut our mouths for good!"

As Pictree and I run quickly along the moonlit sandy path between the hedges, Tom floating above us, I wonder three things: Who or what waits for us in this part of the maze? How much does Tom want to take charge of this Quest? And *why*?

23

Deep in the maze, there's nothing but sand, darkness and hedge. And it's getting colder. We march on for ages until, around a tight dogleg turn, we find ourselves in a long wide lane lined with short leafless trees. As soon as we step past the first stunted tree, two things happen. It begins to snow and Tom vanishes.

I cry out. "Tom? Are you here?"

His answer is a scattering of snow swirling into a funnel.

"Looks like Huw's owl cunning has lost its power," I say. "Maybe it's just as well you stay hidden for now, don't you think? We don't know what's ahead."

From the snow funnel comes a single word. "Agreed."

"Great, you still have your voice!" I exclaim. "I thought it would disappear like it did in Waeter."

"So did I," Tom says. "Hey, look down!"

Two sets of footprints are clearly outlined in the snow. Suddenly a bigger set appears under the funnel, and moves away, and as they turn around, the snow funnel scatters.

Tom laughs. "Come on, let's keep going."

The maze curves left — then to a right angle — and then left again. We're in a hexagonal space. Six leafless trees are evenly spaced around the walls.

A small gray figure creeps from behind one of the trunks. He's about four feet high and dressed in a brown tunic and pants with white designs slashed across them. His dark skinny arms and long feet are bare and dotted with decorative scars — circles within circles. His large head is covered in a tight fitted hood with slits for his ears, which are so long they fold over the top of his hood. His face and broad nose are covered in a thick pebbly paste. But it's his tiny deep-set eyes that startle me — a shocking light blue.

"It's a Gnomus," Pictree whispers. "There are Gnomus tribes in the Tag-A-Long Isles where I am from. They work in caves underground — guarding treasure and other buried things for various clanns. They can be very quick — and nasty when angered."

"Does he mean a gnome?" I whisper to Tom. "Like in Earth fairy tales?"

"Gnomuses were once plentiful on Earth, but like everything magickal, they were driven out. Humans got rid of every form of intelligent being different from them."

"And now they're working on getting rid of *themselves*," I mutter.

The Gnomus, after sniffing the air, walks right up to me. Up close, I see his eyes are rimmed with red as if the muck smeared on his face has irritated them. I don't move when he touches my arm. Then he nods.

"You are Ena," he says in a voice as dry as powder with a Scottish burr to it.

"Yes."

The creature screws up his face into a grin, showing blunt brown teeth. "I am Spriggan. Of the Elfsig Clann. We guard the barrow of the great Gernac. I've received a message from Mennow. You found the Wand of Waeter. Well done, Ena."

I nod graciously and say, "You have your clann with you? How many? We need protection from Eefa."

He grins again, and this time his eyes are mischievous. "We are many — but Elfsigs are good at hiding. That makes us efficient at surprise attacks."

"Where is Gernac?" I ask.

Spriggan crooks his finger at us, walking backward. I follow, Pictree and Tom right behind. The Gnomus leads us to the tree he was hiding behind. He touches the back of the trunk and the bark crumples to expose a rough opening.

Spriggan grins nastily. "You wish to see Gernac? Follow — and be quick about it."

He drops through the opening. I look at Pictree, who shrugs and leaps after him.

"I'll go next," Tom says.

"Oh no you won't!" I step into the hole. My feet fly out from under me and I'm on a giant slide! I land with a thump on a pile of snow-covered leaves. We're on a high treed ridge overlooking a snow-hazed valley of trees with a clearing in the middle. There's a moon above — a three-quarter creamy moon, bathing everything in dull milky white.

In the middle of the clearing below is a grass-covered mound, thinly covered with snow. Lying across it is the figure of a giant — like a child's drawing — outlined in large blue stones that are eerily luminescent in the cold night air.

Have we found the second confiner and the Regent of Erthe?

ERTHE

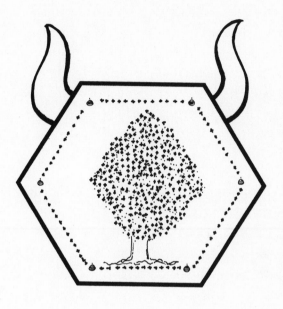

24

"That hill is a barrow," Tom whispers.

"A *what?*"

"You have them on Earth — old burial mounds. You call them barrows, too."

"That thing is a *grave?*" I squawk.

Tom chuckles. "The giant figure means this barrow harbors a *sleeping* king, not a dead one."

"Is a king sleeping there?" I ask the Gnomus. "Is it Gernac?"

He nods. "Ena must sound a Wood-crier to open the entrance."

I whisper to Tom, "A wooden whistle? I have one. Cill gave it to me."

"Let's see what he's up to first — you can tell him once we can trust him."

Spriggan frowns at me. "I think at first you have two voices, Ena. Then I see prints in the snow. You have a third being with you."

"We weren't trying to hide him," I say defensively. "He's my Watcher, Tamhas. He's lost the ability to be seen sometimes ever since he came through the border cave. We don't know why. The other is Pictree Bragg — of the Hobyah tribe."

Spriggan sneers at Pictree. "Hobyahs are no our enemy. You are fortunate. I'd have to kill you otherwise."

Pictree grins. "You'd have to catch me first."

Spriggan leers at him, then stares at me intently. "Once the door to Gernac's confiner is open, I will give you a clew and you will throw it into the opening. Follow it to Gernac's resting place. When you find our great Regent, blow the stone horn at his feet. This will wake him, but ... it will also signal to Eefa that the barrow lock has been opened."

"Will Gernac tell me where the Wand of Erthe is?" I ask, trying not to panic.

"Listen!" Spriggan says. "On the small table beside Gernac is a stone sword. Use it to cut the silver chain. That is the one that keeps him from speaking. Do not cut the gold chain. To stop Gernac from fighting Eefa, Moraan removed his voice and half his strength and put a sleep cunning on him." He chuckles. "Takes a lot to shut up the great Regent of Erthe."

"Will he come with us to fight Eefa?"

"He will want to. But you must take what he offers and leave quickly to find his Wand. He will sleep again."

"Easy, no problem," I murmur glumly.

Spriggan glowers. "No. *Hard!* As you leave Gernac's confiner, roll up the clew. You *canna* leave it behind. Remember, Eefa is readying for attack."

A trickle of fear threads in and around my gut. "How do you know?" I look over my shoulder half expecting to see Eefa screaming toward us through the air. "Maybe she wasn't able to follow me."

"Tambro, my clann listener, hears the thud of hooves — Eefa's mighty Heorots gathering. That's how I knew when to meet you."

I manage to squeak, "Heorots?"

Tom says, "Giant deer with huge antlers. Harts. I think you'd call them stags today."

"Th-that doesn't sound *too* scary."

Spriggan sniggers. "Wait until you see what rides them. Come. Follow me. Quickly."

He leads us into the forest, leaving no footprints. Now and again I lose him, because he blends so well with the brown trees and white snow. I think about gliding above the ground but decide it doesn't matter. Pictree and Tom are leaving enough of a trail. What does one more set of footprints matter?

It's silent and unnerving in this forest of leafless oak and tall pines. A haze of frozen mist lies low to the ground. I open my ears and nostrils, allowing my skin to absorb everything. Faint rustling movements keep pace on either side of us. With them come the same odors of wet animal skins, clay and soil that surround Spriggan — his clann is well hidden.

As we descend the slope, the smells of pine needles and cold wet snow bring back memories of the early spring day Tom and I went back to the bee farm to find my father, who was being held prisoner by Fergus in my old room in the barn. I hadn't seen him in almost a year. He was in terrible shape — filthy, emaciated and unable to remember me. It was in order to save him that I had to go on my Seeker's Quest. After we won the Quest, we took him to Argadnel to recover. Now I've put his life — *all* of our lives — in danger.

Will I see him again? My link with my Earth mother, Leto Sweeney, is strong — if she was dead, I'd know. But I'm not sure about Dad. My eyes fill with tears and I stumble. I feel as weak-limbed and frightened as a lost kid.

Spriggan frowns at me, his blue eyes full of doubt.

I touch the Waeter sphere in my pouch and feel a tiny surge of confidence. "Don't worry," I say to him, "I won't let you down."

I straighten up. I will not give into the fear. I *can* get through this. I have to, for my family and for Fadanys.

25

We race across the clearing to the barrow. As I follow Spriggan around the base of it, I feel as small as a bee zooming past an enormous hive, but there's no sign of an entrance in its thick, grassy hide.

"Are you ready?" Spriggan asks. "Remember, Eefa willna know where you are until you blow the horn of stone at Gernac's feet. Then she will know."

"But how can we fight her troops when they *do* arrive?"

He cackles without humor. "Fight them? The Heorots will be ridden by Sifs taken from the Boggen Moors. They were once Elfsigs like me and miners of silver." His laughter grows louder, the brown paste on his face cracking. "But then, I used to be twelve hands tall — look what the mines did to me! However, I lived — the Sifs didna!"

"You mean they're *dead*?"

He nods, still laughing. "Riding dead!"

I gulp. "Ghosts?"

"Not ghosts. Boggys. Your best chance is to out-run them. Most of the time they'll be only a flutter in the air or the sweep of a sword. But you'll see the Heorots well enough, even in the dark — just remember they're not alone!" Spriggan laughs again, but then his face slams into a grim stare that scares me. "I have good ears. I heard you say you have a Wood-crier."

"My friend Cill of the Barroch tribe gave it to me. She said —"

I stop. I'm expected to Call someone in every Element. Cill said if I blew into it, she'd hear me. But there's no way she can — not where she is now.

"Let me see it," Spriggan demands.

I show him the wooden knot. He holds it between his palms, then gives it back. "Use it."

I look at Tom, who nods. With a shaking hand I put the whistle to my mouth and blow. No sound comes out. It didn't work! As I stare at it with dismay and relief, a hole opens in the side of the barrow with a loud clattering of stones — and Cill drops out of the sky, landing face down in a puff of snow. "Eee! Eee! Where is I? Where ... who ... eee!"

Spriggan leaps on her, a knife in his hand.

"NO!" I shout. "She's the friend who gave me the whistle! She said it would bring her to me but I didn't think — Oh, Cill. I'm sorry."

Spriggan points at Pictree. "Is this the one you Called when you were with Mennow?"

"No. Pictree came through the border cave with me — as did Tamhas. The one I Called in Waeter died in Fomorii."

Spriggan puts away his knife and spits on the ground. "Fomorrians! Pshaw! How do we know this leaf being won't fight us — stop you from winning the Wand of Gernac? How do we know she's no one of Eefa's Players?"

"She's my friend," I say loudly. *Winning. Players.* Game words. But this is a Quest, not a Game. Or is it?

Cill clutches my arm in a death grip. "I be loyal to Emma. She be my friend. I never betray her."

Tom's strong voice growls, "The entrance to Gernac's barrow is open. We're wasting time!"

Spriggan looks startled, but heads for the entrance.

Cill, close on my heels, says, "Who Eefa? Where we be? How I get here?"

I turn to her, "Cill, I can't ask you to stay and fight with me. I'm sure Spriggan and his clann would protect you until this is all over."

She pats my arm. "I remember Pictree. He help us at Cymmarian Market. If he stay, I not leave you, either. Now be quiet, Emma. Tell me what I to do."

I sigh. It's a waste of time to argue. "Just remember that those who look like Spriggan are on our side. Any other being is the enemy."

"Ooo-kai," she says, still holding tightly to my arm. She's afraid, but I know how brave she is under the fear. A fiercely loyal friend, Cill risked her life many times in my Seeker's Quest, defying Fergus to fight for our side.

Clods of earth and stones are falling into the barrow's gaping hole, which is crisscrossed with tangled roots.

Spriggan shoves a ball of gold thread at me. "Toss this clew inside and follow it," he snarls, "but first tie the end firmly near the entrance. Quickly! I will whistle when Eefa appears."

I stare into the black hole. I take a deep breath, wrap one end of the clew firmly around a rock at the entrance, then throw the golden ball into the darkness. A sizzling sound echoes back at us. I push aside the roots and, with a shaking heart, climb into the hole.

26

Pictree, Cill and Tom crowd in behind me. When I take hold of the gold fiber lying on the ground, it glows with bright blue light. We follow the light down a stone passageway with many entrances leading off it, while the clew ball rolls along the ground ahead of us. Cill and Pictree whisper in amazement as the light slides over carvings of mountains, valleys, trees, caves, animals — lions, antelopes, deer, rabbits, snakes, toads, gromands, mousels, roderes and more. We crunch along the gritty floor. Suddenly the clew rises in the air and turns down a passage. It does this half a dozen times, guiding us deeper and deeper into the barrow.

I mutter, "If it takes this long to get back, Eefa, her Sifs and those giant deer will be waiting for us at the entrance, bored out of their minds."

Cill and Pictree giggle. Tom doesn't. Finally, a few yards on, we stop. The remaining ball of the clew — about one inch in diameter — lies in front of a stone door. In the center of the door is a carved hexagon with two animal horns protruding out the top of it. In the middle of the hexagon is a tree covered in bees. I press my right forearm against it, in case I need my hands for fighting.

"Yow!" I pull back, blowing on a smoking burn as the door creaks open. "I wish there was an easier way than *branding* me!"

"I'm sorry, Creirwy." I feel Tom take my hand, and his breath is cool as he gently blows on the burn. With my other hand, I touch his arm.

"Why didn't you say you're *solid* again even though you're invisible?" I whisper.

"It's easier for me," he says gently, as his fingers tenderly touch my skin. Why does he do things like this? It's so ... I'm sure he doesn't realize ...

"You must roll up the clew to return, remember?" Pictree says, bringing me back to reality with a bump.

"Yes, yes," I say irritably. "I remember."

I pick the tiny gold ball up and hold it on the palm of my hand. I stumble through the doorway, still feeling Tom's breath on my skin. The clew lights up a small hexagonal room. In the middle, a heavy stone slab rests on four stone legs, each in the shape of huge beelike insects with open wings. On the table lies a figure covered in a thick layer of dust. What did Spriggan say to do? *Blow the horn at his feet?*

Tom whispers, "Wake him. *Hurry*, Emma!"

I push my right hand through the soft dust at the body's feet and feel around. There! The shape of a curved horn. I grab it, shake the off the dust and blow into it. An eerie high-pitched wail pours out into the dusty air. The body on the table leaps to its feet, its head almost touching the ceiling. It shakes itself like a dog and the air boils with dust.

I sneeze. One by one, the others follow. Soon we're all covered in fine silt — even Tom is outlined in it. A giant stares down at us, his great head swiveling. So this is Gernac. His hair is thick and woolly, dashed all over with gold and silver leaves. Just above his forehead is a tall crown of twigs covered in crystals and colored gems in the shape of bees, ants and other insects and edged all along the bottom with crumpled copper leaves. Below his waist he wears a wide apron of striped gold and silver.

But the rest of Gernac looks as if he's two men joined down the middle by a thick ribbon of solid gold. The right side of his torso, covered in gold paint, is brawny and thick, his coppery colored leg as wide and solid as a stout oak. The left side is painted with silver. It's emaciated, the ribs sticking out, the arm stunted. That leg is knobby and chalky white. Even his face is divided down the middle of his nose, the right side covered in gold paste, the left in a silvery veil decorated with small stones. His right eye is dark under a heavy brow, but I can see only a gleam of dull gray behind the veil. So that's what Spriggan meant when he said Moraan took away half of Gernac's strength.

Around his neck is a plain gold torque with two thick chains. The silver chain is welded to a ring of steel set deep in the stone table, the gold chain wound around one of the table's stone legs to another steel ring on the floor.

He stares at each of us in turn. Then he points to his throat and mouth. That's when I remember what I have to do. I find the small table and, under more dust, a sword. I raise it and bring it down on the silver chain. It clangs, the chain drops open, and the sword breaks in two.

Gernac coughs loudly, spewing clouds of dust. We all duck. After a few deep gasps, he bows toward me. "I .. was …dreaming of your return … Ena." His voice is deep and full of gravel.

"G-Gernac," I choke out, "we must find your Wand quickly. Eefa is on her way! I need to know how long I —"

"Quiet!" He blasts out a cough, waving his arms through another billow of dust. "Cut the other chain. I will come with you. I have dreamed of a young woman we will come upon in our travels. She is in a small space — waiting for me to find her." His bizarre face takes on a dreamy look. "I will rescue her and make her my life partner."

Gernac's fallen in love with a dream! Is he nuts? I shake myself. Why shouldn't this Regent of Erthe be nuts? I am, too!

I say through dry lips, "Spriggan explained that Moraan insists you stay here."

He bellows, "Moraan is dead! Chose the coward's way out. Left our fate to ..." He scowls at me. "... a mere younger who doesn't look strong enough to fight her way through a gorse bush! Why didn't Moraan fight a proper battle? We could have beat Eefa. We still can. She's all wind —"

How do you shut up the Regent of all the land, trees and animals of Fadanys — who's now a captive in a barrow? A crazy being who dreams of damsels in distress, for crying out loud. His brains must be dust, too!

Finally Gernac sighs gustily and leans against his table, arms crossed. "You won't go against Moraan's wishes. No point in arguing with you."

"No — Sire ..." I say, my knees trembling. "Mennow explained that if any of you took control of Fadanys without your Wands — chaos would occur."

"So you've seen Mennow. Did you find her Wand?"

"Yes."

"Excellent!" We look at each other consideringly. Then he says, "When you find my Wand, I will have some mobility. Moraan can't hold me back forever. Meanwhile, Eefa will soon be upon you. Your way out is through my hand."

He opens his closed fist. On the palm rests a thin hexagonal stone tablet. As I reach out to take it, Gernac closes his fist over it.

"Remember, Ena, that Erthe is strong and weak. But, when it is attacked, those of Erthe always fight back. You must be like Erthe and Waeter, Ena. Do not let your emotions take over. But do use them and your inner strengths when you feel your weakest, and you may discover a power you did not realize you had."

He opens his palm again and, as I take the tablet, his weak hand covers mine. In the middle of it is the symbol that has been burned on my arm. A flush of energy floods me, making me feel stronger, less afraid.

"I am doing nothing. It is all *you*, Ena. Even in weakness there can be power," Gernac says, a sudden warmth in his gravelly voice. "Now, take the tablet. Remember, you will find the next portal through my hand. Your inner spirit and new physical strength will help you — *if* you overcome your fears and anxieties, Ena."

I put the small object in my pouch. I'll read it when we get to a safe spot.

"The portal is through your hand?" I ask as a shrill whistle echoes down the passageway and into the room.

"Spriggan's warning! Eefa!" Pictree exclaims.

"Gernac! How much longer do I have — how much time have I used?" I cry.

Before he can answer, Gernac crumples to the floor.

"And how is the way through your hand?" I demand, shaking his arm. "Please, Gernac!"

He whispers, "...my hand, to find the Wand. Time? I cannot think — I do not —" He closes his eyes and falls into a deep sleep.

"Emma, start gathering the clew. Let's go!" Tom orders.

I have to leave Gernac on the floor. I run after the others — the door slamming behind me. As we race along the passageways, I wrap the clew's thread as fast as I can.

Tom cries, "Faster, Emma, faster!"

We reach the entrance to the barrow, my hands shaking so badly I can hardly wind the last few feet of thread. As we stumble out into the open air, Spriggan is dancing up and down, pointing.

"There they are! There they are!"

27

I throw the clew to Spriggan and follow his jabbing finger. Snow-white stags, impatiently tossing their antlered heads, stand shoulder to shoulder in a semicircle along the crest of the ridge. I focus in on them. Only two riders are visible — a thin female with short red hair that stands out from her head like an exotic bird's and a slender male wearing black. The female is dressed in brown leather, a metal breastplate over her narrow chest. Her face is calm, her eye sockets sooty, her forehead decorated with a weblike veil dotted with gems.

Eefa.

The male rider has long black hair, but his face is covered with a red mask. Is this Arawn, the son of Aibell and Clust? Is this my brother?

I feel a flutter of fear and excitement. But I force it down. "Spriggan, the stags fill the ridge up there. But there are more than two riders, right?"

"Och aye, the others carry Sifs," he says. "Invisible now."

"But there's no one on the crest right behind us. Is that the way out?"

Spriggan shrugs. "No one is there because Eefa has been stopped by the wide gorges my clann dug into each ridge. They'll have two ravines to leap over if they want to get here. On my next whistle, my clann will distract them and you can run."

Cill looks up the ridge. "Or Eefa just come down across barrow field."

Spriggan snarls, "She'll know I have my clann throughout the area, full of nasty surprises. Become invisible, Watcher, and climb high."

I say, "Pictree and Cill, if I hold hands with you, you'll also be invisible. But our footprints will be seen — and if we get separated —"

"Emma!" Tom says. "Stop talking! Move!"

"I need to ask Spriggan — do you know what Gernac meant when he said the way is through his hand?"

"No, I don't! He's talking nonsense! Leave me now!" As he runs toward one end of the barrow, he shouts, "Elfsigs will be all around you. Be strong!"

We take off into the woods. Holding Pictree's and Cill's hands makes climbing slow. The snow is deeper here and Cill is floundering. I know I'm strong enough to make it on my own, but I can't leave them exposed. We finally reach a ledge of rock overlooking the valley.

"Wait!" I call. "I need to see what's going on."

Pictree pulls on my arm. "Emma, keep going."

"No," Tom says. "Emma's right. We must see what's going on."

Finally, he's agreeing with one of *my* orders.

The line of Heorots has separated, one half heading to the left, the other to the right. Only Eefa and Arawn remain, looking across at us. Can the red-haired Druvid see us even though we're invisible? She *must*. Dread flushes through me.

The two groups of Heorots converge at the huge ditches that the Elfsig Clann have cut deep in the ridge. Some turn and head down the hills toward the valley. Many fall, spewing up puffs of snow. Small figures swarm the treetops. Spriggan's clann — slowing the enemy with traps. I let out a yip of excitement. Surely this will give us enough time to escape.

"Let's keep going up," I cry.

There must be a way out on that ridge above us, but what did Gernac *mean* when he said the way out was through his hand? And why didn't I press him harder when he first woke up about how much time we had left?

Cill puffs behind me. "If you let go, I travel in trees. I be more help in high."

Pictree adds, "I'd be faster on my own, too. It won't matter if they see us. They know where we are, anyway."

I agree. Cill is soon in the trees. Pictree keeps pace with me. When we reach another rocky ledge, my heart stops. Some of the riders have made the leap across the gorges. Flashes of white ripple through the dark tree trunks coming toward us.

Suddenly, a riderless white stag pounds down the hill right behind, dodging trees with skill. As the creature leaps over a log, a swirl of gray appears on his back, a flash of a tight gray hood, a red rectangular mask with narrow slits. Just as quickly, it's gone, but not before the gleam of a sword whips the air with a loud whap.

"No move!" Cill shouts from above, and instinctively I do as she says.

Tom's footprints crash past me, aiming for the deer. As it and its ghostly rider hurtle toward Pictree, I push him aside so I can take the brunt of the hit. I wait, ready to run out of the way at the last second, knife in hand, just as a long tendril of vine wraps around the stag's legs and the mighty animal crashes, spewing up the snow. There's the clash of metal against metal as Tom fights the rider, who suddenly screams and vanishes, along with its stag.

Tom and I both call, "Thanks, Cill!"

I peer over the rocky ledge. Can we climb below from here? Oh no! Arawn and Eefa have already ridden down through the forest and are racing across the clearing toward the mound. The beat of Heorot hooves grows louder around us.

There's no way out. I can hear Tom giving orders. I must *think*. I watch mesmerized as Eefa urges her stag up onto Gernac's barrow, scattering the snow off the giant figure. Arawn moves up beside her. Eefa shades her eyes and gazes up at us, a grin across her face. She spreads her arms wide, as if to say, Come down to me. It's all over.

I have to do something. But *what*?

Tom shouts, "Emma! Look out!"

Four Heorots are thundering straight at me. Pictree and I leap out of their way. They turn and charge again, the Sifs slapping the air with their swords. This time, I leap aside, then lunge forward just as quickly, thrusting my knife into a Sif, which dissolves into dust. Tom and Cill go into action, and soon the stags and riders disappear.

"What do we do?" Pictree cries.

"I wish I was an owl again," Tom shouts. "I'd fly down there and claw Eefa's eyes out! Look at her! Sitting on the barrow like a spider waiting for flies."

As the thunder of more stags comes closer, Gernac's words return to me: *Do not let your emotions take over. But do use them and your inner strengths when you feel your weakest, and you may discover a power you did not realize you had.*

I close my eyes. An image appears behind my eyelids. Can I do it? I call to the others.

Tom asks, "What are you up to, Emma?"

"I'm going to try to shape-change."

"It had better be *now*!" Pictree cries. "Look!"

Dozens of white stags move like silent ghosts through the forest toward us, their riders' red masks visible in twists of the cold air.

Grasping the sphere of Mennow, I draw on all my spirit and strength. As I look down at Eefa's smug face, anger boils inside me, swelling my chest, filling me until I'm sure I'll explode. Sounds of excitement from the others bring me back to reality. When I glance down, all I see are feathers, giant feathers everywhere! I look behind me — my head swiveling with ease. A tail, many feet long, fans open. I raise my arms and huge feathered wings spread with a snap and loud whoosh! whoosh!

Cill cries, "That Emma? Emma, you there?"

"Yes, it's me!" I squawk excitedly. "Climb on my back, everyone. Hang on tight!"

I can feel them crawl along my broad back. Now and again a hand tugs one of my feathers.

Tom shouts, "Go, Emma. *Fly!*"

I run on clumsy legs to the edge of the cliff, dragging my heavy wings along the ground — and with a scream that sounds like a red-tailed hawk, I jump off the rocky ledge. After a couple of heart-stopping tumbles, I spread my wings and glide, letting the cold air lift me higher. I wheel up into the sky.

"Be careful, Emma!" Pictree cries. "They're shooting at us!"

Long pointed missiles turn and drop just short of us. As long as I stay high above the valley, we're safe. I laugh at Eefa's furious face with a high-pitched squeal of delight.

I circle quickly, keeping out of range and looking for an exit. There are distant cheers and then a howl of laughter from the forest. In treetops, small creatures wave wildly at us, arms windmilling. I take the hint and keep circling. The top of the ridge where we were hoping to find the exit is crowded with nothing but more woods.

The giant figure is right below us, Eefa and Arawn waiting on the mound near its feet. Eefa raises one hand and a flash of light roars past me.

"Jeez!" I cry. "That was close!"

I dodge and weave to put her off her mark and during a dive, see a silver flash on the barrow behind her. One of the giant's hands is now a silvery blue. As I stare, the hand drops down and a dark hole opens. So that's what Gernac meant by finding the way through his hand.

Look at the giant's hand, I telepath to Tom and hear him gasp.

Eefa, seated on her stag at the left foot of the giant, hasn't seen it. She throws another ball of fire at us. A searing pain cuts through my right wing. I lurch sideways and drop a few feet.

There are shouts of triumph from the two figures below.

Tom roars, "Drop fast and aim for the giant's hand. Ignore Eefa. *NOW!*"

For one giddy moment, I hesitate, and then I hear Gernac in my head: *Your inner spirit and new physical strength will help you* — *if you overcome your fears and anxieties, Ena.*

I swallow down the fear, collapse my wings, tuck them to my sides and drop, steering with my tail. Cill wails with terror while Pictree cries, "Go, Emma, *go!*" Tom's hands tighten on my back. Strength from some deep reserve kicks in, and we zoom with eye-popping speed toward the only black spot in all that gray and white. To the side I see Spriggan waving wildly at us, jumping up and down. Arrows skim past — one hits my leg, but I keep going. A flash of Eefa's furious face and Arawn's stiff red mask, and we go headfirst through the giant's hand.

28

The smell of moist earth and wet bark clogs my nostrils. Tree roots slide over black walls, and ghostly images of boulders are visible in the murky light. I'm lying on my side. I lift my left arm, expecting to see a wing, but my hand wavers in front of me. I feel a pinch of pain above my wrist, and in my thigh, but nothing like the wounds I felt while flying. I run my other hand over my arm and leg. No stickiness of blood, but there's a smear of ... I smell it — beeswax? — where the arrows hit. Odd. I sit up and bang my head on a tree root. Ouch. Where am I? If the others are here, they don't have night vision, so I poke around in my pouch for my light stick and turn it on. Jeez, another cave.

"Tom," I whisper, "are you here?"

The leaves rustle beside me. "You never could do a decent landing, Creirwy! I'm going to talk to your training Master." He's brushing dirt and leaves out of his short black hair. I push him hard and he laughs as he falls over.

"Tom! You're …you're *Tom!*"

He looks down and then turns his scarred face up at me and grins like a lunatic. "I've had no control over my shape-changing ever since we entered that cave portal on Argadnel, so this probably won't last long, either. But — hey, I'm here now!"

We stare at each other in wonderment. He reaches one long arm toward me, his eyes half closed, a smile on his face … when Pictree sits up in a far corner and squawks, "Tom, you're back!"

Cill rustles over, holding her head. "I fall hard. Ooph! My leaves ache. Tom? It *you!*"

"Yes, isn't that great?" I don't care that the others are here, I throw my arms around his big warm body. I've been longing to do that since we left Mennow's waters — when I wasn't mad at him, that is. Gently, he unwraps my arms.

Softly in my ear, he says, "I promised Histal. Rules. Forgive me."

I push myself away. "Right! Histal. *Promises. Rules.*"

He groans. "Emma, I'm your Watcher once again — for a while — I shouldn't —"

I turn away. "Yeah, yeah. Whatever."

Cill calls out from behind a dense tangle of roots, "Emma, come. Something here. What it mean?"

A section of the earth has been cut into a deep hexagon. Inside the space is a masklike face of beeswax.

"I suspect this is a puzzle I have to solve or something will be taken away from me," I reply, a sick feeling in my stomach. "The shape of this space is like the tablet Gernac gave me."

"Have you looked at it?" Tom asks.

"I haven't had much time, have I?" I snap.

I pull the thin tablet out of my pouch and read it out loud, trying to keep my voice steady.

Erthe Pneuma
Strength and weakness combined
like the omar and the Shellan
Caidil-stan the Shellan-magh
into the grave of Finias-er-elder's galad
Come close and once there
Call thy name, and lock the omar masq
Upon the face of Kera

"Doesn't mean a thing," I say. "Unless this wax mask is the omar masq." I look closely at it. Is that movement inside? Yes. Bees — milling and fumbling behind its bland features.

"I think this is the portal to Gernac's Wand," Tom says.

"Like I didn't know that already?" I say sarcastically to hide that fact that I'm scared stiff. I don't want to risk another member of my family. I push him aside and speak to the mask. "I am Ena. Can you let us through your portal?"

The mask trembles, then its mouth opens and a humming whisper comes from it. "Agree to the proffer of our Master and the way will open."

"What is that?" I ask, praying, *please don't let it be like the Waeter's portal*.

"If you fail in your task ... memories of your family that you hold to be true will no longer belong to you. If you fail in your task, your family will not know you. You will not know them."

I am unable to speak.

"Agree, Ena, or the portal will remain closed," the mask says.

Tom grasps my hand. "I heard, Emma. But at least it doesn't threaten your family's lives."

"But Tom," I whisper, "I will forget I ever *had* a family. And they won't remember me. It will be *worse* than death."

Cill wraps her arms around me. "You have Tom, me, Pictree, Gyro and Badba."

I stand dazed with misery.

"The memory loss happens *only* if you can't find Gernac's Wand. We'll find it!" says Pictree.

"Will we?"

"Yes," Tom says. "You must be strong and we won't fail."

"But what if I *do* fail?"

He says sadly, "You have no choice but to try."

I nod, my heart feeling like a lead weight. I look at the mask and say, "Okay! Yes ... I — I agree." An opening appears above us and as the mask falls into my hands, I burst into tears.

29

As we climb out into clear air, the damp earth sludges closed behind us. It's dark out, but there are yellow and gold leaves on the ground. Above, the pale shell of a moon peeks between the branches of surrounding trees. I wipe my eyes and wrap a pad of leaves around the hardened mask, securing it with strands of grass. Then I place it carefully in my pouch.

Tom and Pictree are beside me. "Where's Cill?" I ask.

Her small figure drops out of a poplar tree. "I right here. I be looking around see where we be. Look like *humans* here. Road. We be in small wood. Field all around."

I open my Watcher instincts, listen closely to the air, smell the soil. I walk the path beside us, and in one sickening, joyful, terrible moment, I know where we are.

I say, "We're in Grandpa MacFey's wood. We're on Earth. In *Bruide*."

I run down the path, through the small gate that leads to the wood, across the narrow highway toward the gravel drive that leads to my old home. I have to see it, touch it, *remember* it.

Tom grabs my arm and drags me behind a tall stand of grass beside the road.

"Get off!"

"Emma, your family isn't here."

"How do *you* know? They *could* be here! Prisoners!"

"Fergus still runs this place. It may have a Keeper. Slow down. Let's figure out why Moraan sent us here. We need to plan our approach."

"Always so logical," I snap. "Look, *Tamhas*, I have to see who's living here. It's my memories that are at stake. My life with my family! I don't expect you to understand."

His mouth twists to one side. "Oh, I think I understand. If it means not being allowed to remember someone who is special to your life."

"Are you saying —" But Pictree and Cill appear, and Tom's face shuts down. I must have misunderstood him — as usual.

Cill hisses, "This be your family bee farm? Why we be *here?*"

"For a reason we'll no doubt figure out," Tom says. "I'm trying to become invisible, Emma, but I can't. This could be a problem."

"For you maybe," I say. "You three stay here. If no one's there, I'll call you."

I transmute invisible and run down the driveway before they can stop me. I think I hear a growl from Tom but I ignore it. I'll check out my old room first. The barn stairs are leaf-strewn and a couple are broken. The room has the dank smell it had when they kept my father captive here. I open all the windows to let in the night air. Then I go back outside, my stomach twisted in knots, certain now that my parents are not here. Dad would have repaired the stairs.

As I walk to the house, I realize someone has knocked over half-a-dozen beehives, and a couple have been bashed to bits. My mind is red with the pumping of my blood. The deep hum of bees rises in the distance. Does my being here remind them of Mom? I edge toward the back door of the farmhouse, listening hard. Our old truck stands near the back door. It has three flat tires. A back window on the second floor of the house has been shot out. Local kids, maybe the same ones who wrecked the hives. My skin prickles with anger, but I breathe deeply. *Must* control my emotions.

The back door is locked. I search for the key in a fake stone in the flower border, now thick with dry weeds. It's there, but heavily tarnished. I stare at it, remembering every moment I spent in this house. And I won't forget those moments, no matter what that mask full of bees said.

It takes a few minutes of hard work to turn the lock, but finally the door screeches open on rusted hinges. If anyone's in the house, they'll have heard that. Nothing moves except for a skittering along one of the baseboards. Mom will go mad if she finds out mice have invaded the house. Then I let out a hoarse laugh that hurts my throat. Mice? If only mice were the worst things that had been living here since we left.

I push the light switch. A dim light comes on above the kitchen table. I quickly turn it off again. We don't want anyone to know we're here. I change my eyesight to night vision. Everything is instantly cloaked in crisp green light. I walk down the hall and check the main rooms. The place smells like damp, moldy towels. Mouse dirt everywhere, empty beer cans in piles in the living room. Mom's flowered couch and matching chairs sag, their covers grimy and littered with wrappers from MacGregor's burger stand in town. Candles stuck on saucers run along the fireplace mantle; the grate is jammed with ashes and half-burned wood. A party place for kids. I walk to the front of the house. The door, tucked behind the screened veranda, is ajar, the lock broken. The intensity of the anger building inside my head is scaring me. Calm. Be *calm*.

I transmute visible and climb the stairs to the bedrooms, dreading what I'll see. Fergus must have called that lummox of a Keeper back to Cleave. The house has clearly been abandoned since Dad was released from the barn four months ago.

I sit on the torn, stained mattress of Mom and Dad's bed. A half-empty package of cigarettes lies on the floor, forgotten amid beer and soda cans. How many times since we went to Argadnel have I wanted to come back to this place that gave us such an ordinary, *safe* life for almost a year. And when we lived here, how many times did I used to complain there was never anything to do in the country? Now, if I don't find Gernac's Wand, this could end up being my only memory of the farm.

I open the window and wave my light stick in the air. In the shadowy darkness, I can see the other three running up the driveway.

30

"So this is a human house," Pictree says. "I can't see much, but it smells ... strange."

Cill rustles around, her little red eyes glowing in the dark. "Smell *bad*."

Tom says, "That Keeper must have lived like an animal."

I growl. "Maybe. But now it's clearly a local kids' hangout."

"What's a *hangout*?" Pictree asks.

"A place to drink booze — alcohol — and party ... and who knows what else. If we're going to stay here for any time, we'll have to clean it up."

Tom shakes his head. "We'll only rest for a bit. Eefa will find her way here eventually. We'd better locate that Wand fast. Which means we need to translate that tablet — figure out who Finias and Kera are."

"There might be someone in town who could help us," I suggest. "Someone who knows what it means."

"Good idea," he says. "Who?"

"The only people I know — the MacIvors. Last time I saw Mr. MacIvor, he was yelling at me to stay away from his family. Mrs. MacIvor was the mid-wife who took away my parents' child, Ailla, and put Summer in her place. What kind of person does *that*? Later, when my dad was being held prisoner, MacIvor brought groceries to the farm for that jerk of a Keeper. He's one of *them*."

Pictree says, "If he's so bad, will he tell you any-thing?"

I shrug. "It's our only hope. If I can get him mad enough, he'll yell at me and maybe blurt something out."

Cill says calmly, "If MacIvor wife once stealing Ailla, we talk to her first. She know something of names Finias and Kera on tablet."

Tom puts a hand on my head and says in a father-ly tone, "You need to rest and think, Emma. You're too wound up. Pictree and I will go into town to see the MacIvors."

He's taking over again. "Oh no you won't. I'll talk to them."

"We'll all go," he says kindly, and I have a sudden urge to hit him. "But you'll have to stay here, Cill. I don't think humans are ready for a pile of leaves that talks." He laughs. "Although I'd love to see their faces!"

I shrug off his hand. "Nice that you can laugh. My parents' house is a pigsty, Mom's beehives are wrecked. Hilarious, isn't it?"

Without warning, bright lights slide through the room, followed by the low growl of an engine — a vehicle, coming toward the house at high speed. The light goes out, the engine is cut. Everything is dark again. Cill, Pictree and I scramble to the window and peer into the yard. A truck has stopped about twenty feet from the house.

My teeth clench. "I'll handle this. Don't come out unless I call you."

The driver and a passenger get out of the truck, talking and laughing. There are four other kids sitting in the flatbed of the truck — three girls and a boy.

I bang open the screen door of the veranda and wait, hands on hips. I rein in my anger. I'm a Watcher. I'm in ... *take a deep breath* ... control.

The driver is a stocky kid with a thatch of black hair. He's wearing sneakers, jeans and a T-shirt. Ryan MacIvor. His sister, Lacey, was Summer's best friend and spent a lot of time here on the farm playing with Summer — until those final few days, when Mr. MacIvor refused to let her come near us. Ryan was always nice to me, even when the other kids teased me about my pale skin and white hair, calling me names like Icicle Face. They didn't know I longed for friends, yet had no time for them — I had to watch over my family. No idea why — just knew I had to.

I recognize the passenger as well. Benny MacNab, whose head is so full of muscle there's no

Margaret Buffie

room for brains. The people of Bruide are all
stocky, dark, quiet, hard-working, mind-your-own-
business folk. Like Ryan. Benny is different. He
was always in your face. A bully. Odd that Ryan's
hanging out with *him*.

Ryan strolls toward the veranda, talking over his
shoulder. Before he puts a foot on the step, he
jumps back. "Whoaa! You scared the crap outta me.
Who —" He leans forward. "Hey, is that you,
Emma? Emma Sweeney?"

"Yeah, it's me, Ryan. What have you been doing
to my family's house?"

Ryan holds up both hands. "Hey, don't be mad,
Emma. We were told you weren't comin' back,
okay? And the creep who lived here after you left
took off and never came back so —"

"So you figured you could turn it into your own
little party nest? Who told you we weren't coming
back?"

He shrugs. "My dad. Look, I'm sorry, Emma,
okay?"

A girl with long black hair calls out, "Hey, Ryan,
this your old girlfriend from Sunday school or
somethin'?" There are splutters of laughter from
the rest of the kids.

Benny moves in front of the truck. "Hey,
Blondie! This is our place!"

"Shut up, Benny," Ryan says. "She used to live
here. Her grandpa was Keeper MacFey."

"I don't remember *either* of 'em."

Of course not — because Fergus wiped out the town's memory of my family. Will my memory of them be next?

"Wait a minute." I stare at Ryan. "How come *you* remember me?"

He lowers his voice. "My whole family does, but we can't talk about it. Not since you left and especially not since Dad got so weird." He shrugs again.

"Hey, Blondie, you on your own here?" Benny's eyes glint like a gromand's in the dark.

"My mom and dad are coming in a day or so," I say, wishing it were true. "I came ahead — with my friend, Tom."

Tom steps out from the shadows and Benny edges back behind the hood of the truck, sneering. "Hey, you two been watching too many Star Wars movies. What's with the getups?"

The other kids are straining to see Tom. I'd forgotten he was wearing his chiton and leggings, and I'm wearing my green Watcher suit, both a little worse for wear.

Tom folds his thick arms over his chest. "I'm a black belt of Gharanda. Emma's wearing the latest stuff from — er —"

"Montreal," I say quickly. "Where we've been living."

A splutter of laughter and Benny jeers, "So what's a black belt of Ghar-whatever do? Dance around in his little tights on his little tippy-toes?"

"It's like karate. Come here. I'll show you how it works."

Benny's eyes swivel to Ryan. "Come on, let's go. Waste 'a time here."

Ryan moves up a step. "How did you get here, Emma? I don't see a car."

"We — uh — hitched. Why did you say your dad's becoming weird?"

"Nothin' really. Just he's been acting kinda strange the last while."

"Are we going or what?" Benny shouts.

The long-haired girl calls out, "Shut *up*, Benny. Come on, Ry, let's go."

I ask Ryan, "*How* is your dad acting strange?"

He glances over his shoulder, then back to me. "Maybe *you'd* know. Right after you left, I heard my dad telling my mom he'd met a guy named Keeper who'd moved onto the bee farm. He said Sweeney — your dad — was in the barn, some kind of prisoner. Dad was told to bring groceries to the farm every week and keep his mouth shut."

"Fergus's Keeper," I mutter.

"Few months after that, my dad was so stressed I couldn't stand it. So I came over to see if I could help *your* dad — but he was gone — and soon, so was the Keeper guy. Do *you* know what was going on?"

"Does your father ever mention *my* father — or me?" I ask.

"He just babbles. Says that what happened here was partly his fault but soon he might get a chance to make amends. Since the Keeper guy left, Dad wanders off, and I always find him here. Hey, is your dad okay? Did he get away safely?"

"What did your dad mean about making amends?" I ask, dodging Ryan's question.

"Crazy stuff, Emma. Says a yellow ghost told him what to do."

"A yellow ghost?"

Ryan nods. "Says it told him to wait here for someone. Dad keeps saying he should've taught Lacey and me *the old ways*. Whatever they are."

My chest tightens. The old ways. I heard Ryan's mother say those words to my grandfather when he was arguing with her in our kitchen. It must have been right after she switched Summer for Ailla. They didn't know I was listening. Mrs. MacIvor was upset, but Grandpa MacFey told her she was doing the right thing and finally she'd said, "You're right, of course, Ewan MacFey. But the old ways are not easy."

I found out later that, once before, Mrs. MacIvor had placed a changeling younger from a different world with Leto and Dennis Sweeney — after their first baby died at birth. That changeling was me.

Ryan breaks into my thoughts, talking quickly. "Dad's always checking the beehives. Repairs them all the time. Like he's suddenly a beekeeper! He'll go ballistic when he sees how Benny rammed those hives with his truck."

I scowl at the muscle head.

He scowls right back. "Come on, Ryan — move it!"

Ryan holds the truck keys in the air. "Benny's not a bad guy," he says, as if reading my mind. "He's got a big mouth, but he's a good friend. Had a rough life. He's always wanted to get out of Bruide — be a pilot — but his parents won't let him leave the farm. He told me he was sorry about wrecking the hives — knew it was stupid. Besides, the bees paid him back."

"How?"

"After he knocked 'em over, a huge swarm came after him and the other guy in the truck. It being night and real quiet, he said the swarm sounded like a jet plane. They had to close the truck windows and drive for miles to get away."

He looks over at the fallen hives. "Makes me wonder if there *is* something weird going on here, like my dad thinks. Benny was really freaked out. Still is."

"Why do you come here to party?" I ask. "Knowing your dad wouldn't like it?"

Ryan jerks his head toward the truck. "*They* come here to party. I'm trying to prove to Dad this place is just an empty farmhouse — no yellow ghost, now or ever." He throws up his hands. "It's

just that sometimes I think my dad *actually* did see
something. Now my mom's getting freaked. She keeps
Lacey away from here, watches my dad all the time.
It's creepy."

"Hey, Ryan, we going or what?" a girl with short,
spiky hair calls.

He glances back at his friends. "In a minute."

"Ryan, would you ask your dad if he'd be willing
to talk to me? Tell him I might be able to help him
sort this stuff out."

He looks at me intently. "Really?"

"Just ask him, okay?" As he turns to leave, I say,
"We arrived without any food. Could you get us
some? We're *starving*."

"Got just the thing." He walks over to the truck,
reaches through the open window and comes out
with a large, grease-stained paper bag.

"Hey! That's ours!" Benny shouts.

"I'll buy us more."

"When?" Benny snarls.

"There's a social over at the Rosebank
Community Club. I'll pay the entry fee and you can
stuff your faces all night." Ryan hands me the bag.
"Talk to you later, Emma. Gotta go."

"Don't forget to ask your dad, okay?"

"I won't forget."

Benny jumps into the driver's seat, demands the
keys from Ryan and drives the truck in a tight circle, spitting up gravel. As it cruises by, he shouts, "If

you or that ugly friend of yours says anything about us breakin' into this dump, it'll be the last thing you do!"

"Shut up already. Just drive," Ryan says.

Benny kicks the gas pedal, and the truck weaves down the drive in a cloud of dust.

Suddenly the anger inside me spills over. "Jerk!" I shout. I raise a hand to return Benny's final rude gesture, and a crackling light flashes off my fingertips, snapping like a whip against the truck's tailgate.

One of the girls squeals, "What was that? Was that lightning?"

The truck brakes, its taillights flashing, then roars onto the highway.

31

I gape at my hand like it belongs to someone else. Tom pulls me back into the house.

"Did you see that?" I gasp.

"You've got some sparks coming off you, all right," Tom laughs.

"You mean it *was* me?"

"Oh yeah, that was you!" He puts one hand around the back of my neck and pulls me toward him in a friendly bear hug. I can smell the biscuity warmth of his body through the chiton. His heart suddenly sounds loud and fast in my ear. I push away. "Why do you do that?"

"Do what?"

My cheeks are hot. "You know what. Just *don't*, okay!"

I walk away on shaky legs to find the other two while Tom mutters, "How can I stop if I don't know what I'm doing wrong?"

Pictree and Cill are in the living room by the window. I pull the curtains and light two of the candles; then I ask Pictree, "Do you feel danger around us? Right now?"

He stands still a minute, eyes closed. "I don't feel any danger. But I'm not sure if it's because there *is* none or because I've lost my abilities as a Sensitive. I hate feeling *muffled* like this. Ever since that fog fell over Argadnel, I haven't felt like *me*."

"You and me both," Tom says, looking at me funny.

"Never mind. Let's eat." I lead them to the kitchen with one of the candles and look in the cupboards for some plates. There's a crusty pile in the sink, but a few clean ones remain at the back of our old china cabinet.

I say to the three of them, "Ryan gave us a bag of fast food."

"How fast?" Cill looks at the bag warily, no doubt expecting it to leap away from me and zoom around the kitchen.

I laugh and peer inside the paper bag. It smells of vinegar, fries, yeast and hot dogs. Once a week, Dad would go into town and buy hot dogs and fries for the family — double fries for me — as a treat. The memory hurts, but at least I still have it.

I say brightly, "There's something here you might like, Cill. But first —"

I turn one of the taps in the sink and a gush of rusty water pours out. Thank goodness they didn't turn the water off. Suddenly I'm as thirsty as if I've swallowed a handful of sand. I let the cold water run clear, root around in the cupboard for glasses and fill four to their brims. We drink them down and refill them.

I look at the gritty tabletop, thick with smears of old food and mouse poop. "Let's eat on the veranda. I don't think they'll be back tonight."

I don't tell them how the filthy kitchen makes my heart long for my family. And I try not to think that this dark and dingy room, once so full of light and activity, could soon be lost to me forever.

32

Cill and I eat the fries while Pictree and Tom gorge on everything, including the wieners. Pictree declares them as tasty as roast rodere. I shudder to think of anyone eating flesh, even one of those nasty rodents.

Cill loves the greasy fries, smacking her lips and making little oooh sounds of satisfaction and asking me if I can teach her how to make them.

"When this is over," I say, "I'll get Mom to plant potatoes on Argadnel and then show you how to grow them on Cleave."

The thought of Mom makes the oily potatoes turn to sludge in my mouth. I spit them out onto a paper napkin and toss it into the empty bag. While they're finishing their food, I slip into the house and run upstairs.

Under the stairs to the attic is our old linen closet. It looks like part of the wall, the small turn-lock hidden in the deep shadow of the overhanging stair treads. It's still filled with blankets and sheets, and

Mom's little lavender sachets are still scattered about. The kids didn't find it and, from the look of it, the Keeper didn't either. He was such a dumb ox, he probably slept on the floor or outside on a pile of rocks.

I drag out bedding and pillows and put some in each room in case the others want to rest. Setting myself up in Mom and Dad's old room, I push the bed close to a window, where I can keep an eye on things. I make the bed with a mattress cover and two bottom sheets, a top sheet and a woolen blanket, then squeeze a pillow into a flowered pillow case. After that, I open the window to let in a wash of cold night air that smells of mown hay and the heady scent of mature Nicotiana plants.

I sit on the edge of the bed, my knees against the windowsill, and stare at the blue darkness of the night. A headache stabs at the back of my skull and my eyes are burning with fatigue. It's been just over a year since I was last in this room — my parents were reading in bed, Mom's glasses perched on her nose, Dad poring over a set of blueprints for his Plexiglas "henge."

I'd said, "I'm just off to the barn," and they'd looked up, smiling, but then Mom took her glasses off and said, "You shouldn't worry so much, sweetie. Get some sleep. I know you keep watch ... for some reason. But nothing's going to happen to us."

But something *did* happen. A week later, Fergus came to Earth to steal Summer away from us. And we all ended up living in Argadnel. And, despite Fergus and Rhona, Huw and Bedeven, my family created a *home* on that misty island. It wasn't perfect, but at least we were together. Where are they now? In Argadnel? Or locked in a confiner somewhere?

All my life I've dreaded something happening to them. Twice I had to fight to keep them safe. Now I must do it again. Since the fog fell, I've tried so hard to hold back the feelings of fear and anger, but here, in Mom and Dad's room — smelling of lavender sheets and fresh air and full to bursting with memories — I'm overwhelmed by them. Even good memories aren't always a good thing. Sometimes they hurt worse than the bad ones.

A movement makes me look up, blinking back tears. Tom stands in the doorway, one shoulder against the jamb.

"You okay, Emma?"

"It's a mess, isn't it? I have no idea where Moraan has hidden the Erthe Wand. And if I don't find it, I won't be ... *me* ... anymore — and time is going by and I can't tell how fast."

He sits on the edge of the bed and brushes my short bangs off my damp forehead. "I wish I could help, but my powers —." He shrugs. "But you can do it, Emma. And I'll always be here with you."

I push him away. No, he won't. Having Tom so close hurts almost as much as losing my family. "I won't give up," I murmur. "You don't need to worry. I'm just feeling sorry for myself."

"You have every right to feel sad and angry."

I stare up at him. Why can't he ... Oh, what's the *point*? I feel my heart harden.

He says, "Cill's taking first watch. I'll wake you when it's your turn."

I nod and look away. "Don't forget."

"There's a chair in the attic right by a window that overlooks the wood. I'll be up there. I know Cill will be conscientious, but a backup watch is good."

I nod again and let my head fall onto the pillow, dragging the bedding over me. When his footsteps disappear down the hall, the tears threaten again, but I refuse to let them fall. Ironically, I must close off all memories of my family, for I know they'll interfere with my Watcher's abilities to find Erthe's Wand. I must stay focused. Plan. Concentrate. I have to talk to Mr. MacIvor before anything else. I try to plan, set out strategies, but my brain melts like soft caramel.

I'm shocked awake by Tom pulling me to a sitting position. "Someone's here," he says in a strangled whisper. "Follow me. Quickly!"

33

I stumble up the stairs into the moonlit attic. Cill and Pictree are standing in the middle of the room.

"Who — who's here?" I choke out. "Eefa? The Sifs?"

Tom points to a corner in the attic. Huddled together are an old man and Ryan MacIvor.

"This is my dad," Ryan says while staring at Cill with frightened eyes.

I look at the old man. This *can't* be the loud-mouthed jerk who'd shouted at me to leave his family alone. *That* Mr. MacIvor was stout, full of energy, with a bald dome surrounded by a thatch of black hair. This man is thin and hunched, his hair white. He stares at Cill, his body shaking like he has a fever.

Ryan puts a protective hand on his arm, giving Cill another fearful glance. "I told Dad I'd talked to you, Emma. He says you were taken away to another world. Maybe you can convince him he's wrong." He pauses and looks around warily. "Why has Tom brought us to the attic?"

"We can keep an eye on … the outside from here."

The old man mutters something to Ryan, who sighs and says, "He claims the yellow ghost's name was Moraan and he told Dad to wait for Ena, the one with a special mark on her hand."

MacIvor, with some of his old aggressiveness, growls, "I knew it was Sweeney's kid here as soon as he told me about her! I knew you was trouble the first time I laid eyes on you bundled up beside Leto Sweeney. I knew you wasn't one of us. And now you've brought freaks with you from some-place. I heard 'bout other worlds from Moraan — that's where you been. Ain't ya?"

Ryan interrupts. "Dad says this yellow ghost told him that a Druid named Eefa would be stalking Ena, to take some kind of Wand from her. Dad says in the old legends there are people called Druids who have supernatural powers. The yellow ghost — Moraan — is one. This is … *crazy!*"

I have to smile. "Oh, believe me, this is *nothing* —"

As I speak, MacIvor begins to rock back and forth, chanting words over and over. It's the riddle on the Erthe tablet Gernac gave me.

"Moraan told you that, right? Do you know what it means?" I kneel down beside him. We stare at each other for a few moments and then he nods and says, "Yeah, okay, I can translate it for you."

He closes his eyes and in a singsong voice, says, "Erthe power, strength and weakness combined like the wax and the bee, sleeps below the field in the barrow grave of Finias the Elder's brave maid. Come close and once there, Call her name, and lock the amber mask upon the face of Kera."

"An amber mask? Do you mean made of beeswax?" I ask him.

"Yeah, that's what it means."

I stand up. "Barrow? Whose bee field?"

"Not far from here," he says.

"You must tell us where. But quickly, who is Finias the Elder — and Kera?"

"I was told as a kid that Finias was the one who led our clann from Scotland to Manitoba and built the town of Bruide. His wife, Moiren, died givin' life to their daughter. Finias named the baby Kera — which means 'honeycomb.' It was Kera who caused the end of the old ways."

"How?"

MacIvor rubs his bristly cheeks with both hands and sighs. "Kera wasn't anythin' like her parents, who were dark and short — like most Bruidites. She was tall and thin, with pale yellow hair. But she had a way with the bees. Like your mother. Except Kera had no interest *but* her bees. Word was, she always had a far-off look in her eyes — as if she was waitin' for something or some*one*. Some folk said she was simple in the head. Anyway, it was said she would walk through the little town wearing a crown of bees on her head, saying nothin', just lost in her own thoughts. A swarm followed wherever she went. By the time she turned sixteen, she had her own farm — *this* farm."

I gasp. "She was an ancestor of Grandpa MacFey and my mother?"

"Keeper MacFey and she were of the same line. But Kera had no children."

"What happened to her?"

"Not many young men were interested in Kera, beautiful as she was. Most thought her a bit off her head, like. But there was one young fella, it seems, thought he could get through to her. He was the blacksmith, see, and could offer her a good home. But she refused him three times, even though her father gave his blessing. This young fella grew obsessed with Kera, followed her everywhere, watched her every move."

"He stalked her!" I say.

MacIvor shrugs. "One morning, he went to the bee field where she was workin' and asked her a fourth time. I guess she told him to give up, she'd *never* change her mind, because suddenly the blacksmith struck her down and killed her."

"Ooh, ooh," Cill cries. "The *bees*! I bet they get mad."

MacIvor doesn't look at the strange leaf creature, but says, "Yeah. The sky was dark with bees. Like night, they say." He looks at me suddenly. "I don't know if it's true. I'm just telling you the story as I was told."

I shiver, but nod for him to continue.

"When the villagers arrived at the field, nothin' was left of the young man but his clothes. Kera was lyin' on her back, her hands folded like she was laid out in a funeral home and … and she was encased in a clear casket of beeswax. If anyone tried to get near her, the bees forced 'em away."

"How terrible," I breathe.

MacIvor says, "Finias wanted to bury her, but the bees fought him off. Then a young cousin of Kera's, who often helped her with the bees, talked to the huge swarm."

Mom used to talk to the bees. So did Grandpa MacFey.

"No one could hear above their thunderous roar," MacIvor continues. "But they could tell she was listenin', as well as talkin'. She told the villagers what they had to do — dig a deep wide hole and, in the hole, build a wooden hive with a rounded top and place the casket inside. Then they were to cover it all with earth, leavin' one small hole. The bees would preserve Kera until the time for her return."

"Her return?" I gasp. "Wasn't she dead?"

He lifts his shoulders. "No one knew. The townsfolk were told never to go to the field again. That's when Finias decided it was time to leave the old ways, let their knowledge die out, and to blend with the other folks around them. The people tried, but I gotta admit, we've always been seen as a bunch of inbred oddballs."

"My grandfather MacFey and your wife knew about the old ways," I say. "But most of the townsfolk don't, do they?"

MacIvor shakes his head. "Nah. Now and again, I get a glimpse — it's like we have it inside us to remember, but fight it. The strange thing is, that Moraan ghost knew all about Kera. He said he picked this place for you to live because of the ties between your Earth family and Kera. And he told me that I had to guide you to Kera when you arrived."

"He's responsible for me being sent to Earth?" I was right! Mennow hinted at it and now Mr. MacIvor's confirmed it.

"I'm only tellin' you what he said." He lowers his head into his thick hands. "Last year, before you disappeared, I yelled at you to stay away because the sight of you made me want to remember. After you were gone, I felt responsible for what happened to your family. Your dad was kept hidden in the barn, and I knew somethin' terrible had gone wrong. After he vanished, I worked hard at forgettin'. I thought I'd managed it. But then the yellow ghost came and told me the story of Kera and showed me where her grave was. He said I was to guard it until the *one* with the sign of Erthe on her arm arrived." I show him the mark on my forearm. "And that's you, Emma ... that's you."

34

"Shush! Quiet!" Pictree whispers. "Danger. All around. Moving closer."

"Oh jeez," Ryan says. "I hope it's not that idiot Benny!"

I turn on him. "You told *Benny* I wanted to see your dad?"

"No. But he kept harping on and on about you. He phoned me just as Dad and I were leaving — said that some weird-looking woman's been asking about a blond girl named *Ena*. He thinks you're selling drugs and this redhead is your supplier or something. Benny watches way too much TV. He won't —"

I interrupt. "And the woman told Benny to contact her if he saw me, and that's just what he did."

Ryan growls, "I told him that I'd knock his block off if —"

"Let me think!" I command.

So Eefa is already here, but it seems she can't track me without a local's help. Moraan must have set up a protective cunning on the farm. But now she *knows* where we are, thanks to that jerk Benny. I transmute invisible and move to the attic window. The light outside is muted. The sun will rise soon. I can't see anything except the yard, the gray ribbon of the old highway and the distant copse of Grandpa MacFey's trees.

I whisper over my shoulder, "Danger still coming, Pictree?"

"Very close now."

Cill lets out a small squeak. Ryan and his father cower from her. I change my eyes and try a few night visions. When I click into a gray one, I suck in a sharp breath.

Tom asks, "You can see them?"

I can hardly breathe. "Yes."

A semicircle of riders on ghostly stags surrounds the front of the property, the riders' slitted masks like red flags over their eyes, their heads dark gray.

Standing on the driveway are Eefa and Arawn. Eefa's wearing brown leather, a copper breastplate and a helmet with a silver scorpion on the front, its tail covering her nose. The boy is in black, the same red mask covering his face. Behind them, two white stags shift on their long legs, waiting for their riders.

Eefa looks up at the house with a cat-curl smile of satisfaction. She will take this house apart and fling pieces of it through the air before we even know what's happening.

"Is that Arawn with her?" Tom asks.

I nod. "According to Mennow, he's devoted to Eefa. Some brother he'd make, huh?"

"Some *what*? Whose brother? Hers?"

"I'll explain later," I say.

Pictree says urgently, "Entities very close to the house!"

Three gray cloaks swirl toward the veranda. I open my ears as wide as they will go and project my range out of the attic. There's rustling along the main floor hallways, and harsh breathing rises through the floor.

I transmute visible. "So that's why she's smiling! They're already *in* the house!"

Cill rushes to my side and pulls out a long thin knife. "We must fight!"

"No. We're bound to lose. I think she wants to get rid of all of you. On my own, I'd be easy to trick or blackmail."

Mr. MacIvor is on his feet, terrified. Ryan's face is all eyes.

I can hear the Sifs sweeping through the rooms below. It can't be long now.

I whisper frantically, "She's sent them in as tracking dogs to locate us."

My small band of beings is in danger because of me — I have to do *something*. I stopped the waterfall in Fomorii and I became a giant bird in Erthe. What can I do here? The Sifs surrounding Eefa and

Arawn are clearly visible, their crossbows trained on the house. They're expecting me to fly away — so they can bring me down.

We're trapped.

Suddenly Gernac's voice echoes again in my head, as clear as if he is standing beside me. ... *Erthe is strong and weak. But, when it is attacked, those of Erthe always fight back. You must be like Erthe and Waeter, Ena ... and you may discover a power you did not realize you had.*

I close my eyes tight, gathering all my emotions and physical strength together. I imagine a thick impenetrable wall gliding under our feet, up the sides of the room and arching high above the roof. A wall that we can move through, but no one else can enter.

When I open my eyes, nothing's changed.

Tom hands a sword to Pictree. I take my knife from my belt. Cill gives Ryan a knife, and he stares at it like he's holding a snake. We wait.

Nothing happens. I listen hard. Still nothing. I look at Pictree. He shrugs.

"Can you feel them?" I whisper.

"Yes. But more distant now."

Tom growls, "That can't be!"

He strides over to the wall and, with his back against crumbling plaster, inches forward and peers out the window. He frowns, opens the window, pushes his hand out, then laughs.

"You did it, Emma! You put an invisible wall around the attic. Look, Eefa's in a frenzy! Amazing! Even at my best, I could never do *that*." He looks at me as if he's seeing a new Emma.

I run to the window as streak arrows bounce off an invisible barrier a few feet from the house. Eefa throws long orange lights at us, but they veer off in all directions. The Sifs and their Heorots ride around her and, as she screams orders, they swirl faster and faster, until the whole pack vanishes in a puff of dust.

The sun rises above the trees, but its first burst of rays soon vanish behind a thick layer of storm clouds, trimming their edges in yellow.

"They'll be back," Tom says. "They're just hiding until we make a move — but we'll have to go out there, Emma."

I turn to Mr. MacIvor. "I need a detailed map from you. We must get Gernac's Erthe Wand, and only *you* know where it is. You can stay here with Ryan, but my band and I have no choice but to try and outrun Eefa again."

"*Again?*" he cries. "You've dealt with her — it — before?"

"Twice. And beat her both times."

He grabs my hand. "I'll show you. We'll use my truck. It's at the back. Ryan can stay here until I return."

Ryan cries, "No way, Dad. I'm coming with you."

Tom says firmly, "Right! Let's go!"

35

Tom, Cill, Pictree and I climb onto the flatbed of MacIvor's truck, which is nose to nose with our old wreck. As MacIvor starts the engine, Ryan beside him, a blue truck roars around the house and almost hits us. Benny climbs out of the cab.

"Back up!" I shout. "You've blocked us in!"

He ignores me. "What's goin' on? Hey, Ryan, where you been? We gotta —"

Mr. MacIvor leaps out of his truck and charges at Benny. "Move that damn truck! We'll all be killed if you don't!"

No doubt Benny's seen the rough side of Mr. MacIvor before, so he hustles into his truck and backs away in a cloud of dust.

Pictree cries, "They're coming! I can feel them!"

"Let's move!" Tom shouts.

Mr. MacIvor aims his truck over the grass verge, and it roars across the rough pasture, turning to avoid gopher holes and a scattering of beehives. Thank heaven there's no fence. I look back. The road in front of the farmhouse flickers with white and gray shadows and flashes of red.

Benny stares after us, arms wrapped around the steering wheel. Soon his truck is surrounded by white stags, the Sifs visible now and again in the spiraling light. Suddenly, his truck lurches forward and he drives hard after us, the Sifs ignoring him as they race past. I shout through the cab's small window. "They're here! Where's the barrow!" Mr. MacIvor points to a hill of yellowing poplar trees in the wide field.

"They coming fast," Cill wails.

Benny's truck stops in the middle of the field. The frantic *reow, reow* of the choking motor echoes through the air. Why was he driving toward us and not away? Our truck bucks like a wild horse, but we finally reach the grove of poplars.

Tom, Pictree and I leap out and race for the trees. Mr. MacIvor and Ryan stay in the truck.

"Look for the hive barrow! Hurry!" I shout to the others.

There's a shout from Cill, high in one of the trees. "Here!" she cries out. "Wax shape in earth. Go to middle!"

Pictree cries, behind me, "Too late!"

A force like a giant magnet pulls Tom, Pictree and me out of the grove. We land on the ground in front of two sets of feet, one in black leather, the other in orange eelskin covered in gold studs. Eefa grins down at me, her white face and sooty eyes bright with interest. A silver canine shines among her yellowed teeth. Beside her stands the masked young man. I raise my hand, trying to send a flash of electricity at her, but Eefa spins the blue light into the air, laughing.

"Not quite got the hang of it, have you?" she gloats. "Oh, this will be too *easy!*"

I look up at Arawn. "Afraid to show yourself?" I gasp. "Only cowards hide behind masks."

He stares through the slits without moving. Eefa swoops down a long sinewy arm, grabs a handful of my hair and pulls my head back. "I could kill you right here. But it seems you are the only one able to find the Wands ... at present. You will find Gernac's Erthe Wand and you will come back out and give it to me, along with Mennow's Wand, which you have."

"Never," I say, staring up at her.

"Then I will kill your little band of helpers one by one, starting with the Bruide folk and ending with your beloved Watcher." She smiles at the fear I can't hide. "Oh yes, I know all about you, Ena."

I gasp. "If you harm them, I'll destroy the Wands!"

Her eyes spark with a terrifying intensity. "Moraan chose *you* to find them, but I will have them. We can negotiate or you can die. I intend to win this Game."

"It may be a Game to you," I whisper, "but not to me. And you can't kill me, or the Wands will be lost."

She laughs and points to a cluster of Sifs. Everything — their red masks, tightly hooded cloaks, bound legs and boots — is made of dust. When they move, it flies around them like millions of tiny insects. She then points at the truck. "Take the old one and younger and ... let's see ... yes, the Hobyah younger."

Mr. MacIvor, Ryan and Pictree are dragged past me and forced to kneel in front of Eefa. Mr. MacIvor is trembling but grim, Ryan wild-eyed with fear, but Pictree stares calmly up at Eefa. "Don't do what this creature wants, Emma. Do what *you* have to do," he says.

Eefa slaps his face with a loud crack. "Take them away!" In a whirl of gray, the Sifs, Pictree, Mr. MacIvor and Ryan are gone.

I shout, "You won't win your pathetic Game! And I won't be a Player in it!"

She laughs her high-pitched screech. "I've set this Game and you're *in* it whether you like it or not. Moraan's maze is now *my* Fidchell. You have no choice."

"Oh yes, I have!" I cry.

"I'll keep things simple for you. I have your friends. If you don't give me the Wands, I'll turn them into dust." She grabs my arm and hauls me to my feet.

I push her away and, to my surprise, she releases me. The weird thing is, she looks shocked when

I growl, "Oh no you *won't*! Because if you hurt them, you'll have nothing to negotiate for the other Wands."

Eefa narrows her eyes. "So we can come to terms down the road, is that what you're saying?"

I shrug. "Who knows? I'm only interested in keeping my friends and family safe."

"But I could beat you to the next Wand. Then we'll see how well you negotiate." She grins. "I'll just keep your friends for now."

"You'll never beat me to a Wand," I say firmly, hoping she can't see the doubt in my eyes. "Only I can open the portals. You can only follow me."

"Ah, Watcher, don't forget who I am! Moraan couldn't get rid of me on his own because my power was growing too fast. His portals and cunnings are not invincible." She leans close to my face. I can smell her rancid breath. "Never underestimate me. Not *ever*. Meanwhile ..." She sweeps her arm through the air. " ... find Gernac's Wand. I'll wait for you here — and after that, I'll be with you every step of the way!"

36

Cill drops from the trees right in front of us. "Eefa take your friends, Emma. I sorry."

I nod, unable to speak. Poor Pictree. Ryan and his dad must be terrified. Eefa said she'd wait for me to find Gernac's Wand. Then what?

Tom calls out, "Emma! Look! Cill was right. A beehive."

In the middle of a grassy clearing is an old-fashioned beehive sculpted in wax. On top is Gernac's symbol. Quickly, I press the matching mark on my forearm onto it. The hive melts and the Earth widens beneath it. A sweet burst of fragrant warmth rises up and surrounds us. Inside the hexagonal opening are wax stairs. I step carefully onto the first one. It gives a little but holds. Tom and Cill follow.

We descend to a deep chamber of wheat-colored wax. Large decorative bees swarm across honey-combed walls and ceiling, hanging in loops at the tops of six tall pillars. In the middle of the room is a wax sarcophagus. The lid is thin and I can see a blurred figure under it. Kera's arms are folded across her waist. Tucked between her hands is the Wand.

"Man, this is like Snow White's bedroom," I say.

"Snow White?" both Tom and Cill ask.

I'll explain it to them later. Right now, I have to get that Wand. "So, do I tear open the lid and grab it? Hey — maybe you should kiss her, Tom. Never mind. You're no prince, that's for sure." Then I mumble, "Mine neither, apparently."

"What *are* you muttering about?" Tom is irritated. "We have a crazed Druvid waiting up there!"

The casket is sculpted with pale translucent clover, wild roses, climbing vines and hundreds of tiny wax bees. Cill has been examining it while Tom and I carp at each other. She points at the foot of the coffin and says, "There be six-side shape here. Maybe put your symbol here?"

She's right. In the middle of a circle of bees is a hexagon with two small horns above it. I press Gernac's symbol against the soft wax and the casket's lid melts away.

Kera is dressed in a long blue shift. But there's no handsome prince for her. Just three ragtag misfits who want to grab the Wand and run. The Wand is as long as her arm, a wax ball on the bottom and a carved wax oak tree on the top, covered in tiny animals, birds and plants of every kind, like a Japanese ivory.

As I reach for it, a *real* bee floats in front of my face, veers away and lands softly on the Wand. He's followed by another ... and another, until the Wand is teeming with gently humming bees.

I look down at the clear smooth face of this lovely girl who died so many years ago but is still so young. I gently lift the earth cave's mask from my pouch, unwrap it and place it over Kera's face. I clear my throat and manage to squeak, "Bees? I have come to rescue this — er — Wand. May I please return it to its rightful owner, Gernac, the Regent of Erthe, in order to bring balance to a world in chaos?"

Nothing happens for a few seconds, but the buzzing grows louder and slowly the Wand rises up. When it reaches eye level, the bees part, allowing my fingers to grasp it. In a flash I'm in the field above. *I am Kera, collecting honey from one of the hundreds of hives dotted throughout the clover. Suddenly a figure rushes at me from behind a tree. Confusion, bewilderment and terrible pain flood me as a young man with a tortured, furious face thrusts a knife into my side. I look deep into his eyes before I drift down through warm, scented air.*

I'm back in the hive. The girl hasn't moved, but the mask has melted into her bloodless face and now there's soft color in her cheeks. But unlike Snow White, she doesn't wake up. The bees fly to her and form a floating ring around her body.

"Thank you," I say.

As the final bee joins the circle, the Wand melts in my hand and becomes a heavy ball of green stone veined with dark red. I stare at it, feeling more focused and alert than I have since we arrived at the farm.

"Blood-gem," Tom mutters. "Spirit and substance."

I put it into my pouch with Mennow's sphere. "I wish we could help her."

"The bees will know when the time is right, Emma."

"It just doesn't seem fair to leave her!"

Cill pats me gently. "Bees care for her. We go now. Have to get past Eefa. How get away so she not know where we be?"

My gut lurches as I stare up the wax steps.

Tom puts a hand on my arm and I feel its warmth through my jacket. "Remember the night this all started? I asked you what would happen if you fell, who would be there to catch you?"

"Yeah, and I said I'd just have to catch myself," I say bitterly. "I *should* be doing this on my *own*. Huw is dead and I don't know where Mr. MacIvor, Ryan or Pictree have been taken. Soon you and Cill could be ... and my family — if I lose this Wand to Eefa — I'll lose you all forever." I choke out the last few words.

He tightens his grip. "Your training didn't prepare —"

Cill interrupts. "Not true, Tamhas! Since I arrive, Emma get stronger in all ways. *You* keep on go, *Emma*. We help you. You draw from deep inside self. You not lose Wand!"

Tom looks at Cill. "But, even so, Emma is still an untrained Watcher while I —"

Cill says angrily, "You want command Quest, Tom. But you cannot. *Emma's* Quest. This *untrained* Watcher become huge bird, put strong cunning around farmhouse!"

Tom smiles. "Yes, you're right, Cill. I keep wanting to guide you, Emma. It's hard for me —"

"You didn't act this way during the Seeker's Quest." My inner voice stops me. *But he did keep information from you — stuff you should have been told. He betrayed you, in a way.*

Almost instantly my guard is up again. "We have to run — *now*," I say firmly. "Agreed, Cill?"

"Agreed!"

"Tom?"

His face is as smooth as the wax mask I put on Kera's face — but he nods.

We run straight up the stairs to whatever waits for us.

37

When we reach the top of the stairs, the atmosphere outside throbs with a strange silence.

Tom whispers, "Take time to think, Emma. Do we try for the truck? Head back to your grandfather's wood?"

"*Now* you're asking my advice?" I whisper, my heart going like a jackhammer. "Eefa will be waiting beside the truck. I don't know —" I stop, eyes bulging. "*What is that?*"

A heavy thrumming under our feet grows steadily louder. The branches of the bushes and poplars dip and sway from the vibration. I can barely stay on my feet. Eefa is shouting to the Sifs, her voice taut and shrill. We duck behind the underbrush along the edge of the small hill, the rumbling vibration shaking our bones. I can see Eefa through the leaves, seated on her Heorot. She lifts her head like she can smell us. With stamping hooves the Heorots move forward in our direction.

"Aiyeee!" Cill cries, pointing up.

A column as thick as a giant redwood trunk rises from the woods with a roar. It branches out, then separates into black bundles that swerve in wild patterns before joining into large swarms that plunge toward the meadow. In seconds, Eefa, Arawn and the Sifs are smothered in bees. Shouts, screeches and dust fill the air. Running hard, we break from the wood. I look for Pictree, Mr. MacIvor and Ryan, but I can't see them.

"We have to get to Grandpa MacFey's wood!" I shout. "The exit *has* to be there!"

In the field, MacIvor's truck is burned black. We veer toward the farmhouse. From our right, a blue truck bounces toward us grinding to a stop ten feet away. A bearded man leaps out.

"Ena!" he gasps. "Go with the younger. He will take you to the exit." He's a giant of a man, his beard brown and hair full, his cotton shirt roughly sewn, leather pants tucked into knee-high boots. Two swords are strapped across his chest, and the nose of a streak rifle sticks up behind his left shoulder.

I stare at him. "Who are you?"

He holds up his hand to show me the mark on it. "Gernac?"

He hands me a small sword in a gold scabbard. "You released the gold chain when you found my Wand. I have restricted powers, but I can still fight. Take my Wand and this sword. The bees will stop Eefa for a while, but soon her powers will drive them away. I will take Kera to Erthe and keep her safe — for she is the one I dreamed of. I wish I could go with you, but I cannot."

He draws out the streak rifle and runs toward the writhing figures of Eefa, Arawn and the Sifs, calling over his shoulder, "You asked about time in my barrow! You now have less than two Earth days left to find the other Wands!"

I stare after him trying to take it all in. Less than two days left? But how *much* less? And I only just found the second Wand! How can I find two more Wands in less than two days?

"Emma!" Cill points behind me.

Benny is leaning out of the truck gesturing wildly. Cill and I squeeze into the cab, while Tom leaps into the flatbed and crawls quickly to the open back window.

"Where's Ryan and his dad?" Benny shouts.

"I'm sorry, Benny. They've been taken as prisoners. We can't help them. Drive!"

He stares through the windshield, then punches the steering wheel. "Shit! That guy told me to get you to safety or he'd wring my neck. What's this all about?"

"Just move it!" I shout. "Or they'll take you too!"

He turns the truck in a wild circle and we crash and thump over the field.

Tom calls out, "Look! Gernac's knocking them off, one by one."

"And look!" Cill cries, peering out the back window. "Other being fighting them, too. Like outline of light. Maybe two beings, maybe one. Hard to see."

I try to see past her leaves. "Is it Pictree and Mr. MacIvor?"

Tom blocks the window with his broad back. "I don't know. *Good work, Gernac!* He's winning. Uh-oh — wait! Some Sifs are getting away. Eefa's with them. Arawn's beside her. The bees are thinning. She's driven them off — you'd better move this thing!"

Benny's truck roars past the house just as a long swarm zooms overhead, blocking the light.

"Follow them!" I yell.

Benny looks at me as if I'm insane, but does as he's told. The swarm leads us to the woods, as I knew they would. Benny crashes through the old fence around it. The bees hover in the air about ten feet in front of us.

"Stop!" I shout. "We'll get out here!"

As we tumble from the truck Benny calls out, "I have to go back — to find Ryan and his dad."

"No, leave that to Gernac, the man you brought here!" I gasp. "Benny, go home! You have no way of stopping them. Go home. *Please.*"

He's about to back the truck away without answering when we hear the clatter of hooves coming across the highway.

"Benny! Out of the truck," Tom orders. "Come on!"

With a howl, Benny bails. The bees fly farther into the wood, and the four of us follow on the run. The thud of hooves and the snap of branches build behind us. A yelp of pain, then Eefa's now familiar screech of fury. I look back — Eefa's head and shoulders are covered in bees. Arawn is thrashing at them with both arms. The Sifs and their Heorots are black with insects. Still, they thunder toward us.

We race to the spot where we climbed out of the earth cave, but there's only a mass of bees draped around the base of a thick oak tree. They separate as we aim for them, and a gaping hollow is exposed. Cill goes through first, dragging a protesting Benny. I think he's more horrified by her than by Eefa chasing us, but she's wrapped her vinelike fingers firmly around his chubby body. As soon as they're gone, I push at Tom to go next, but he picks me up and stuffs me through the hole. I bang my head as he drops in behind me. Flashes of light spark in my brain just before I land hard, try to sit up and fall back into swirling darkness.

AIRE

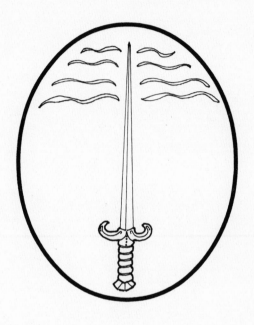

38

How long have I been out? My head hurts. But I got the Wand! That means — yes! — I remember my family!

Suddenly light floods through my closed eyelids, making my head pound harder. I cover my face with my hand. When I try to open my eyes, brightness slides between my fingers like a knife.

"Emma?" Tom's voice is right beside my ear.

"I can't open my eyes," I say. "Horrible *light*. Must be from hitting my head."

"No," he gasps, "I've got the same thing."

"Me too," Cill whispers. "I cover with my leaves."

Benny grunts, "Turn off the lights! Did we really go through a *tree?*"

"Keep your eyes closed," I say. "I'll adjust my vision, find out what this is."

Tom says, "I'm back in owl form and can't change out of it!"

"Hang on." I concentrate on putting a film of darkness over my vision, then sit up and open one eye. The piercing light is diffused, but bright enough to whiten everything, even the hedge on either side of us. My head feels as if someone is banging it with a rubber hammer.

"We're back in the maze."

"I figured that's where we'd end up," Tom grumbles.

Cill is a bundle of leaves curled in on itself. Benny is on his stomach, his head in the crook of his arm. Tom is standing, his feathery head tucked under his wing.

"I'll see what's ahead," I say. "Maybe it's darker there."

Tiny colored lights dance through the hedges, race in front of me with a plinking sound, then zoom into the core of light. Nearby I hear soft music.

"Who's there?" I call.

A breeze brings more lights, which gather to form a yellow sword in the air. From behind it, a single note sounds repeatedly. A second note is added, then a third, followed by a wash of notes, creating a plaintive melody. Each time a new note is added, the sword expands and transforms, folding itself into a birdlike shape with long twisting wings, becoming a moth with a tail that spirals into another winged creature — slowly spreading, turning and changing, each new creation more beautiful than the last. Then the music fades, the images grow smaller, and I'm standing in silence.

"Who's there?" I ask again.

The voice is breathy and low. "I am Nuit."

"Is this — am I in the realm of Lilith, the Regent of Aire?" I ask, taking a guess.

"I know that you are Ena. I will take you to Lilith."

"I have friends with me. They must come, too."

"Your servants are welcome in Lilith's court, as long as they do not speak."

"They're not —"

A tall, slender creature moves slowly into the light.

"Welcome, Ena." The white face, surrounded by a pearly iridescence smiles down at me. The breathy voice is deep, the face a blend of arched masculine nose, thin lips and large slanted feminine eyes.

"We can't go with you until this light is reduced and my friends can see."

A long milky arm covered in bangles that *ting* like thousands of tiny chimes sweeps through the air, and the light dims to a soft haze.

I call out to the others. Tom flies straight to my shoulder, but Cill approaches more cautiously. Benny stays where he is, sitting cross-legged on the ground, gaping at Nuit.

Nuit leans down to him. "You are a — human. How did *you* get here?"

Benny mumbles, "I — uh — I ..." then he crumples backward in a dead faint.

"And you are of the Aire," Nuit says to Tom, ignoring Benny's inert body. He frowns at Cill. "A Barroch. I do not like Erthe. It is dark and heavy."

I prod Benny with my toe. He groans. "Okay, Blondie, explain the joke."

"You've heard of the old ways, right? From Ryan?"

He nods, his face white as flour. "Yeah, bunch of crap."

"Well, welcome to the *old* old ways, Benny."

He sneers. "I'm in a traveling freak show. A leaf creature and a guy who turns into an owl. And now a giant cross-dresser with built-in lights."

"Hey! I can leave you right here."

He stands up. "No thanks. I'd end up like Ryan and his dad. *Missing*. Besides, I *know* I'm not awake. I probably knocked myself out getting out of the truck." He frowns. "But I *did* see those white deer and the bees and — never mind. Just don't leave me here, okay, Blondie?"

"I'll turn you into a mouse with no tail if you don't start calling me Emma!"

Benny says, "Okay, okay! *Emma*."

"Listen, Benny. Tom, Cill and I are partners. If you start pushing your weight around, we'll —"

" — turn you into a toad *with* a tail," Tom finishes.

"I make him into leaf stew," Cill adds.

Benny smirks. "Yeah, okay, I get the point."

I pat him on the shoulder. "He thinks we're kidding."

Benny looks from me to Tom to Cill. Good, he's worried. I laugh, then turn to Nuit. "We're as ready as we're going to be."

39

We follow Nuit through the vaporous light. As he moves, he rings, pings and chimes the same curious tune over and over.

My feet are moving across *nothing*. Cill, who is always terrified of things she can't touch or see whimpers to herself. Benny is quiet except for a cuss word of amazement now and again. I stay close to Nuit, whose cloak's designs keep changing shape, like the sword's light. Finally he stops, takes my hand and presses my right palm toward an oval symbol that suddenly floats in front of us. It has wavy lines around the point of a small blue and yellow sword. My hand drifts right through the symbol. No pain, to my surprise. A black oval swishes open in the soft mist, releasing a shockingly cold wind that almost knocks me over. Tom curses and bats my head with his wings to keep his balance.

"Quickly," Nuit orders. "Inside!"

We rush past him through the black opening. A clear door slides shut behind us. Nuit remains on the other side, his profile toward us, his arms crossed. I recognize something about the shape of his head and his posture — but what?

Benny lets out a whistle. "What a room!"

We're in a dim round space with a curved ceiling and a blue glass floor. On the far wall is a spherical window, pale light shining behind it, but not reflecting into the dark interior. I look out the window and see nothing but clouds racing by.

In the gloomy space, the only furniture is a high-backed chair of velvety black moths' wings and a small table piled high with black bound books. Spread around the chair are more books, some open, some stacked like bricks. From the floor to the center of the spherical ceiling are rows of bookshelves. All the books have black spines. I wonder why the ones above our heads don't fall, but a sound distracts me.

From behind a black curtain emerges a powdery face with red painted lips, a narrow nose, black eyebrows, sharp black eyes and two milky white hands covered in ornate rings. The chalky face and long neck are surrounded by a ruff of black lace covered with drops of ebony jet. The bodice is a tightly fitted triangle of velvet, with a full skirt of heavy brocade. The sleeves above ruffled wrists are tight to the shoulder. Near one eye is a tiny black patch in the shape of a moth. Her hair is strung with jewels, one blood-red stone hanging over her white brow.

"Welcome ... Ena."

"I'm pleased to meet you, Regent of Aire."

"I am so happy ... to see you. Moraan was ... angry with me, for I was the last to agree to his ... scheme. I live in ... closed semi-darkness now. I thrive on light and ... fresh clear air. It is ... hard for me to keep up my scholarship ... when I must struggle for every breath." The voice is wheezy and high-pitched, as if every breath hurts.

"I'm sorry you are not well," I say.

"I ... manage," the painted mouth says with a small gasp. "I visited Eorthe ... many spancrests ago. You are from Eorthe ... so I wear ... the clothes of your world."

She looks like something out of the first Queen Elizabeth's court. It's definitely been awhile since *she* visited Earth!

"You look beautiful," I mumble, giving her a curtsy — which surprises me and makes Tom snort with laughter.

"... I know you will find the Wand of Aire ... Ena ... and release me to my ... winds and light ... and life." Lilith sucks in a breath, and her eyes roll back as if she's about to faint. She snaps open a black lace fan and waves it in front of her face until her eyes focus again.

"I will try very hard to find your Wand," I say earnestly. "Do you know Eefa?"

The fan moves rapidly in the air. "A brilliant and ambitious ... Druvid. I wondered if she might ...

259

be good for ... Fadanys, but I was not allowed to ... think this way. The others in the Tetrad ... agreed with ... Moraan. I was ... *outvoted*."

"You really thought Eefa might do good?" I ask, surprised.

"Sheer madness!" She laughs behind her fan — a breathless wheeze. "... I know you feel you have out ... witted this great Druvid, but she's ... simply *allowed* you to win ... so far — and soon it will be very ... dangerous for ... you to be anywhere near ... her."

She's right. Eefa followed us to Fomorii, but on Earth, she arrived the same time we did and used Benny to track us. How fast will she get to Aire?

Anxiously, I ask, "How much time do we have left to find the last two Wands? Gernac said less than two days but he didn't say exactly —"

Lilith interrupts, "Oh much less than *that*. Gernac always was a bit of a ... dunce about time. Oh no ... my dear, you only have one day left — or less. I cannot be more specific than that. I have no doubt you will do it in time."

I gape at her. "It — there can't be less than one day! I'll never make it!"

"Oh ... but you *must* find my Wand of Aire ... and keep it safe," Lilith breathes.

I choke out, "I will do my best, Regent Lilith." I want to add, "but I wouldn't bet on it." I can't believe we've used up that much time. I feel like throwing up.

"Eefa is so ... clever," she says. "She knows she'll win the Game ... in the end, so she can ... play cat to your ... mousel. You must be cautious, yet quick. You must use your intellect ... your logic ... to outwit her ... if you *have* any logic!" Her fan covers half her face. She lets out another wheeze of laughter. I decide I don't like her very much.

"You call it a Game," I say. "Mennow called it a Quest."

Lilith's shriek of laughter behind the fan ends with a choking cough and rolling eyes. She falls back into the moth chair, grasping the black arms with bony fingers. When she gets her breath back she says, "Dear Watcher. So ... naive. Mennow believes Fadanys can survive without the ... Game, as does Gernac." Her red lips thin in a sneer. "They call this a ... Quest? But what is a Quest — except the Game? Oh yes, to Eefa, this is a ... Game. Make no mistake, Ena."

Her words make the hair on my head prickle. I'm collecting Wands for this Tetrad of Waeter, Erthe, Aire and Fyre, but who's to say that when they have them back, they will make a world free from the horrors of the Game? Am I being led through this Game by some idealistic vision of a perfect, impossible world? Or did Moraan hide their Wands for other reasons? Did he kill himself — or did they kill him? Maybe Eefa works for *them*. And does she have my family? No. If she did she'd use them to blackmail me into giving her the Wands as I collect them. My head is spinning.

"Game or Quest," I say, "I'm here to finish it."

Lilith nods. "Yes ... you must."

Tom says, "Eefa's a nasty piece of work, Regent Lilith. If this is a Game to her, not even you are safe."

Lilith looks as if a blob of slime has spoken to her and looks at me. "Instruct your servant to be quiet. I do not ... speak with attendants."

Tom mutters something rude, then telepaths to me, *Ask her for Aire's disk so you can read the puzzle for the Wand.*

Okay, but don't you think this is a little too easy? I telepath back. *Where's Eefa? Why aren't we running around trying to escape? It doesn't feel right.*

Once we leave and follow Nuit to the portal, that's when Eefa will show up, I bet.

Lilith is watching us with narrowed eyes.

I clear my throat. "I was hoping you'd have a disk for me."

She peers at me over her open fan. "You will go with ... Nuit. He will guide you to the ... portal." She flutters the fan and a breeze swirls around the room, lifting my hair. "Aire is a place of breezes, winds, electricity, the very ... breath of Fadanys. Aire is a place of the mind, of invention ... imagination ... the search for knowledge and ... wisdom. You must use logic and intelligence to find your ... way."

She leans toward me and opens her powdery palm. Lying in it is an oval silver disk. When I take it from her, a small zizz of electricity goes up my arm. I look at the words but, as usual, I don't understand half of them.

Aire Pneuma
Foaghar, smuain and anale
Take ruag to the drochaid
And in the waeters her meamna will tell
of Queen Wynda's galad
Come close to the Darach and
through the geall of Taffine
it will be fadail.

I let my mind open. Slowly the words dissolve and begin to reform, but then Lilith lets out a loud wheeze of laughter and I'm distracted from them. She walks over to the outside door and strikes it with her fan. Nuit enters with a swish of light.

Lilith turns to me. "You may Call one who will accompany you on the ... *Quest* through Aire."

"No," I say. "I won't risk anyone else's life."

Lilith taps her chin with the folded fan. "How ... commendable of you, Ena. But it was set by ... Moraan and cannot be broken. Call a ... friend. Someone who searches for ... knowledge and knows the ways of ... *aire.*"

I look at Tom, who nods. We both know who I must Call. I close my eyes and in a tight voice call out, "Gyro!"

Sharp black shadows zigzag around the room. Something bangs against the wall, knocking books out of their shelves. A black feathered headdress rises above the pile of books.

"Badba," I cry, "what are you doing here?"

Gyro's head rises next to hers.

"Oh no!"

"Not *both* of you!" Tom exclaims.

Badba leaps to her feet, draws two long knives and slashes them through the air. "Emma! Stand aside. I can kill them all!"

"Badba," I shout, "put your weapons away! *Now!*"

She does as I command, but stands, legs apart, long yellow nails curled ready to re-arm.

Gyro creaks to his feet, muttering that his eyepiece is out of alignment. He straightens it, stares around, then clomps over and puts his hands on my shoulders.

"Emma, my dear! Are you — all right? Where are we? Who — " He points at Lilith and Nuit.

"Silence!" Lilith demands. "Nuit, show them the portal."

"A portal?" Gyro exclaims. "Is that wise? Emma, do you know where it leads? I've never liked portals — they go to the strangest places — when one doesn't expect it —"

Badba shrieks at him, "I'm worn out waiting for *you* to do something exciting with your inventions. Finally, we get to *do* something!"

"But where *are* we?" Gyro asks. "It isn't good to act hastily —"

"Silence!" Lilith shouts again, then gasps heavily.

I look at my team — Benny, flushed and scared; Cill's leaves bristling with fear and determination; Gyro, bewildered; Badba, ready to fight just for the fun of it; and Tom, calm, yet coiled for action. I've lost Huw, Mr. MacIvor, Ryan. And Pictree Bragg — how will he save his youngers now? Will I lose some of these friends, too? My chest tightens until I'm sure my ribs will crack. How can I keep Calling friends, knowing they may vanish — or die?

40

Nuit says, "Follow me."

I fall in behind the others, Tom's owl weight on my shoulder. Nuit leads us past the chair in which Lilith is sitting, then to the black curtain, which dissolves as he touches it. In front of us is a door with a single round window. Lilith's chair swivels with a soft whoosh. Her eyes bore into my back.

Nuit touches a dot in the middle of the window and the door shushes open. He gestures to us to enter.

"I'll go first," I say.

"No, no," Gyro says. "I will go first. Please, Emma."

"All go together," Nuit says, growing impatient. His face is tight — anxious — and he's avoiding my eyes. Why?

As we all huddle near the door, I say, "I must —"

"Go!" shrieks Nuit, a long silver pole appearing in his hands. He pushes us through the door.

Was that a giggle? Lilith is still in the moth chair, her white hands gripping the arms, but suddenly her face melts into an unguarded mixture of rage and rapture, her eyes narrowed, her lips drawn back, exposing dark yellow teeth and one long silver canine.

"Eefa!" I shout, and before I can push my way past Nuit, he knocks me back.

Tom flies over him just as the door shuts with a loud bang. This isn't a portal, it's a prison cell — and Tom is on the other side.

"*No!*" I shout, pounding the door. The silver disk clatters under my feet, but I don't care.

"Tell me what has been going on," Gyro says, holding me still. "Tom can take care of himself. Tell me slowly and logically so we can all decide what to do."

Badba nods vigorously, the tall black feathers on her leather helmet flapping. Cill's concerned face and Benny's flushed cheeks flash between the snapping feathers.

I explain as quickly as I can, with Cill adding bits I've left out. Gyro nods, tapping his silver nose with a thick fingernail. Tap. Tap. Tap. "So, she isn't the Regent of Aire, but your enemy, Eefa? And the creature Nuit? Could that be —"

"Yes. Arawn!" I run to the door and peer out its window. "Eefa's pointing at Tom — flying around the room! Arawn is himself again and chasing him. Oh no! Eefa's throwing light streaks at Tom — she'll blow him up!"

Jabs of electricity burn through books. The black moth chair explodes as Eefa tries to hit Tom, who is skimming behind it.

"We have to do something! Wait. There's another being — no, *two*!" I focus on them, but it's like trying to trap a flickering light. "Tom's flying in circles. Now he's diving at the ghosts. He's ... *gone*!"

I shush the babble of voices behind me and press the side of my head to the door, opening my ear's deepest channel. Didn't I see two ghostly figures in Rhona's sanctuary? Is one of them Moraan? Is he alive? If not, who *are* they?

I hear Eefa screech, "Where is that blasted bird?"

Arawn answers, "He vanished. I'm sure someone else was here. I saw —"

"Who could you see? No one can come within ten paces without my knowing. I felt no one. That Watcher, Tamhas, is still here. I *smell* him."

"Eefa," Arawn warns, "calm yourself. You were so intent on the bird, you didn't notice anyone else. You know you can't think straight when you're this angry!"

Eefa lifts her hand and sends out loud cracking bolts of light randomly around the room. Books spew off the shelves.

"Eefa, stop! This is madness. The owl can't harm us now. But you — NO! Don't do it!"

For a moment there's silence. Eefa — dressed now in her brown Player's outfit, her bright red hair sticking up around her small head — is staring at my door, her smoky eyes like a gromand's after its prey.

She grinds out between her teeth, "I'll *kill* her. I'll kill *all* of them!"

"No. Eefa! You *know* that Ena must live until she finds all four Wands. All we have to do is stay close to her. It was just luck that the channel remained open so we got to Aire the same time they did. We beat her to Lilith. Remember that!"

She spews out, "Luck had nothing to do with it, you fool! I know how Moraan's mind worked."

"Yes, of course, Eefa," Arawn says in a light, fawning voice. "But think, dear friend. You can't kill Ena. We must stick to our plan. Don't ruin it by suddenly losing your —" He stops dead.

"Losing what?" she jeers. "My *mind*?"

"Divine Eefa," he pleads, "time is running out. We have to gain the Wands before Fadanys is destroyed by Moraan's final cunning. We *must* keep our heads and let Watcher Ena find the Wands! If you had been able to read that disk, we could have jumped ahead of her again."

Eefa's face is dark red. I realize she's laughing. "Of course I was able to read it, you idiot! I know what she must do." She thumps her chest. "*I* will be in control from now on. I may not be able to take the Wands *yet*, but I will break Moraan's cunning!"

She looks at the window again, our eyes locking. "But then again ... why not kill *her* and take the two Wands she already has. Why not?" She takes one step forward. "I can find the other Wands on my own!"

"No!" Arawn cries. "Moraan's cunning may hold, and then what?"

She sneers. "Why do you go on and on like Moraan's fool? I don't have to do it the way he *planned*. I am *Eefa*, more brilliant than Moraan ever was. I'll break his cunning! But first —" She points a bony finger at my window.

I duck, shouting, "Hit the deck!"

Bodies hit the floor as a thunderous crack tosses us around like clothes in a drier. Cill grabs me just as everything stops, and I make a soft landing on her. Gyro and Badba slide to the floor in a tangle. Benny lands with a thud beside them, holding his head.

I look around the cell and at the door. Nothing has been damaged or broken. That's when I notice for the first time there's another small window on the far wall.

"What *happened*?" Benny moans.

The small chamber is still rocking as I crawl to the door and look through its window. Books are flying through a gaping hole in the wall. No sign of Eefa or Arawn.

I cry, "Arawn must have pushed Eefa's arm, so instead of blasting us, she's punched a hole in the wall and got sucked out!"

As I speak, I realize that my brother just saved my life. *But,* my inner voice reminds me, *only because he wants you to find the Wands so he can steal them.*

I point at the door, and light sizzles from my hand, but bounces away. I can't open it! I bang on its window. "Tom! Are you out there? Tom!"

"You think he dead?" Cill asks. "They all dead?"

"No. No, Tom can't be dead. I'd — I'd *know* if he was dead!"

"Eefa and Arawn?" she persists.

"I doubt *they're* dead," Gyro says. "If Eefa is as great a Druvid as they say ..."

Someone taps on the window on the far wall. A heart-shaped face is peering in at us. Tom!

41

Emma, there's someone here who can help you once you get out.

Tom moves aside, and a long gray face with immense pale eyes stares in at us. It appears to have no nose; its mouth is tucked in on itself. The face slides up and the window is darkened by a moving soft grayness splashed with silvery arrows.

Emma, Tom telepaths, *listen to me. This is the real Nuit. Eefa took him and Lilith prisoners. When Eefa went nuts, she knocked a hole in their wall, too.*

Where's Lilith? I ask.

Free of her confiner. Not what Moraan intended, I'm sure. Nuit says Lilith won't show herself. Ashamed of being duped by Eefa. Nuit will guide us to the portal. But hurry!

Who were those ghostlike beings that helped you?

He shouts, *Never mind that! You have to get out of there — now!*

You saw them up close, didn't you? Was it Moraan? Is he alive?

I know he's lying when he claims, *I don't know. I was being shot at, remember?*

But you flew straight at them, Tom. They saved you, didn't they?

He is angry. *Now, Emma! We still have to find Lilith's Wand — and Pillan's. Wait! Nuit says he just saw a group of Duggs fly near us. Eefa probably Conjured them.*

"Duggs?" I say out loud. "What are they?"

"I know Duggs!" Cill cries. "Dugg tribe once live in Barroch. Fergus drive them out when he take over my world. Not even he want Duggs around."

"What do they look like?"

"Ugly. And bad. Very greedy."

"Duggs, eh?" Badba sneers. "I've had run-ins with that tribe. They're a nasty bunch!" Coming from Badba, that's saying something.

Tom impatiently taps his beak on the window.

I find the disk and hold it up to the window. *Ask Nuit if the disk I have is the right one. Eefa read it and will be heading wherever Lilith's Wand is.*

A long three-fingered hand presses against the glass, then vanishes.

Tom appears again. *It's the right one. Now how do we get you out of there?*

Wait — I must read it first — if I can. I go inside my head and concentrate hard on the disk. The words dissolve as they did before and this time, I can translate it all!

Aire Pneuma
Sound, thought and breath
Take flight to the bridge
And in the waeters her spirit will tell
of Queen Wynda's daughter
Come close to the Oak and
through the pledge of Taffine
it will be found

But I still don't understand what it means. What bridge? Who's Wynda or —

Emma! Tom shouts. *Concentrate! Hurry!*

I put the disk away and say to Gyro. "I can only hope Lilith — Eefa — lied to me about how much time we have left. But the important thing now is for us to escape. I don't know how we'll stay together or even if we'll be able to breathe out there, never mind *fly*! But we've got to try. The window's too small."

I close my eyes and try to imagine a hole in the wall. When I open them again — nothing. I throw my blue light again and again. Still nothing. "I can't seem to make even a dent in this material. Do you think you could try, Gyro?"

Gyro taps his nose in thought. "Yes, I have something that goes through anything. And I have resila cordage; it will keep us tied together. I can live in most climates, as can Badba, but I don't know about Benny — as he's human."

Benny sits on the floor holding his head. "I've gotta wake up!"

"Any ideas?" I ask. We stop and think. At least, I hope *they're* thinking because I can't get a spark of an idea, except a stupid one that would never work. I'm still trying to figure out why I can't get through the wall. But then I've always been bad at walls.

Cill says, "I can be like resila rope, too." She flutters one hand, and four long tendrils wrap around Gyro, who laughs and says, "Of course!" Then he sobers. "But that just means we'll fall together, doesn't it — in a way, really? Emma, you can grow wings, but you wouldn't be strong enough to keep us all airborne."

"No. But maybe, just *maybe* …" I twirl my hand. "Stand up everyone. Turn your backs to me."

Badba mutters that she's not above cutting me up if I do anything bad to her. Benny turns slowly, like a sleepwalker. Once they're all in position, I try to think how a skillful Druvid like Mathus might think. I go into Watcher mode, hold up both palms toward the group and croon, "Wings for everyone."

Of course, nothing happens.

Badba looks around and snorts, "Wings? My clann lost their wings a thousand spancrests ago. Besides, you're just a Watcher — what magick can *you* do? You can't even get through this wall!"

"She *special* Watcher. She turn into bird," Cill says. "You make yourself giant bird again, Emma."

Gyro stares at me through his eye lens. "Surely Cill exaggerates, Emma."

"No. But if I tried again, I'd fill this whole space and never get through a hole no matter how big it was. Any smaller and I couldn't carry all of you."

Badba sneers. "We'll die of hunger here. But I'll be the last alive!" She looks at Benny and smacks her lips.

"Shut up, Badba, or I'll turn you into a bug!" I shout.

She mutters disdainfully, "If you can't make wings or open a hole in this wall, how can you turn me into a *bug?*"

"Shut up, Badba! Everyone stand as before!" I close my eyes, imagining bright red and blue wings for Badba, metal gliders for Gyro, moth wings for Cill and a double set of big butterfly wings for Benny. I imagine mine large and strong, green with splashes of bright red. I keep the images strong in my head. There's a sharp tug between my shoulder blades and cries of shock and amazement from the others.

It worked! Everyone admires their wings, except Benny, who has fainted again. He's lying on his side like a fat butterfly just out of its chrysalis, two sets of dusty white wings gently stretching open on his back. Cill pats his face. He groans and looks up at her.

"I'm really here, aren't I?" he says. "And — and I've got wings on my back. Right? And you're real, too, aren't you, Cill? And you've got brown wings, right?"

She nods and gives him a drink from a vial she's produced from under her leaves. I don't know what's in it, but Benny sits up, face flushed, points at Gyro and says, "Cool. I wish mine were metal."

I grin and tell Gyro to get going on opening the wall, while the rest of us tie ourselves together.

Gyro pulls a metal tube out of his pouch and runs to the wall with the small window. I loop the last of the rope around his waist and tie it tightly. We don't want to lose *him*. He ignites the tube with a crackling sound and slides it over the wall. It cuts the metal like a knife slicing air. A screaming whistle of wind slides in the first fissure and roars around the room. Gyro cuts a hole big enough for us to get through. Like parachute jumpers, we get ready to leap.

42

"Badba, you and Gyro go first. Cill, you grab Benny. I'll go last!" I shout, my hair whirling around my head. "Everyone ready? Gyro, you tell us when we should go!"

Tom dives and whirls, shouting encouragement.

Gyro stutters, "I believe we can — er — it looks as if we might be able —" With a curse, Badba grabs Gyro's arm and leaps through the opening. Benny's wild-eyed face passes me, followed by Cill's.

"Yeeeow!" I cry as I fall out the hole behind them, the rope tight around my hips.

We fall like five lead balloons. I work my wings hard but can't slow us down. Suddenly, a gray creature with enormous wings and trailing silver tendrils floats below us like a graceful sea ray, creating an updraft that slows our descent.

"Nuit is helping you. Flap your wings!" Tom shouts, zooming back and forth.

I pull on the rope as hard as I can. Badba is gaining, Gyro not far behind. But as for Cill and Benny ...

"Cill! Open your eyes!" I shout.

"You won't get your bearings if you don't look! I've got you!" Benny yells. His white wings ply the air in slow jerky movements. I thought Cill would be helping *him*, not the other way around. She opens her eyes and squeaks.

"You gotta help me, Cill," Benny shouts. "I can't do it by myself!"

She finally unfurls her brown-spotted wings, and together they hitch and wobble toward us. The rope links us far enough apart to stay clear of one another's wings.

Nuit glides under us like a silent alien spacecraft, then suddenly swoops up, so close I can feel the force of his wings. He smiles, his face both gentle and terrifying.

He telepaths, *It won't take long to the portal, Ena. You will have to use your mind to win the way through.*

He does a slow somersault, as if underwater, straightens and flies straight ahead, his ribbonlike tendrils touching each of us now and again, as if making sure we're all accounted for. Once we hit our stride, I look around.

"This must be what heaven looks like," I call. "Blue-tinted clouds."

"Heaven what you make it. Mine in trees!" Cill puffs. "Where butterfly take us?"

Tom calls, "To a portal to find Lilith's Wand."

Gyro creaks along behind me, crying over his shoulder, "Stop that, Badba, or I will cut you loose — if I have a mind to!"

Badba is turning cartwheels, a huge smile splitting her face. "This is almost as much fun as riding Lycias!"

Lycias is Badba's drakon — a gentle beast with leathery wings, lots of feathers and a face like a giant crocodile. He saved our lives at the Battle of Moling Bridge by dragging our wounded enemy, the grisly Yegg, over the side of the ship to drop to her death.

Benny points to clouds on our right and shouts, "Hey! Over there! Now they're gone! Did you see 'em?"

In those few seconds, I caught a glimpse of a sharp green face, and the flash of orange wings. "Did you see them, Tom?"

"Yes! Duggs all right. Eefa's using them to keep track of us. But there's no point in chasing them down. Too many clouds."

Nuit keeps going, leading us toward a circular opening in a dark yellow cloud. It's a twisting funnel — like a sideways tornado. Its force tugs on our wings.

Nuit beats slowly toward the opening. Is this a trick? Will he move aside as we get closer and get us sucked into the vortex to be killed by the Duggs? He gestures for us to come, then falls backward, his wings tight to his body. Instantly, he's sucked into the churning whirlpool of clouds.

43

Tom is gripping my shoulder. In a tight bundle of flapping wings, we all fly closer. I stop. Benny and Cill bump into me. Even Badba looks uneasy as she comes alongside.

"I think we'd better untie ourselves. This could be dangerous if we get tangled in the force," I say. "But we'll hold hands as long as we can."

They all agree except Tom, who says he'll go on his own. Holding each other's hands, we tighten our wings as Nuit did and wait for the churning clouds to suck us in.

At first the pull is gentle and pleasant, then it grabs us like a huge hand and we're off! I can't breathe. I'm sure my hair is being torn out of my scalp. I don't know who's yelling the loudest — Badba, I think — as we roar through the funnel. Suddenly we stop for two breaths — before, with a final lurch, we're thrown against something hard. I smack my elbow just as Cill lands on me, followed by Tom. There's a metal crash, then thumps and thuds as the others land.

We're on a surface of pink marble, surrounded by the yellow cloud. Standing nearby is Nuit, his giant wings held wide and high. His body is almost human, the legs long and thin, the torso narrow at the hips and wide at the shoulders, his skin layers of minute gray scales. He has long feet and hands. His fingers and toes have rounded tips, like a tree frog's.

He opens his strangely folded mouth and speaks in a curious musical whisper. On his open palm is a sword of dark blue with a yellow handle. As I take it from him, he says, "Althane, the sword of Aire, for your task. Time is running out. You must pass through the portal, which has been breached. Perhaps Moraan's cunning will compensate, but there is no guarantee. Especially when the major Player is writing her own rules."

So Eefa's moved ahead of us again — she *did* translate the disk.

Nuit folds his wings. Behind him is a smaller funnel cloud. "You must fly to the portal."

I say, trying not to let my voice quaver, "Thank you for guiding us here, Nuit."

"Take care, Watcher." As he speaks, his gray face dissolves into a smooth round head with small delicate features partially obscured by a veil of misty light. Two cerulean eyes look at me with interest. In a thin piping voice the face says, "The portal will call on your reason, your intelligence and your instincts, Ena."

"Do you know how much time I have left to find the last two Wands?"

"You have close to one and a half Earth days left."

I don't know whether to be relieved or horrified. Eefa's lie was terrible, but — a day and a half isn't much better.

Before I can say another word, the creature is gone in a swirl of gray.

Cill asks, "Was Lilith? Or Eefa?"

"It was Lilith, I'm certain," Tom answers. "Can you all fly on your own now?"

Everyone nods. Benny flaps his wings and rises a few feet, a grin on his round face. "This is so cool."

I stare into the tunnel. What's down there? What if I can't open the portal?

"Emma!" Tom says. "We've got to get going. Come on!"

He flies straight into the small tunnel. I lift off. Behind me I hear the creak of Gyro's wings and the rapid beat of the others, along with a few shouts of excitement from Benny and Cill. The force is much less in here, but still pretty scary. We land with only a few bumps in front of a wall with a crystal oval embedded in it and carved with the symbol of Aire — wavy lines with the small sword cutting through them, tip up. It slides open to my touch. On the other side is a small smoky space with lights darting in and out of the vapor.

"What be that?" Cill asks.

I try to put my hand in, but the mist solidifies into a tiny silver gate. When I pull away, the mist and blinking lights return.

"Here," says Tom, landing on my shoulder, "let me try."

"No," I say. "I have to do this. Don't push me!"

Everyone moves back a few steps. Tom flies over to perch on Gyro's shoulder, glowering at me. I ignore him and stare at the vapor. I try to touch each light as it appears, but every time ... clank ... the silver gate closes over it. When I move back, the misty vapor returns. I chew my lip. Lilith said to use my intelligence. Good advice if my brain didn't feel so fried. Wait. There was a picture of the sword in the corner of the oval door when it appeared — maybe the sword Nuit gave me does something.

I hold it close to the mist, tip up. At first, nothing happens. Then the sword pulls my hand closer to the smoke, through the gate, which dissolves — exposing a small clear dome. On its surface, a dozen or more flashing lights blink on and off at different times. I touch the sword tip to one of the lights. It makes a soft musical sound and the other lights go out. Now what?

I touch the light again and it emits the same tone, but two other lights flash. When I touch them, each has a different musical tone. When did I hear music before? Yes! I close my eyes and think back to just before we met Arawn posing as Nuit. I can see the lights in the maze. A melody comes back to me. I try to visualize the pattern in my head. But what was the *first* note? I took music in junior high — and piano lessons — until we moved to the farm. I know the basics, but that's all. I hum the tune. I think the first note is D.

I touch the lights, setting them off randomly, trying to memorize the sound each makes. I find the note that I think is D, then touch the other lights, searching for the melody. I try to proceed logically, and yet think intuitively. I'm close, but ...

Cill says, "One sound you make not right."

"I know," I sigh and try again. And again.

"I think the third note is this one." Tom points to a soft yellow light, not the green one I've been touching.

I run through the sequence again, but it's still not right. Wait, that blue light sounded like the one I'm looking for. I substitute the blue light for the green one, and as soon as I touch it, I know I've got it. The lights pulse in unison, and the melody plays again and again. Then the colors converge, forming a long, smooth face of azure light, the eyes filled with tiny stars, the hair pale yellow clouds. There is no mouth or nose. I hold my breath and wait. Who or what will it ask me to give up?

44

The voice is soft, like Nuit's. "You will lose your powers if you do not find the Wand of Lilith."

That's it. One sentence and the face is gone, and a portal door opens in the wall. I can't see anything through the opening but air.

My mouth is dry as dust. "At least I won't lose my family."

Gently Tom says, "But if you lose your powers, Emma, you can't fight Eefa. And your family …" He doesn't finish it. "Time is running out. We must keep going."

He's right. She'll destroy us all if I lose my powers. It's like I'm standing on the edge of Histal's ravine and I'm going to have to jump and keep dropping until I find out what lies at the bottom.

"Stay where you are," I tell the others, pushing away my fears. "Tom and I will check things out."

I fly out through the open portal, Tom right behind. We're in a gorge of green and black granite, the air a cold greenish haze. Above are gray-green clouds and far below, a froth of green river. Dark shapes rise out of the water, huge tails slapping the surface.

I call to the others, "We're in Moling! Come on!"

They soon catch up and like a string of geese, we fly, following the course of the river.

Tom telepaths, *I'm glad we don't have to cross the bridge to get to the hermitage.*

The disk said there's a spirit I'm to talk to. Maybe it's one of those ghost beings who helped you fight Eefa and Arawn in Lilith's confiner.

No. It has to be Dierdre.

I glance over. *Tom, tell me the truth. Did you recognize those beings?*

He evades by calling out, "Look, there's Moling Bridge!"

It appears in the distance, a long trestle swaying in the wind. The disk mentioned a bridge. We're on the right track for sure! As we get closer, Baudwin's hermitage looms up through a layer of cloud like a picture of a Tibetan monastery. I met Baudwin on my Seeker's Quest. He had once been a powerful, dangerous Game Player but had sworn off the Game when he met the beautiful Dierdre. But giving it up had been harder than he thought. He planned a secret attack on the world of an old friend of Dierdre's father. Dierdre followed him, but was killed by Freelooters on the way. Her father had been killed, too, while visiting his old friend.

Horrified by what he had done, Baudwin buried Dierdre in a small temple room in a hermitage where he remained as a reclusive Scholar and a poet as penance. In order to keep out Game Players eager to pick his brain, he set up a Bridge of Leaps at the hermitage, which no one had been able to cross — until we came along. I spoke to Dierdre's spirit in the temple room before Baudwin died in the Battle of Moling Bridge, saving my sister Ailla and me. We buried him beside Dierdre, so he could be with her forever.

I'm brought back to the present by exclamations of surprise. Everyone recognizes where we are, except Benny, who keeps saying, "It's like some kinda video game. It can't be true. This place! It's amazing!"

On the bottom step of the hermitage, we land — well, some splat, but we're all okay. I remove the wing cunning to sighs of relief from Gyro and Cill. Badba looks a bit sulky, while Benny shouts, "Hey! Why'd ya do that? That was the *best*. Think we'll fly again soon?"

I shrug. "Who knows?"

He hitches up his jeans, ready for action.

"Meanwhile," I say, "let's find out why we're in Moling."

As we climb the stairs, Tom, on my shoulder, stiffens with tension.

"Emma," he says in a low voice, "you've managed well up to now. But you should think about letting me handle things. I'm more experienced. Try to understand — you're going to need more help than —"

"*Why* do you want control? Because I'm a Noviate Watcher? Because you think you know better? Or because you've got your own agenda, and you're holding out on me?"

"So far, luck's been on your side, but now Eefa's well ahead of us. We have to figure out a way to move past her."

"And you can do that," I huff. "And I can't?"

"Emma, look —"

Cill cuts him off. "Emma. Something wrong. Look at door."

While Tom and I were arguing, the cloud thinned, revealing the full building with its sweeping pagoda roof. The designs of fighting men are still on the door, but the center picture of the beautiful Dierdre has been blasted off. The door is ajar. I run up the stairs and through the opening. Bedeven, a vicious Player for Rhona of Fomorii, deliberately destroyed the place just before the Battle of Moling Bridge. Afterward, we'd lovingly repaired it in honor of Baudwin and Dierdre. Now it's been destroyed again.

In the middle of the temple room should be a pool of green water. Above should be a slowly spinning sphere with two faces — the beautiful, serene Dierdre and the scarred warrior Baudwin.

Now the pool is only a few feet of murky water. Pieces of the mural wall lie broken beneath it. Only one small piece of the shattered sphere — Dierdre's eye and part of one cheek — hangs suspended above the pool.

"They done bad thing!" Cill cries. "We avenge!"

"Yes!" shouts Badba, slashing the air with her knife.

I kneel at the edge of the pool. Am I responsible for this, too? Of course I am. I can only sit and stare. The fear of losing my powers sweeps over me. If I lose them, this kind of monstrous devastation will occur again and again.

"I'm sorry, Creirwy," Tom whispers. "I don't think we'll be able to talk to Dierdre. But now perhaps you see you might need guidance —"

"Leave. Me. Alone," I grind out.

Someone pats my head. Benny's round face looks sadly down at me. "This musta been a beautiful place. I know all about masonry — I could fix the wall for you."

"When all this is over —" but I can't finish the sentence. A tear falls into the water, forming radiating circles.

"Look," Cill whispers beside me. "There."

Two faces waver just below the surface of the water. Benny jumps back with a yelp.

"I'm so sorry," I say to the faces, my voice choked. "It's my fault. I promise to fix the hermitage as soon as I can."

The water changes, becomes smooth and shiny as a mirror. The faces lift like glass carvings.

A sweet voice speaks. "Welcome, Emma. You have come far."

"I'm on a Finder's Quest, Dierdre," I say. "I'm —"

"We know what has happened, Emma. The others are waiting for you."

"Who?" I ask. "Eefa and the Duggs?"

Baudwin speaks. "No. The others wait for you. I am sorry that I cannot go to battle with you this time."

"*Battle?*" I cry, suddenly realizing with a jolt that we have few weapons. "We — we're not prepared for a battle!"

"Hey! I am!" Badba snarls, clattering her knives.

"The ones who wait for you wish you to fight Blackabrot, King of the Unseelies," Dierdre says. "He decreed a payment of a thousand gold pieces to any being who would steal Taffine, the youngest daughter of Queen Wynda of the Faerseelies. It should have been impossible to find Taffine, as she was brought secretly to the Faylinns to be Sarason's bride."

"Taffine's name is in the message on Lilith's disk," I say. I hold it up for them to see.

Dierdre begins to speak. "Aire Pneuma — Sound, thought and breath — take flight to the bridge — And in the waeters her spirit will tell of Queen Wynda's daughter — Come close to the

Oak — and through the pledge of Taffine it will be found."

"Yes," I ask. "But what oak?"

"Perhaps the one that you must go through to find Taffine," Dierdre says.

"So she was taken by the Unseelies?"

Baudwin nods. "They tracked Taffine to Gray Sara's clann and stole her away. She will be taken to their fortalice, where she will be forced to become Blackabrot's life-mate."

Cill whispers, "I know Unseelies. I know Blackabrot! Badder than Duggs."

"You must save Taffine," says Dierdre, "for Blackabrot is not her destiny."

Tom says, "And is Taffine the answer to finding the Wand of Lilith as well?"

"Yes. She carries it with her."

45

Stunned at this news, I ask, "Does Eefa know this?"

"She destroyed our temple to try and make us tell her everything. We told her nothing. She already knew from the disk that Taffine is the *link* to the Wand. But not that she *has* it."

"So you're saying Druvid Moraan gave *Taffine* the Wand? And now she's been kidnapped?" I want to pull my hair out. I pace back and forth in the small space. "Dierdre, where have they taken her? I have to find the Wands of Aire and Fyre in less than a day and a half in Earth time. But how do we know this Blackabrot hasn't found Aire and already given it to Eefa?"

"Taffine doesn't know she has it. If Blackabrot finds it he won't know what it is, only that it has great power."

"Oh wonderful!" I growl. "This is just *perfect!*"

"Gray Sara and Sarason must have some idea where she's been taken," Tom says calmly, giving me a warning look. "They'll remember us from your Seeker's Quest, Emma."

"Yes," Dierdre says, "they can show you." And her image fades.

"We'll have to go to the oak forest and find them," Tom says.

"No need," Baudwin replies softly. "They are here."

I whisper to his fading image, "I'll come back one day. I promise. We'll fix the temple again."

I hear Cill's squeak and turn to find a group of beings behind us. I recognize Sarason with his red hair and snub nose. And how could I forget his mother, Gray Sara, leader of the Faylinns? Everything about her is gray — the long woven cloak, her hair, her skin — even her eyes. I also recognize the rough auburn hair, woven leggings and jackets of dull maroon and green tartan of four other members of the Faylinn tribe. This is what they wear when they're not tiny dancing creatures draped in wisps of fabric with flowers and jewels in their hair. They're what humans would call Faeries, but they're nothing like those mythical beings.

With them are six female beings — small and slender, with long copper hair, narrow dark faces, black eyes and pointed noses. They're dressed in dark orange, from their loose shirts to their silk-wrapped legs, which end in soft boots encrusted with beaded leaf patterns. On their right shoulders they carry bows and quivers. On their left, strings of colored stones. These must be the Faerseelies.

They scowl at me suspiciously, their black eyes glinting with malice.

Gray Sara says, "Yee 'ave return, Watcher. Once more a younger 'as been taken from we. Taffine be promised life-mara of Sarason. Blackabrot taken Taffine. Yee must go with Sarason and Faerseelies. Fetch er back 'ere." She points at a Faerseelie who looks older than the others and wears a copper band around her neck. "Er be leeds of clann. Dradia."

Dradia stares at me with savage hostility.

"Do you know where they've taken Taffine?" I ask Gray Sara.

"Troo fire. Eefa follow. I 'ear leaf drop. I 'ear er talk. Eefa speek 'bout goin' where Blackabrot hide-lair be."

"They went into a fire?" I ask. The disk doesn't say anything about a *fire*. Something's wrong.

Gray Sara says, "Wee show where fire be. Sarason, my clanna and Faerseelies go with yee troo't. Sara will 'ave revenge!"

Dradia walks up and leans close to my face. Her language is a series of whistling sounds, but easy to translate. "I warn you, Watcher. If Taffine is harmed because she is unwittingly carrying your Wand of Aire, I will kill you and all your Players."

"I — they're not my Players. They are my friends. We're on a Quest and your threatening us doesn't —"

But she turns her back on me and walks away.

We follow Sara, scary Dradia and the others to the back of the hermitage. In the distance, part of the oak forest belonging to Sara's tribe is covered in dense smoke.

"Blackabrot burned your forest!" I cry.

"Partlee burn-ned. Eefa come and trick us to say where Blackabrot go. Er make magick cunning and go troo fire where Blackabrot takee Taffine. Eefa say — where Eefa go be Emma desteeny. And Eefa laff like crazed giff. Er make manie of my tribe sick — give my familees foods that urt em. I muss elp with 'erbs and poultice. Dradia warn-ned me. I not 'ear er. Dradia's tribe not getee sickly."

Tom says, "Eefa beat you here, Emma, and, as Sara says, it's your destiny to follow *her*."

"*Eefa's* not my destiny! But of course we must follow where she went — if she went after Taffine."

He doesn't answer. Just glowers.

"So Game reverse now," Cill says solemnly.

Badba snarls, "We'll get that Eefa and cut her head off!"

Benny asks, "Doesn't the disk say what to do?"

"The disk led us here," I answer. "But things have changed. The disk is useless now."

Gray Sara touches my arm. "Ifin yee tell me what ona disk, mabee Sara help yee."

Tom, on my shoulder, says, "Might as well read it again, just to be sure."

I give him a sour look and take the disk out of my pouch.

"Look!" I cry. "The message has *changed*." I read it aloud, tripping over some of the words.

Aire Pneuma
released by Waeter and Erthe
Fuels the predator Fyre, yet
is consumed by it
To the fior truen will Pillan
release his disk to find the twin
So use the lann of Althane
Upon the heart of smuid
Then strike the spor to enter

Gyro asks, "Does this mean you have to find the Wand of Fyre first? Why else the reference to Pillan? Is he not the fourth of the Tetrad? You may, possibly, have to backtrack later to get Taffine."

"No!" Dradia whistles. "Taffine first!"

"But the disk has changed," I say to her. "I should follow it."

Her face hardens. "You will find Taffine first or you will all die."

"We can't risk losing sight of Taffine," Tom says. "Emma, you're out of your depth now. Can't you let me —"

I reply, sarcastically. "Solve it all? Sure. Go ahead!"

He glowers at me, but I ignore him.

"Pleeas. Emma," Gray Sara says, "letee Sara hear disk once egin?"

I hold the disk out for her to see. She shakes her head, so I read it out loud and say, "I understand that 'lann' means sword but what is 'fior truen'?"

She nods solemnly. "It mean hoo be trulee brave."

"And 'smuid' and 'spor'?"

"'Smuid' mean smokee — the other, 'spor,' be the one that starts fire. I call er flint. Make a lick'a fire."

I feel the familiar tightness in my chest. "See? It's leading us to Eefa anyway. We have to go to the fire, use the sword of Althane on its heart of smoke. That's what this means. But can we find both Wands in less than a day and a half?"

Badba sneers, "You've never let a *time* challenge throw you off. Don't start now."

I can't help it. I grin at her.

Gray Sara points to a group of small ponies eating grass and says. "Ride back to forst. I give mea pony to Emma. Two extree for her tribe."

Sarason nods and runs down the wooden walkway that leads to the meadow beyond. The others stream behind him but not before Dradia throws me a sour, suspicious look.

I look to Sara for reassurance, but she waves her hand. "Go-ee now, Watcher! No' to wastee time! Go!" When I next look back, she's gone.

As worried as I am, I have to laugh, watching Cill, Benny, Badba and Gyro trying to squeeze onto two small white ponies. I drop down into Watcher mode to make myself small, and call Cill to share Sara's pony with me.

After some loud debate with Gyro, Badba cries, "Just take the blasted horse. I can run faster anyway. Give that useless human, Benny, the other one."

Tom's ahead, flying low and steady. When we reach the forest, I change back into Emma mode. Sarason and Dradia take us to the center of the smoking woods, where Dradia points at a pile of red coals and announces that this is where Eefa vanished. The smoke is dense and foul. Benny is coughing badly, his skin pasty. Cill holds her leaves up and away from hot spots on the ground. Gyro's metal sections have waves of heat coming off them.

"Are you sure?" I ask.

"You don't trust what I tell you?" Dradia jeers.

"I'm only asking."

Sarason's four Faylinns and the six Faerseelies gaze at me silently. I point at the coals and ask if everyone is sure this is where Blackabrot and then Eefa went through. They all nod, nervously glancing at Dradia.

Tom, sitting on a burned branch, telepaths, *Ease up, Emma. You're questioning a proud leader in front of her clann. You can't show you don't believe her.*

I know he has a point, but I'll never admit it to him. Instead I sneer, *Surprise! There you go, doubting my leadership again. Dradia is very hostile. I want her to understand that as long as she acts this way, I don't — won't — trust her, okay? She must earn my trust.*

Or you could simply trust her and gain her respect that way. You still have a lot —

Yeah, right, I know ... a lot to learn! But I'm going through this fire portal and you can come or not. And so can Dradia. Now, I have one question for you. Are those ghosts of yours following us right now?

I don't know. But it might be someone who is willing to help you — as I was helped.

Why won't you tell me the truth about them? You're keeping something from me. Deliberately. My friend and Watcher, eh? Out loud, I say to everyone, "I'm going through this portal. With luck, I'll find Taffine before Eefa does. Those who wish to come, follow me."

When I pull the Althane sword from my belt, its yellow blade shines brightly in the smoky gloom. I point its tip over the circle of embers, hold my breath and stab into the center. The coals shatter, an orange shaft opens, and I'm sucked into the portal's searing red heart.

FYRE

46

To my right is the dim outline of the hedge. The black air smells like burning rubber and gives me an instant headache. My hair is singed a bit, and my clothes have scorch marks on them. A second later, Tom hops onto my shoulder, batting at a few smoking feathers. "Here I am, O leader of the Quest. *Now* what?"

A blue light cuts through the darkness, Gyro's voice following it. "Are we all here? All except for — oh no! — Tom and Emma!"

"We're over here!" I shout.

The light slides over the maze hedge. Cill cries, "Oh, Emma! Thank Oaklah!" Gyro creaks out of the darkness, a bright light shining from his helmet.

Benny says, "We're back in that maze, right? Whew! What's the awful smell?"

"Gyro, turn that light out. We'll see better without it," Badba orders.

The light goes off. The maze is cast in a dark greenish glow. Dradia, Sarason and their tribes emerge from the gloom. Dradia's hair is singed, too. She nods sharply at me. I nod back. Not friends, but a sign of respect, I think. Good.

"Okay, everyone," Tom announces. "Keep your eyes peeled — for Eefa, Duggs, Unseelies, or anything else not right, and tell me immediately — or Emma, of course."

"Yes," I say, frowning at him. "Meanwhile, you fly ahead a bit, Tom — as lookout. But keep to the right. That worked before."

He gives me a slow nasty owl blink, then takes off, with a disdainful flapping of wings. The rest of us trudge on for ages. A few times I have to tell Badba to quit griping, but other than that, everyone is pretty quiet. Just when I'm wondering if we've gone the wrong way, the smell of burning rubber grows stronger and we come upon two rows of vaporous red lights suspended along the hedge. Each light is caught in a round metal cage like a captured moon. I call Tom back to my shoulder. He lands fast, his talons digging in hard. He's still miffed.

At the end of the path is a stone wall inset with two metal spheres made up of overlapping silver "petals" joined in the center. One has been destroyed and then closed over with blackened fused debris. There are deep burns and gouges on the second one. Dradia looks at Tom for an explanation, but I beat him to it.

"Eefa must have opened one and wrecked it before going through the other, but was in too much of a hurry to totally mess up the second one," I say.

Tom adds, "There are silver studs in a smaller circle in the center, as if its petals have been nailed shut. I think it's a portal."

"Gee, you think?" I sneer.

"So how the heck do we open it?" Benny asks.

"Disk say strike flint and enter," Cill says.

"Yes," I say, "but who carries around a flint, for crying out loud? I didn't think to —"

A dozen hands push under my nose, each holding two sharp-edged stones.

"Aaah," Gyro says, "we don't appear to lack for flints."

Sarason says, looking at the sphere with interest, "Firee needis woods to spark."

I examine the portal. One of the studs is dark blue. "Let's try sparking a flint at this," I say. "Dradia, you try first."

Dradia looks at Tom, who nods. I swallow my irritation. With practiced movements, Dradia sets her flints sparking. They hit the blue button with rhythmic splats. Slowly the button turns red and sends off an intense heat that spreads to the other "nails" on the sphere. The first one pops, just missing me. When the last one pops, the steel petals try to open, but Eefa's weld holds them closed. Dradia sparks her flint at them, but nothing happens.

"That *stupid* Eefa," I growl. "Stand back!" I can feel the anger pulsing through my body and into my hands. I aim my right hand at the swirl of petals. Blue sizzling lights arc and zap the portal again and again. Finally the petals creak open. Behind them is a wide metal tunnel.

Dradia stares at my hands, a half smile on her dark face. The others edge into the tunnel. When I stay rooted, exhausted and still shuddering with anger, Badba gestures at me.

"You're the leader, Emma. Do some leading here! Or I'll take over."

Will I lose my powers as soon as I enter the world of Fyre? After all, I didn't find the Wand of Aire. I step forward. My knees feel about to buckle.

Badba crows, "Thought that would get you moving. Make way for our leader!"

The others stand aside for me to pass, then clatter along the steel walkway behind me. It's not far to a metal circle ahead — no doubt *another* portal. Like a mass of dark cloud, a silent stillness fills my head.

Tom telepaths, *Emma? Are you okay?*

I can't say it. I can't tell him how afraid I am. I can't tell him that I can't go on because I'm scared I'll lose my powers — and everything else with them. I can't tell him I don't trust him anymore, that I know he's lying — keeping secret the identity of the ghosts, trying to take control of the

Quest. He was my soulmate, my *split-apart*. Now we've split so far apart we'll never join again. The air between us blurs. I can feel myself teetering.

"Okay, everyone, let's take a break," he calls. "Sit down, Emma. You need to unwind."

I can't *unwind*, I want to shout. If I do, I'll fly apart into a million pieces. And then you'll finally be leader, Tom. I start to laugh and can't stop.

His voice rings out. "Has anyone brought food? Water?"

Dradia says something in her sharp whistling language. Soon, food wrapped in small oily bundles and water in leather pouches appears. Cill organizes it.

"I forget you *human*, Emma," she says. "You need food, rest. Sit, please."

Hiccuping, I sit down and accept a scoop of mashed sweet berries and a piece of honey cake, not bothering to point out that I am not, in fact, *human*. I almost throw up the first mouthful. Am I that tired, that *afraid*?

Cill whispers, "I know you worried about time — and about lose powers. Eat first. Get strength back. Then see if powers gone. Take little bit time, Emma."

"I have no idea how much is even a little time, Cill," I choke out. "I don't know how much time we have left." I want to cry, but can't — not in front of Tom and Dradia. I try not to eat too fast after that and when the first gush of water fills my mouth, it's positively ambrosial.

Benny shoves a squashed chocolate bar at me, but I shake my head. He *is* human and needs the sugar for energy. Soon, he's sharing it with a young Faerseelie called Whim, and from the bliss on her face, she likes it.

I rest a bit, then decide on a simple test to check my powers. I wait until everyone seems asleep, then I try to go invisible. My heart leaps when I see my hands vanish, then the rest of me. I immediately return to Emma mode. Cill reaches over and grips my arm. I smile at her.

Tom is sitting nearby on a piece of scrap metal. "This is great, Emma! As long as you don't ... over-react to — er — things."

"Oh, don't worry, I'll do as I think fit."

He looks away with a scornful snort.

I glance at the round door. I can't sit any longer. In the center is a small triangle, and inside it the outline of a bird's head, its wings touching above it like two flames. I know I'll have to press that image into my skin in order to enter what lies beyond. I hold the back of my left hand to the symbol but can barely work up more than a low groan when the fiery pain goes through my hand and up my arm. The metal gate squeaks open.

The first thing that hits me is the stench. It reminds me of a school visit to a blacksmith's at a

Manitoba historical site. But this is a thousand times stronger — an intense, oily stink of sulfur, tar and brimstone. A few of the Faerseelies are coughing and Benny is throwing up. Poor human Benny.

Our tunnel is high in a wall of a huge triangular room. Below, at the meeting of three metal walkways — one attached to each wall — is a big egg-shaped metal cage. Under the walkways, a crust of black goo heaves and bubbles, exposing molten cracks of red.

"Dangerous down there," Tom says grimly.

"Boy, you're observant," I say, and his talons tighten. "Ow — ease up, okay?"

The light in the chamber comes from five, hovering, caged red moons. Nine birds with black feathers and yellow tails and crests fly slowly around the lights, now and again wafting silently past us — as if unaware of our presence.

"How we get down?" Cill whispers over my shoulder.

"How beautifully designed," Gyro breathes, waving a small glowing rod in the air. "I am reading an admixture of metals — an amalgam of great complexity — but I'm sure it includes palladium. Only a High Alchemist could produce such a balance!"

I peer over the edge and answer Cill's question. "There's a ladder leading down to one of the walkways."

Tom says, "I suggest you and I go first, Emma, followed by —"

I say firmly, "I'll decide, thank you. Just give me a moment to think."

Dradia pushes to the front. "Sarason says Tom is *your* Master Watcher. We must allow one of his status to lead us."

My face grows hot. "This is *my* Quest. It is not Tom's. Moraan set the … Game … for me — so I am the leader."

"You would be wise to listen to Tom's expertise," she says. "You are willful. Whatever anger you feel for him must not cloud your judgment. We have a right to a clear-thinking leader."

"Emma save me and others in Seeker's Quest," Cill says. "She be good leader. She think of others' safety."

Sarason interjects. "Emma be a goodly friend to Faylinns — but wea musut makee cleer. Who bea leeder, Tom or Emma?"

"I think Tom should lead us," Dradia says. "I don't trust this Eorthe human's abilities. She listens to no one."

Gyro speaks up, "Now, now, you haven't had much of a chance to judge. As it happens, she is *not* human — not that this is bad thing … but I can — er — almost guarantee that Emma is an excellent leader. Mind you, Tom is also —"

Badba elbows him. "You're not helping, Gyro!" Then she slaps her chest and crows, "I will be leader!"

That sets everyone off. Cill, for the first time since I've known her, is shouting with the others. Dradia is right. I haven't been listening to anyone. I've only been following my own way. I must ... the noise gets louder. I try to speak — to explain and apologize — but the arguing is escalating. Tom sits to one side, listening. When I look directly at him, he looks away.

That does it. I raise my hands and send a blue light down the length of the tunnel like a jab of crackling lightning. Everyone shuts up and gapes at me.

Cill breathes, "Emma not lost powers! They *growing*."

Dradia steps up to Tom and says, "Someone must be leader. Will you do it?"

Tom is quiet for a long time. Then he says, "I cannot be the leader. Only Emma can lead this Quest. It's what Moraan arranged."

She whirls around and glares at me. "Then *you* will find Taffine or —"

"I know, you'll kill me. Look ... I apologize to you and to Sarason. I will listen to whatever ideas any of you have. And I will also pay close attention to Tom's. We will work as a team from here on in. Agreed?" Except that I know Tom has his own agenda and will do whatever he likes eventually. I just wish I knew what it was.

Dradia narrows her eyes, then nods. Sarason answers, "Agreed."

"So we must plan how to approach the cage below," I say. "I looked along the top of the wall above the metal walkways. There are two other openings on a level with ours. One is closed and one is hanging askew, kicked or blown open. Eefa, no doubt. She may have captured Pillan and be posing as him. We must be cautious —"

Tom arches his wings, ready to fly.

"No," I say urgently. "Those birds might attack you." I turn to the others. "Tom and I are going down the ladder. If I raise my right arm, it means it's okay for you to climb down. Agreed?"

Dradia nods curtly. "Agreed."

Badba pushes her way to the front. "I'll come as well."

"No —" I begin.

She holds up a dark blue hand. "I've been patient, Emma. Even you would agree with that. I've followed orders, even though I am a Ravan. In case of bird attack, I can fight them off."

Gyro says, "She's right, Emma. Let her go with you." He smiles at Badba proudly.

"My tribe will be ready to take them down if Badba has to fight them," Dradia says. "We must work together ... for *now*."

Cill squeezes my arm.

I nod. "Okay. Badba, you follow Tom and me down. Keep your knives hidden and your big mouth *shut*." She glares at me. "I mean it, Badba. Or

— or I'll turn you into one of those," pointing at the birds.

"Fine, fine," she says, but I know she could be trouble.

"Everyone else be on alert," I say. "Take action, *only* if I give the signal for attack. I'll raise my left arm — and it will hold the sword of Althane."

I climb down the ladder, Tom as stiff as a stuffed owl on my shoulder. I keep an eye on the birds, expecting them to attack when we reach the walkway, but they keep swirling and diving like fish in an aquarium, uninterested in our presence.

I walk cautiously toward the cage. The stink below us is eye watering, lung rotting. I close my nostrils and breathe through my mouth.

The cage is finely wrought with thin vertical rods of silver and gold. I let out a small yelp when a chalk-white hand grips one of the rods, then moves to another a few feet farther on. Once I see the flash of a pale yellow eye. I hope this creature is leading us toward Pillan, not Eefa.

47

The "egg" sits on a triangular platform. As we walk
around it, we come to a triangular window covered
in gold screening as fine as a cobweb. Behind it, a
humanoid lounges, arms and elegant legs crossed as
if he's leaning against a building waiting for a bus.
He's tall, hairless, pure white and naked except for
a loincloth of sparking metal threads.

"You took your time — considering it's running
out ... *fast*," he drawls. "Ena, the Watcher, destined
to save Fadanys, I presume? A trifle out of sync,
aren't you?"

"Pillan?" I ask.

He snorts. "Who else would be caught alive
inside a ridiculous metal eggshell? Moraan said that
I would be like the Phoenix, rising out of my confiner. Those absurd birds are supposed to remind
me of that promise. Moraan didn't much like me,
even though I pledged allegiance to his plan. I
didn't like him much, either, but I liked Eefa even
less — the devious hag." He sniggers. "She's ahead

of you, by the way. She thought she was following Blackabrot to his lair, but ended up in the maze and found her way here. She demanded to know why she'd ended up in *my* confiner. She needed to find some being called Taffine. Of course, I told her I had no idea who this being was. She was very, *very* angry when she left, devising all sorts of punishments for you. I particularly liked her idea of roasting you in Moraan's laborare fireplace. Admit defeat, Ena. She'll find whatever she's looking for before you do. You're not *evolved* enough to beat Eefa."

"*Excuse* me?" I say, hands on hips.

He smirks. "I don't think I *can* excuse you! Eefa told me you've *lost* Lilith's Wand, and now she's going to have to find it herself, after she locates mine!" He pushes off his wall and moves gracefully toward me. Red and yellow lines slide under his white skin. "I bet she's already *found* Lilith's Wand." He winks and a small flame licks his eyelid.

"How long ago did she leave?" I ask, not rising to his bait.

"Not long." He touches the webbing and flames roll around it like lit alcohol spilled across a table. "Hasn't come back this way, either."

I swallow hard dreading his answer, but ask, anyway. "How much time do I have left to find the Wands?"

He laughs. "In Earth days? Less than one."

"You're lying!" I yell. "You must be!"

"I assure you I am not. I have no reason to lie. After all, even I want you to find the Wands."

My heart sags in my chest. I'll never make it now.

"Giving up, Watcher?" He grins at me maliciously.

I glare at him and to my own surprise, growl, "*Never.*"

"Did you give Eefa your disk?" Tom asks Pillan.

Pillan snarls, "Don't be a fool! I would never give the disk to that horror!"

I frown. "How do I know you *aren't* Eefa? She locked Lilith in one of her own rooms and then pretended to be her."

He laughs, smoke curling out of his mouth. "Lilith is supposed to be so bright, so intelligent, so *informed*. Yet why am I not surprised Moraan was so afraid Lilith would drift out of her confiner — birdbrain that she is — that he made her solid as ... well, as a *human*. He didn't think it through, did he? It made Lilith a *sitting* bird, easy for Eefa to pluck." He laughs again then blows a perfect O of flames at the webbed window. They lick through, almost burning my skin.

"Now," he croons, "all Eefa has to do is watch you find both Wands — if you *can* — and steal them. Looking at you, I think she has a good chance!"

Badba lets out a growl, but I glare at her and she reluctantly subsides.

I say, "Just give me the disk."

Pillan shrugs and tosses me a triangular red object. It slices through the webbing, and as I catch it, he says, "Don't forget you've got to Call some-one to help you, though what good it will do, I *don't* know. You've made quite a mess of things. And that pile of beings with you! Look at them up there, crowded around the tunnel opening, like baby birds in a nest!"

"I have no one left to Call," I say. "I can't risk more friends or any of my family. I can't."

He leans close to the webbing. "Ena, even though it may not seem so, I am on your side. Call *me* as your next Player."

"You have no powers," I say, standing firm. "And it must be someone I trust."

"Well then — just remember, the Regency of Fyre depends on you. When you reach the portal, you must know that Fyre is both the heat of destruction *and* the light of creation. Use your brain, your strength, your emotions and the dual forces of Fyre to gain entry. Too much to ask of such a puny little being, perhaps. How you got this far, I *don't* know."

I snarl, "Just show us the way out."

He points to the hole in the black wall where the metal door is hanging. The ladder up to it is bro-ken. Oh great. I lift my right arm to let the others know they can climb down.

As I turn to go, Pillan calls, "Are you so sure that one among your Players has not already betrayed you?"

48

We're all standing at the bottom of the broken ladder leading to the wrecked tunnel. Except for Tom. He's sitting at the mouth of the tunnel we just left, and by the movements of his head, it looks as if he's talking to someone. Pillan is watching, too, and sniggering.

"Tom!" I shout. "Who's there with you?"

Immediately, he flies to us. "I thought we left a few weapons up there."

I don't want to argue in front of the others. Instead, I ask for ideas for getting to the mouth of this tunnel. Gyro suggests making a rope ladder and sending Tom up to loop it over something in the tunnel. It doesn't take long for him to create a makeshift ladder.

"Eefa's destroyed part of the tunnel wall. There are some sharp metal pieces I can hook the rope over," Tom shouts a few minutes later. "Okay. It's in place!" And we scramble up to the narrow opening.

Inside, Tom says, "Read the red disk before we go any farther."

When I look at it, words and symbols appear, vanish, appear again, dissolve. "It can't make up it's mind," I say, bewildered.

When it finally settles, I study it. And to my relief I can read it.

> *Fyre pneuma*
> *Blood, spirit, healing, wisdom*
> *The secret of Jowan is revealed*
> *The galad holds the other*
> *All in hand the Phoenix will fly fyre-winged*
> *The Aire will feed the passion*
> *Through the maze will Waeter flow*
> *Into the Erthe's womb*
> *Where She will find her homeland*

"It doesn't actually *mean* anything yet," I mutter reading it again, this time out loud. "Who's Jowan?"

Cill looks at Tom uneasily and says, "I know, but forbidden to say name out loud."

I don't press her. I know she'll tell me when she can.

I look at Dradia and Sarason, but both shake their heads in bewilderment.

I ask Tom, "Do you know this Jowan?"

His eyes are narrowed and furtive. He knows something, but he says, "I'll fly ahead and see what's there."

He takes off down the tunnel and returns quickly. "We're high above a forest. You'll have to use your wings, Emma. Can you make some for the others as well?"

"Yeah!" shouts Benny.

Dradia gives me a doubtful glare. "You can't create wings for us — can you?"

I look at the Faerseelies, the Faylinns and my own group. "I don't know. It probably won't work, but if it does, don't be alarmed — you'll feel them sprout out of your shoulder blades."

Can I do it? I close my eyes and gather all my strength. I imagine orange wings for the Faerseelies, blue for the Faylinns and the same ones I made before for the others.

The oohs and aahs and soft yelps of surprise tell me I've succeeded. When I open my eyes again, everyone is smiling — and winged.

I say, "I'll go ahead and call out if anything is wrong. Otherwise, glide down any way you can. While I'm gone, practice flapping them so you don't fall too fast."

As I run down the echoing tunnel my own wings tug at my shoulder blades. There's no cover over the exit, so I fly straight out. Tom follows right behind. We're high above a dense jungle. I drop quickly, landing on layers of moist leaves. Suddenly, a crackling sound, followed by warning shouts, makes me roll out of the way. One by one, the others float, drop or crash out of surrounding trees. Everyone lies where they are, catching their breath. All are wingless now.

Gyro says, "Not too bad a drop for most of us, I think, but the wing cunning didn't last too long. Still, you did your best, considering how many you had to make. And no one seems the worse for it."

Benny grins widely. "I love having those things. Hope we get to have 'em again."

Cill is walking around examining the trees. I dissolve my own wings. I'm sitting up against something warm. It stirs suddenly, and with a yelp I try to get away, but a heavy hand grabs my arm.

"Don't be afraid, Creirwy," a voice whispers. "It's only me."

Tom's smiling face looms close to mine.

"How can you be Tom again?" I ask, trying not to grin back at him.

He shrugs. "I don't know, but I much prefer arms and legs. Especially arms." He slides the hand up my arm and around my shoulder.

I push him away. "I think you change shape whenever you want to. And when you're Tom, you know you only confuse me, so you do it deliberately!"

He says, "I wish!" but lets me go.

Cill cries, "Ee! Eeeah! Emma, we be in Cleave!"

Flustered, I look at the heavy tree trunks, the huge leaves on looping vines. "You're right! We're in *Cleave*! *Damn* it!"

Tom stands up, and when they see him, the Faerseelies grab their weapons, but Sarason calls, "Donna be frightee. This be ee Owl. Watcher Tamhas." He turns to me. "Why ee changee?"

"Good question," I say, looking at Tom. "Claims it's a mystery to him."

Tom looks at me, his eyes wide. "You don't believe me, Emma?"

Behind him, a face appears in the foliage, then vanishes. *I know that face.* Tom is staring at the same spot.

"Did you see him?" I ask.

"Who?"

"You *know* who!" I snarl.

He flushes dark red. "Just what are you accusing me of?"

"You've been lying to me and you're still lying to me. Did you *know* we were coming to Fergus's world?"

"The lair of Fergus, Sover-reign Game Playee!" Sarason breathes.

"Why Cleave?" I turn on Tom. "You couldn't have controlled the disk — to bring us here! Could you? How did you *know*!"

"Think, Emma. Where have you been in your Finder's Quest? To Argadnel, to Earth, to Moling, to Fomorii? All the places you *yourself* have been to — places that you *know*. There aren't many other worlds that you've already visited. We — uh — I made a logical assumption."

He's right. The two Wands I've found were in places I've either lived in or visited. The only other worlds I've been to are the Rebuff area in the

Tag-A-Long Isles, where Yegg once lived — but she's dead; Cymmarian Market, which really isn't a world but a place — in a desert I don't even know the name of; and Hafflight, where Gyro is from — but he's here with me. And ... my heart sinks ... the only one left is Fergus's stupid world of *stupid* Cleave.

I shout, "You made a deal with Fergus, didn't you? Once we got to Cleave, he and Mathus could strike a separate Game and eliminate Eefa. Then you could all help *me* find the Wands so Fergus could take them from me. Right? *Right?*"

Tom growls, "Don't be ridiculous! We've only been making sure you're on the right track. Fergus is an experienced Player. And I'm a —"

"Oh, gee, remind me again! You're a Master Watcher — *demoted* — while I am a mere Noviate?"

"That's not —"

I yell, "No more lies! Fergus has always wanted Fadanys and he's using you to get it!" I turn to Sarason. "Will you and the Faerseelies help me find Taffine? Will you fight Eefa? Will you fight Tom and Fergus and their Players? Fergus will surely fight *us* for the Wands, even if it means Taffine's life!"

Dradia's black eyes never leave Tom's face. In a low-pitched whistle, she says something to her troop. Strings of colored stones fly through the air, binding his arms and legs. He falls with a crash.

"Dradia, you're mistaken! Emma!" he snarls. "Don't let them do this. Untie me!"

I stand over him. "Go into Watcher mode and get out of it yourself." I laugh. "Still no Watcher powers, eh? Poor you! Gee, I wonder if Fergus wants a useless Watcher to help him take Fadanys?"

He telepaths, *Okay, you're right — Fergus wants Fadanys, but, Emma, let me explain …* He stops when Sarason puts a long blade to his neck.

"And you were helping him — you *really* were helping him?" I ask, horrified. Sarason growls, but I say, "Let Tom answer — if he *can*," my chest so tight each word comes out in a short sharp burst.

"Emma, before you and Pictree went into the cave portal on Argadnel, I spotted Fergus and Mathus. They'd somehow escaped capture. I followed them through the portal cave, so I knew they were ahead of us. Once you, Pictree and I went through, I figured I could monitor their actions, so they didn't mess things up."

"Why didn't you tell me?"

"Because you had enough to worry about. And because I *am* your Watcher. For some reason, like me, they lost their solidity when they entered the cave. But now and again I'd catch a glimpse of them. They couldn't do much damage as they were. They could follow and watch you, that's all. When you had all four Wands, if Mathus had regained some power, they might have made a move — I just had to keep watch in order to prevent it. And that's what I've done."

"And what about when we were in Aire? When Eefa was attacking you — they saved you, didn't they?"

"By then, Mathus got some power back. Yes, they saved me."

I cry, "Didn't you realize that if Mathus was getting his powers back, we were in trouble? Why didn't you warn me?"

"Emma —" Tom's dark eyes are pleading. "You must listen."

"*What?*" I shout.

Tom clears his throat. "Fergus asked that as soon as we got close to Fyre, you Call *his* name — to be one of your ... Players."

"He *what?* Why?"

"So he can gain full solidity. No one knew for sure you'd end up here in Cleave. But if you Call him now, he could offer real help. He said he wouldn't Call his own Players until it was necessary. They could easily beat Blackabrot and Eefa, I bet. It's better to have Fergus with us, under our watch, than off on his own. I think you should do it, Emma. I —"

"You can't seriously be asking me to Call Fergus to be one of my Players? As if he'd accept any other leader!"

"Emma. *Think.* You'll be terribly outnumbered by Eefa and Blackabrot's Players. Fergus helped us before — in your Seeker's Quest. We can work out a deal."

"A deal? Are you *nuts?*" I screech. "I — I —" I babble to a stop, staring in shock and disbelief at Tom. "How could I *ever* have believed you cared about me — or my family? All this time, you've been working for Fergus. He is your *true* Obligation. Now I know for *sure*. Well, I've already chosen my next Player."

I walk around the small clearing, ignoring Tom's pleas to *just listen*, trying to catch my breath. I don't know if someone who is Eefa's prisoner can be freed, but I shout his name anyway.

"Pictree!"

In front of me, an image appears, fades, then emerges again.

"Pictree! Hold on!" I cry.

He holds out his hand. Mine goes right through it.

"He fading!" Cill howls.

I shout, "Look at me, Pictree. Don't take your eyes off mine!"

I focus on his eyes, holding my hands out to him. Then I pull him forward, using my mind, my will.

He grows clearer, then suddenly he's solid. With a loud slash of light, he's free.

"It worked!" Gyro crows. "Emma! Splendid!"

"Yeah," I breathe. "Haven't lost my powers *yet*." I scowl at Tom.

Benny asks, "Maybe he led Eefa here?"

Badba slaps him on the back, almost knocking him over. "Don't be a dunce, human! She's already way ahead of us!"

"Did you see my family, Pictree?"

"No, Emma. I was kept alone in a gray space. I don't know what happened to Mr. MacIvor or Ryan, either."

"You coulda Called them!" Benny cries at me. "Whyn't you Call *them*?"

"They would have been no use to me," I say shortly.

"Not worth saving, right?" Benny pushes his face into mine.

"We'll get them back, Benny." I put my hand on his shoulder, but he shakes it off. "At least they won't die in battle."

He gapes at me, and I can see reality dawn on him. "Oh. Jeez."

"We'll try to protect you. But, Benny, none of us knows what lies ahead."

His round face goes a sickly white with red stains around his lips and nose. He's going to be sick again. He rushes away.

"We can leave you here with Tom," I offer. "Keep him company."

Tom growls, "You'd better be kidding about leaving me behind, Emma."

Benny wipes his mouth and shakes his head. "I'll fight, don't worry. I just can't seem to keep down the strange food, that's all."

I know he's fibbing, but I nod. "Well, let's get organized and get out of here."

49

I give Pictree a quick briefing about everything that's happened since he was taken prisoner. While he's digesting this, I pull Cill aside. "There's only one name on the disk — and that's Jowan. Is that who —?"

"Shhh! Emma, not say out loud!" she whispers back, red eyes darting. "We must protect him. Keep safe. I take you to him."

"Good. The disk indicates *he* has the Wand of Fyre. Maybe he has some idea how to find Blackabrot and Taffine."

She takes a small wooden whistle out of her leaves and blows into it. A shiver of wind sets the trees and ropy vines swaying. The Faylinns and Faerseelies mutter. The wind grows stronger, twisting the treetops into corkscrews, before veering down and pulling at our hair and clothes. Just when I'm sure it will snap the trunks, everything becomes suddenly hushed.

A whisper of sound filters down. Above us, gray clumps of foliage hang from ropy vines, gently swaying. Cill, a look of joy on her leafy face, calls out in her strangled, crackly language. Mewling clicks and croaks answer, and the leaf bundles drop to the ground. Some are tall, like leafy versions of Big Foot, others are small, like Cill. Benny lets out a shout. Badba is ready to spring into leaf-cutting action.

I call to everyone, "They're Barrochs — Cill's tribe. They're on our side!"

When Tom and I came to Cleave during the Seeker's Quest, Barrochs captured us and took us to Fergus's castel, and that's where we met Cill. As the daughter of the former Sover-reign of Barroch and as the Barrochs' leader, her goal is to free her tribe.

She talks to the Barrochs in clicking croaks. Tom is trying to listen. I stand over him to distract his attention.

"If Mathus and Fergus follow us, it will be your fault." My voice is hard and cold.

"Untie me, Emma," Tom barks. "This is ridiculous! You know I'm on your side."

"Not anymore, I don't," I say.

Tom's voice breaks. "You *must* believe I did all this for you, Emma."

"I did once. Sad, isn't it?"

Cill calls to me and I walk away from Tom's startled face.

"We take you to … one … you want to see," Cill says. "We move fast. Keep *them* from following us."

Gyro, Badba and Benny huddle nearby, wanting to know what's going to happen. I tell Sarason and Dradia the plan. "So, are you willing to continue?"

Dradia looks me straight in the eye. She takes the copper band from around her neck and places it around mine. Her clann steps in behind her, stony-faced. I nod, more honored than they'll ever know. But will I find Taffine? Dradia's eyes tell me I'd damn well better.

"Emma!" Cill urges. "Must go now. We untie Tom?"

I whisper, "How do we find this — er — *being*? Does your clann have that sloop that brought you to Argadnel?"

"No, sloop gone." She glances uneasily at Tom. "We have one other, but easy to follow. Make no wings, Emma. We must go quiet and secret."

Gyro creaks up to Tom and begins to untie him.

"No!"

Gyro says, "But, my dear Emma, Tom is *always* with you."

"We can't trust him." The words are like pins in my mouth.

Gyro looks at me sadly. "Surely, you ... well, you can't mean this, Emma. Tom —"

"Emma ... don't leave me here," Tom pleads. "You'll need me."

"You've lied to me too often. Many lives are at risk."

Tom's voice takes on his Master tone. "Emma, I *order* you to untie me."

"Fergus and Mathus are no doubt hiding nearby. We have to leave all three far behind. Can you do this, Cill?"

She nods. "No worry, Emma. They never can catch us."

As Cill gives orders to her tribe, the three tallest Barrochs walk up to Gyro, Badba, and Benny. They have harnesses with hand and foot loops on their backs. Smaller Barrochs approach the others.

"Climb aboard, everyone," I say, loudly. "Benny and Badba, no shouting — not a peep. We must be as quiet as silence itself."

Badba sneers at her Barroch, while he looks back with amused interest.

"Badba," I say, "do it or I'll make the Faerseelies tie you up like Tom."

Her dark eyes slide over to Tom. She sniggers and climbs aboard her ride.

One of Cill's troop throws her a harness. She slips it on and gestures to me. I change to Watcher mode and put my hands and feet in the loops. The moment I'm ready, she holds her arm up, a vine shoots from it straight into the trees, and we fly upward. The twang and slap of the others flying to the treetops follow. In the distance, Tom calls to me. I look down. He's a speck on the jungle floor.

Emma, what are you doing? His voice enters my head.

Get Fergus to untie you! If not ... I'll come back for you after it's all over.

You won't be able to come back! It's all forward or the Game is lost. Emma!

Game, huh? To him it's a *Game*? And if I'm wrong about leaving him there, what then?

Before I can change my mind, Cill's fingers shoot out, and with a lurch and a swinging dive, we're riding through the dark green wall of forest ahead.

50

Worry about leaving Tom, along with lurching drops and heart-stopping swings, has my head and gut doing somersaults. A Barroch passes us, calm-faced Dradia on his back, then another with a stunned, open-mouthed Benny, followed by a grinning flash of Badba, headdress flying out behind her. We're like silent spiders shooting silk from branch to branch.

We catapult through the damp, cool forest for hours. Suddenly the air is drier and warmer — the cool green light grows dimmer, and there's a faint acrid odor in the air. During an upswing, a dark opening breaks in the foliage ahead.

Cill, now in the lead, shoots her fingers down, and we slowly descend, landing softly on the jungle floor.

"Is this the place?" I ask, climbing off and changing into Emma mode.

Cill nods at a tunnel in the foliage ahead. "Through there be the place of Jowan."

"You can say his name out loud now?" I ask, as the others crowd around us, the leaf creatures standing guard in a wide circle.

"Yes. We be in Jowan's land. We have long time cunning on it to make secret from Fergus. But if Eefa gone through, cunning broken. Mathus find us. In time."

"I think your Barrochs should stay in the trees as lookouts."

Cill clicks at them and they vanish in a snap of vines.

The rest of us walk through the tunnel.

At the end is a metal gate. It stands open, but as I approach, it slams shut.

"Eefa got through the portal," I say, my heart dropping to my knees. Maybe ... could there be a way through the bushes? Metal bars everywhere I look. "Dream on, stupid," I mutter.

I stare at the portal, my troop grouped around me.

"What it mean?" Cill asks. "That portal never here before. Moraan put here?"

I nod. "And Eefa opened it before me. How did she *do* it?"

Cill says, "She be strong Druvid. Maybe powers growing as Game goes on — like yours. Or maybe she find out Moraan's secrets."

Gyro says, "I don't actually understand *any* of this. I don't even know whose side we're on, as it happens. I thought *Tom* was on our side."

I feel a jolt go through my bones. Maybe that's truer than he realizes. I'm helping the Tetrad and the dead Moraan, but are they the good guys? Is anyone a good guy? Or are they all corrupt and I'm — we — are caught in some nasty Game? I shake my head. I can't think like that. I've got to keep going and hope for the best.

The portal looks simple enough. It's just a metal gate with the bird design that's burned on my arm. How did Eefa get it open? It's like she had a key. I explore the gate carefully. Maybe it has pegs, like the first door into Fadanys. No. Maybe just a simple latch. No sign of one. I rattle it. No music, no faces — just a dark metal gate.

I press the burn against the figure of the bird. The metal melts and the bird twists his head and squawks, "You will lose everything if you do not find the Wand of Fyre."

"Everything?" I cry. "What does that mean?"

It squawks again, "You will lose everything if you do not find the Wand of Fyre."

I'm tired, I'm fed up, I've left Tom behind, I've had to work and work to try to keep everything together — I don't even know what I'm doing half the time, and now this stupid bird is telling me I'll lose everything if I don't find the stupid Wand of *stupid* Fyre?

I shout at the top of my lungs, "What is *everything*, you stupid bird!"

When it begins to repeat the same thing, a hot white light flashes in my brain. I don't remember anything except the face of my mother before the white light shatters through me. I smell burning metal before I fall into darkness.

I wake up to loud talking and gentle slapping on my cheeks. I try to sit up but can't. Many arms lift me to my feet and hold me there.

Cill says, "Look what you do, Emma!"

Benny whoops, "It's so *cool*!" while I can hear Gyro saying, "Amazing, truly amazing. We can go through now. But I don't think this is what Moraan intended."

Badba laughs her high screech. "No, it's *much* better!"

I look at the gate. It's no longer there. In the middle of the space is a small metal sculpture. I look closer. Of my *mother*!

"Did I do that?" I ask.

"Yes, yes!" Cill cries.

I lean down to the small figure, and in a choked whisper I say, "I won't let you down, Mom. I promise."

Cill pats my back. "Come, Emma. We go meet Jowan now."

We walk through the overhang of foliage into a large clearing dotted with more metal sculptures — metal plants, animals and a number in the likeness of Barrochs, their leaves thin, oxidized bronze.

Did I do these? No. A real artist did them, building and soldering them bit by bit. Dad would love to meet their creator. I *can't* think about Dad now. Instead, Tom walks into my mind. I should have made Badba his guard and brought him with us. What if Fergus doesn't untie him? He will, won't he? If not, Tom will be left and ... I push that horrible thought away.

At the far end of the clearing is a building with a cone-shaped copper roof. The building is a mishmash of bricks, stone, colored glass, fused chunks of silver, gold and copper as well as scrolled metal plates. It's like a giant piece of jewelry. Gyro and Pictree stare in open admiration.

I've just put my hand on the closed door latch when a series of squeaks and clicks comes from the trees.

Cill says, "Wait, Emma! Barrochs send message. Three beings coming. You want them be stopped?"

Already? I must think quickly. "No, don't stop them. Your tribe will only get hurt. Everyone! Arm yourselves and stand by!"

The Faerseelies are poised, stones or bows and arrows in hand, their sharp features grim. Sarason and his tribe are also fully armed. The Barrochs hold their position in the trees at Cill's command. Benny crouches behind a metal tree. Badba brandishes her knives and streak lights. Pictree asks her to toss him one, which she does with a grin.

A man walks into the clearing. I hold my breath, then let it out slowly, trying not to grin with relief. Pictree, Gyro and Badba crowd around him, patting him on the back.

"Back off, you guys!" I say. "Tom! How did you get here? Or need I ask?"

"Fergus and Mathus are with me. Fergus only wants to talk, I promise. He comes unarmed."

I sneer. "But how many of his Players are skulking up on us as we speak?"

"He says he hasn't been able to contact them up to now — Mathus's powers are too weak. When they passed through the portal just now, they regained full solidity and Mathus his powers. I watched them closely. No one has been Called. *Yet*. You'd better speak to them, Emma."

"I'll give him five minutes, earth time," I growl at Tom before nodding at Sarason's and Dradia's Players to lower their weapons. Cill whistles to her Barrochs. Badba and Pictree reluctantly put their weapons away. They're all clearly puzzled, but I need to know what I'm up against — and how to get rid of them before Fergus's Players get involved.

Tom signals, and Fergus and his Druvid Mathus walk casually into the ring. Fergus wears his thick brown leathers scrolled in green, his hair standing out like black mist. His features are flat and hard, the eyes, under thick brows, solid black. Wide bands of gold, edged with snarling wolves' heads cover his wrists and neck. One dark cheek is sliced vertically by an ugly snake of a scar. He's not tall, but he is muscular and solid. My mother would say he has "presence." I'd prefer absence.

"Ah, Watcher," he says smugly, "you had us biting our nails more than once, I'll tell you!"

Mathus smirks. "But now we have the final two Wands to find."

"We?" I glare at Tom, who looks awkward. "There's no 'we' here. Take *your* traitorous Watcher and ... *go away!*"

"My, my, aren't Watchers supposed to have no emotions?" Fergus grins. "In fact, my traitorous Watcher, as you call him, tried to lead us away from you — here in my own jungle! When he *thought* we were confused, he took off. We caught him just as he reached the portal."

Tom gives him a venomous look, but Fergus only laughs.

I laugh, too. "Oh, I'm sure Tom had no intention of losing you."

Tom tries to telepath, but I shut down immediately. His face becomes rigid, his mouth a hard line.

Fergus looks at Cill, who shrinks inside her leaves. "My personal servant — a traitor again," he says lightly. "You and your renegades will be begging for mercy when we've finished this Game."

"The Barrochs are my Players now," I say.

"They are *my* slaves," he growls. "You did not win them in a Game. But let's not argue such a small point, Emma. Tell me, where have you led us this time?"

"Don't you know?" I ask, and for once he doesn't have an answer.

Mathus, with a growl, nods at the forge door, and it opens with a clang.

51

The stench of smelting, fire and smoke spill out into the clearing. Inside a large room, slips of orange light from a round fireplace flutter over a barred pen hanging from the ceiling about four feet off the ground. To one side, a brazier glows with coals. The room is stifling — spits and sizzles and low squeaks of metal against metal the only sounds. Sheets of brass, steel rods, wood, tools, spears, javelins and shields of copper and gold are strewn everywhere. A blacksmith's workshop — and someone has wreaked havoc on it. Eefa? Did she find the Wand of Pillan? Is she here, waiting for me? And where is Jowan?

Fergus tries to lead the way, pushing past me. As I reach out to grab his arm, a snap of electricity zaps from my fingertips and makes him jump back. He shakes his arm, showing his yellow teeth in a grimace. "Was that *you*, Watcher?"

"Stay back!" I snarl. "Or I'll do it again."

He bows sardonically, but he's *not* pleased — with me or Mathus, who was talking quietly to Tom and didn't see what happened. Tom grins at me. I give him a foul glare and order the Faylinns and Faerseelies to guard the door.

A being covered in soot lies on the floor of the barred enclosure. His blackened features are barely visible, but his eyes follow me wherever I move.

Cill peers into the box, her head barely above its floor. "Jowan? It be you?"

The being struggles to his feet. "Cill! I thought Eefa had returned."

He's short and broad, covered in torn and charred pieces of leather, his feet encased in thick-soled boots. His brawny arms are covered in large red welts and open burns. His red hair and beard under the soot are badly singed. "I'm glad to see you, Cill. Can you get me out of here? Eefa put a cunning on it."

"This be Emma," Cill says. "She fix."

He bows to me, looks over my shoulder and lets out a shout. "Fergus?"

"Jowan? Is it you?" Fergus gasps.

"Yes, brother. It's been a long time. Still ruining civilizations throughout the worlds?" Jowan limps to the bars.

"Thought never to see you again, Jowan," Fergus says casually. "So, you've become a Ceard — a smith? I knew you were in Cleave, but the Barrochs hid you well. I could have had Mathus find you any-time I wished, of course."

Cill whispers to me, "They be doublers — twins
— but Fergus banish Jowan for turning his back on
Game."

Jowan says, "Why are you with *him*, Emma? You
one of his Players?"

I straighten my back. "I am *not*. I am leading this
Quest. Fergus, his Druvid and his Watcher tracked
us here. They'll be leaving soon."

He bows again. "You need the Wand. If you'd let
me out ..."

I pass my hand over the cage. When the row of
bars dissolves, I try not to look too shocked that it
worked. There are murmurs of amazement behind
me, and I can hear Fergus quizzing Tom, who is
refusing to discuss it. Good.

Jowan jumps to the floor, wincing with pain.
"Eefa soon discovered I would take the hiding place
of Pillan's Wand to my grave. The Duggs began to
torture me, but she ordered them to stop. I think
she knew you would soon be here. She said she'd
take the Wands *from you*. Then they left."

Fergus asks, "Why didn't Eefa kill you, Jowan?"

"She wanted me to tell Ena that she knows
where Lilith's Wand is — in Blackabrot's fortalice.
Once I give you the Wand of Fyre, Ena, be doubly
cautious. Eefa will be waiting for you there."

Eefa has found a way to Blackabrot's? That means
we can also find it! But if she can convince
Blackabrot to kill me, he can take the Wands and

sell them to her. A slash of fear cuts through me —
Eefa must know Taffine has the Wand — followed
by a snippet of hope ... maybe Blackabrot doesn't
know yet. I have to beat Eefa to Taffine. Then I'll
have to kill Blackabrot so Eefa can't make a deal
with him.

"When did they leave here?" I ask.

"A short while ago."

"Do you know where Blackabrot's fortalice is?"

He nods. "A general idea."

"I know exactly where it is!" Fergus growls. "I
gave him one of my old fortalices for being lead
Player in a Game some mooncrests ago. It's pru-
dent to keep a close eye on the ambitious ones, I
find. I must send for my Players. They'll bring my
airship, and we can storm the fortalice. He won't
be expecting *me*! Mathus, return with a message
to —"

"No!" I shout. "You won't go anywhere."

Fergus laughs and walks away. I point at Dradia
and, on her signal, the Faerseelies bring him down.
Mathus shouts, and the stones and twine holding
Fergus fly apart. Mathus then turns on Dradia, but
I knock him off his feet with two crackling slashes
of light. He falls to the ground, gasping.

Everyone gawks at me. Dradia nods gratefully.

"I — I won't have anyone throwing their weight
around — unless I order it." My voice is high and
trembling. *Weight*? How about lightning bolts?

Fergus helps his Druvid to his feet. Mathus looks dazed. My small twist of satisfaction melts in the fury in Fergus's eyes.

Tom says, "Emma, you can't beat Blackabrot with this small band of Players, even if you *can* knock a Druvid on his back. Blackabrot has few Players, but they are all seasoned, experienced fighters. And don't forget Eefa's Duggs. Don't be stupid. You *need* Fergus."

"Eefa will probably try to negotiate with Blackabrot," I say. "Maybe we can surprise them. And don't call me stupid again!"

"Or what — you'll blast me with your powers?" he asks, one eyebrow up.

I'll hate him *forever*.

Fergus laughs. "Blackabrot strikes first, *then* negotiates. Usually by chopping up the ... *negotiator*. I know Taffine has the Wand, Emma."

"Tom told you."

"No, I worked it out."

"Fine, if Blackabrot is a hothead, this is good," I say. "If Eefa can't negotiate with him, so much the better. She'll have to fight her way into his fortalice. That will create big losses on both sides."

"And *either way*," Tom says, "you'll be badly outplayed. These Players of yours are not fighters."

"Speak for yourself, Watcher!" Badba screeches.

"Enough!" I command.

Fergus and Mathus walk toward the smithy door, their heads together.

Jowan calls, "You can bring all the Players you want, brother. It won't make a bit of difference. For I have Pillan's Wand and I'll never give it to you!"

That stops them.

I add, "And if you don't do things my way, I'll —"

Fergus bellows, "Fine! We'll do it your way. For now. But you'll lose this Game without me — and *I* don't intend to lose anything. Tamhas and Mathus, take everyone and wait outside. You, Jowan and I need to talk, Emma."

"Tom can stay," I say, just to be contrary. "For *now*." But I have a gut feeling I *should* listen to Fergus. Call it intuition, if you want — Pillan would. Mom would call it common sense.

Mathus scowls, but leaves, the others following.

"Wait!" I say. "Dradia, Sarason, Pictree and Cill. Stay with me."

"And what about us?" Badba says, hands on hips. "Gyro and I —"

"All right, but just keep quiet." Benny looks sulky, but I wave him out.

Fergus crosses his arms over his chest. "We need the element of surprise. To get your Players into an advantageous position."

Jowan nods. "I might have a way."

"Jowan," I say, "we've little time — less than one Earth day. I must find Taffine. I promised Dradia no harm would come to her. So, if you could help ..."

Jowan nods, glances at his brother, then at me. I understand. *Don't underestimate Fergus.* When I nod, he limps over to the forge and sets the bellows to work. Soon the roar in the room is as loud as a speeding train.

He finds a long pair of tongs, pushes them into the forge's fire and pulls out a circle of glowing metal the size of a large pizza and about four times as thick. Grabbing a hefty hammer with one hand, he holds the glowing metal on the anvil and, with three clanging hits, cracks it open. With the tongs, he lifts out a metal triangle from the broken casing and drops it into a nearby bucket of water. The room is filled with steam.

A long shaft of silver with a bird's head rises out of the water. Pillan's Wand.

52

Fergus reaches for the Wand, grinning at me cheek-ily, but Jowan gives it to me. When I touch it, it becomes a small red ball marbled with gold. I don't feel much of anything except deep heat coming from its core, so I tuck it away in my pouch with the other two. One more to go.

Tom's voice unexpectedly enters my head. *Well done, Emma. Our Players must watch Fergus and Mathus like hawks. Fergus is barely able to hold himself back. He's* —

You brought Fergus here. You're one of his Players.

Oh, Emma. When will you —

I shut my mind to him and try to think. Jowan gestures to me and I follow him to a door on the far wall. The others follow. It opens onto a metal bal-cony along the back of the smithy. I expect to see more trees, not rolling hills forming a deep valley as far as the eye can see.

"I didn't realize you were on a hill," I exclaim. "Is that where Blackabrot —?"

Fergus says, "He is far along that valley. Will you let me show you the way, O Great Player?" That chuckle of his makes me want to bash his already scarred face.

"After I lay down a few rules," I say through my teeth. To Jowan I add, "I've got seventeen beings with me. And, if we include, you, Fergus, Mathus and their Watcher, that's twenty-one. Then there are the Barrochs. A lot for a surprise attack."

"Will you stop calling me their Watcher?" Tom growls.

"Yeah ... sure ... *whatever*. Jowan, you said you knew how to get to Blackabrot's fortalice without him or Eefa knowing?"

"Just give us all wings," Badba says. "Like before."

"She gave you wings?" Fergus asks, gaping at Badba. "How —?"

"Never mind that," I say. "As it is, we can't have that many beings in the air without protection. Can the Barrochs take us through the trees again?"

Cill shakes her head. "There be only low foliage and small trees along ridge." Jowan turns to Gyro. "You are the inventor Gyro? I've heard of you. I'd like you to look at something. They've tested well on the whole, except — well, you'll see. They might get a number of us there without the fortalice being aware of us. They may see us coming, but they'll ignore us."

Gyro is alert, his silver nose twitching. "Sounds intriguing. Please. Show me."

Jowan points to a metal ladder riveted to the back of the smithy.

"We'll all go." I say.

When Jowan reaches the top of the ladder, he pulls a lever and the back section of the cone-shaped roof slides open. He strides along a walkway and turns toward the middle of the attic, where five metal troughs lead down toward the open air. Halfway down, sitting on curved plat-forms, are five bronze pods held together by vertical rows of rivets. From the top of each is a tuft of filaments, fluttering in the breeze. They remind me of enormous dandelion seeds.

"They be just like pods of beelspear — biggest tree in Cleave," Cill whispers.

Jowan says eagerly, "Three times every moon-span, the beelspear trees set loose thousands of enormous pods that drift down the valley for miles. They're hollow inside. Each seed's nutrition comes from the top, which also keeps it airborne. So I thought, why not design a floating machine on the same principle?"

Gyro says, "Have you flown one?"

Jowan laughs. "I have. More than once. And crashed halfway down the valley. I just can't seem to get the thrust and balance right. Would you look at them?"

Fergus sighs. "This could take too much time. Emma, let me send for my airship."

"No," I say firmly. "Gyro will make them work."

Tom turns to me angrily, "Are you willing to try these after Gyro's fiddled with them? You could end up with many injured beings. And how many can one pod hold without crashing?"

I refuse to even acknowledge him.

Jowan says, "The pods can hold four beings in each, I'm sure."

"Including Gyro and me!" Badba demands. "He'll have fixed them, after all."

Cill says, "And I call Barroch sloop. Carry five. Leave room for rescue beings."

"The mecha-drone gave you a sloop?" Fergus growls. He gives Gyro an "I'm going to skin you alive" look. Gyro stares at him like an anxious drakon caught in the headlights of an oncoming sloop. But he doesn't bolt.

"Okay. Five can go on the sloop," I say.

I wave Gyro and Jowan to the pods to look them over, then tell the others to follow me back down into the smithy. Once there, I say, "Cill, can you get food? We'll take this time to eat and rest."

After she rustles away, I tell Sarason and Dradia to inform their clanns what's happening, then I go outside and call, "Take time to rest up, everyone! Gyro won't be long."

Tom and Fergus snort. Mathus jeers. Feeling hurt and angry, I glare at Tom. As he takes a step toward me, I walk away. Benny, Badba, Pictree and I find a spot under one of the tree sculptures and sit down. Benny beckons to Whim, the young Faerseelie girl, who nervously joins us.

Benny says. "She's — uh — well, she's —"

Trying not to smile, I say, "You're welcome to sit with us." She crouches beside Benny, a slight glow on the long nose peeking out of the curtains of her hair. He has a goofy grin on his face. If he'd stayed in Bruide, he'd probably have been in jail before long, but here he is, a loyal member of my troop — and clearly in love.

The Barrochs soon return with strange prickly fruits, soft-shelled nuts and wooden bottles of fresh water. After we eat, I'm so weary I can't keep my eyes open. Cill drops a small pile of leaves beside me. "Sleep, Emma. You no good if tired."

I make a face and she cackles with amusement. I roll over onto the leaves. They smell of cinnamon and smoke. Closing my eyes, I listen to the murmur of voices and the wind in the trees, until it all fades away. I'm woken by a touch on my shoulder and look up into dark eyes.

"What do *you* want?" I ask, sitting up and looking around. Benny and Whim are curled up beside each other. I can't see Pictree, but Badba is stretched out on her back, snoring like a back-alley drunk.

Tom searches my face, as if looking for something he's lost. For one moment, I see *my* Tom. I ache to touch him. But then he looks uneasily over his shoulder, and his eyes are wary again.

He clears his throat. "Pictree and I have been up there with Gyro and Jowan. I think Gyro's got it figured out. He's had Jowan stoke up the forge and make five new pieces. They're reassembling the steering mechanisms with them."

"I'd better get the others up and organized."

"Wait. Emma ..." he hesitates. "You can't believe I've betrayed you."

I don't answer.

"After all we've been through, you —"

"Why did you let Fergus follow you here? He didn't know where Jowan lived. You should have left Mathus and him behind."

"I did try. But then I changed my mind. Emma, you're facing a *demon Player* in Eefa. She's a hugely talented and powerful Druvid with the mind of a greedy child. She won't quit until you're dead. Fergus could be our strongest ally in this Game. He has rules he won't —"

"Oh, don't even try to make him out to be a good guy, Tom! *Jeez! You* decided what was good for me without even asking! Or maybe it was just good for *you!*"

"I'm used to being your mentor, your *Watcher*. I can see how you misunderstood my decision to bring them here. But think, Emma. You'll need Fergus's Game skills for this battle."

"I don't need him for anything!"

"But isn't it better to work with the enemy you know rather than the one you don't? You *must* let him bring in a handful of his best players for this Game."

"No! This is not a *Game*. It's *my* Quest. I don't want to *conquer* Fadanys. I want to find my family and save them, and save Fadanys. But if I have to choose, it's *no* contest, okay? But no matter what — when I face *her*, I'll have *all* the Wands! Then we'll see what she offers!"

"You'd give up the Wands? You'd deliberately lose this Game?"

"You're not *listening*. It's not a damn Game! It's real life!"

He towers over me. "What will it take to make you see how much I — how my loyalty to you has never *once* faltered."

"A lot more than you've offered so far!" I snarl, then turn and shout, "Everybody, wake up! We'll be leaving soon!"

53

The Barroch sloop arrives and hovers next to Jowan's balcony. Fergus — under protest — drew me a map to Blackabrot's and a layout of the fortalice, then explained the coordinates to Gyro, grumbling all the way. He thinks he and Mathus are going to take over my command, that they can undermine me.

Not long after, Gyro comes down to the yard with Fergus and Jowan, saying he's set each pod's tracker, as far as he can tell. From Gyro that's a confident statement. I notice that Fergus and Jowan don't speak to each other, but now and again I see Fergus assessing the calm, strong smith.

I study Fergus's map for a while. The way there is easy. The fortalice looks like a castel with towers and walkways. There's no open stretch of land where we can land our pods, just the fortalice's courtyard. I wish I could ask Tom's advice, but I call over my troop leaders and we huddle around the map.

"We must move fast, drop into the courtyard and fight," Dradia says after looking over the map. Sarason agrees.

I chew my lip. "Have any of you heard the story of Helen of Troy and the wooden horse?" They all shake their heads. "Well, she was a very beautiful Earth woman who was kidnapped by a guy named Paris and held in a strong fortress. Her soldiers built a huge hollow wooden horse and some of the soldiers climbed into it. Their comrades rolled it outside the fort gates. Helen's captors were curious, so they pulled it into the enclosure."

Badba shrieks with laughter. "And Helen of Troy's clann jumped out of the hollow horse and killed everyone and saved her!"

I say, "Something like that. They opened the gates so the army could pour in."

Cill whispers, "You want build a wooden horse, Emma?"

I laugh. "No. But I think we can fool Taffine's captors with our pods — get in close before they know what's happening. We'll take one pass and see if there's a battle going on between Eefa's and Blackabrot's Players. Then we'll backtrack. If it looks to our advantage, we'll land. I've chosen Pictree, Cill, Jowan, Gyro and myself as pilots. We'll have no way of communicating. You'll have to follow my lead."

I look at them, my heart pounding. "What do you think?"

"What bout Duggs?" Sarason asks. "Ey flyee. Ey could swarm 'ur pods."

"If they're fighting Blackabrot, we should have time to land before they attack," I say. "I only caught a brief glimpse of the Duggs. What do they really look like? And the Unseelies?"

"Duggs are ugly — dark green with pointed faces," Dradia says fiercely. "Orange eyes. Wings attached to the side of their necks. Unseelies are as black as death, and beautiful. When they turn, they are hollow for a breath or two. Then they vanish. You must always fight them face on."

"Fergus said that Blackabrot uses the same weapons as most Players. What about the Duggs?"

"Like yours," she says, "but they also carry spiked rings with poisoned tips, which they throw with great accuracy."

"But your clann and the Faylinns have no protection!" I say. "Maybe you'd best use the shields in Jowan's forge, although they'll be very heavy."

Dradia smiles, showing pale orange teeth. "We have shields. We gave some to Sarason's clann." She takes a pile of black webbed pieces from her pouch. "Shroud shields. Here … give your team one each." She snaps one with her wrist and instantly she's shrouded by a thin stiff shield hovering all around her body. When she swings her arm out, it's instantly covered in metal rings.

Badba cries, "Yieee! I've heard of these. I want one, too!"

I hand them out, but we're one short, so I skip myself.

Cill argues, but I insist. "No Cill, I'm less vulnerable than you. I have ... powers — which I know little about, but I'm learning — *fast*," I say. "I'll use them whenever I can Conjure them."

I don't tell her that my powers work best when I'm angry. Will I be able to call up *any* magick under the stress of battle? *May as well try now.* There's something I've *got* to do. I close my eyes really tight and set out my inner request, drawing on a sizzle of anger deep in my gut. If it works, I'll find out soon.

I open my eyes and say, "Everyone agree with the plan as it stands?" When they all nod, I continue. "Okay. Each pod holds four, the sloop five. Twenty-five beings. There's thirty-eight of us. Thirteen must either stay here or travel on foot."

During the murmurings, I look at Benny. "You don't need to come, Benny. You've never been in battle — and we need someone to watch the smithy."

"I can't stay behind!" he says. "I'd go nuts waiting! Let me fight, Emma, please!"

"You need to understand, Benny — you could die."

Whim touches his arm, a pleading look on her face.

He folds his arms over his chest. "I'll come, Emma." Whim looks both proud and devastated at the same time.

"Dradia and Sarason," I say, "you must each choose one to be left here."

Dradia nods. "Two of my youngers will stay back. Whim and one other. Sarason has stronger fighters."

Benny smiles at Whim, his tight expression softening.

Sarason agrees. "Olders best warriors."

Whim hands me her shroud shield and I take it, secretly relieved.

"With two Faerseelies out, that still leaves eleven too many. Cill, eight of your beings must follow in the trees and then on foot. We haven't room for all of them, but they know this land best."

Mathus, who has been standing nearby with Tom and Fergus, says, "Wait a minute! That's three unaccounted for. Hey —"

"Yes," I say. "You, Fergus and Tom are *out*."

"What?" Tom shouts. "Fergus and I are your best fighters! Emma, *don't do this*!"

Fergus shrugs. "I'll just call my own Players and we'll be in battle before this pathetic group of Gamers is halfway there."

"No you won't," I say, "because I've put a cunning on you. You will not be able to call your Players. If you wish, you can follow on foot."

Fergus's dark face turns a blotchy red. "You aren't powerful enough for a cunning of that strength!"

He looks at Mathus, who says calmly, "It is as the Watcher says."

I can't believe it worked! I try not to smile smugly, but fail.

Fergus looks like he'll burst. He grinds out, "After I told you the coordinates and drew you that map, you betray me? You'll pay for this, Watcher!"

Mathus takes him by the arm, talking quietly. Mathus will try to break my cunning. I have no idea if — or how long — it'll hold.

"I wish I *could* trust such a great Player to fight on our behalf and not try to steal the Wands," I say. "But it would be like asking a gromand to change his yellow stripes to purple spots. If we survive this Quest, we'll deal with his wrath. Maybe, by then, I'll be able to change him permanently into a toad."

Jowan laughs. "Both pilots and riders must learn to fly the pods — in case a pilot is hurt. You'll have to pick who goes with you in the pods, Emma."

I say, "Okay. Sarason, Dradia and one Barroch will go in my pod. I need good fighters for the first strike."

The two leaders nod solemnly.

There's a loud throat clearing. Before she can screech out a protest, I say, "Badba, you go in Gyro's pod with one of the smaller Faerseelies and Benny. They'll need a seasoned fighter. And no arguing or I'll leave you behind."

While she's huffing to herself, I organize the rest. Everyone seems satisfied — except Tom. His face is impassive, but frustration radiates off him. Now he'll *never* forgive me. Wait a minute — why do *I* need forgiving? He's betrayed *me*. So why does that small annoying voice keep chirping inside my head. *Did he really betray you? Are you sure?* I ignore it. I can't risk listening.

Cill whistles for her tribe as Dradia and Sarason instruct their clanns. Soon, all are assembled and ready to go.

I ask Cill, "Who did you choose to pilot the sloop?"

"I choose Caul, old valued friend and best of renegade leaders."

"Good. Tell Caul to wait until the last pod leaves the bay before he sets off. He must stay behind and out of sight. He may have to pick up casualties right away. I hope a pod won't go down, but you never know."

Jowan turns to the whole troop. "As you go through the smithy, take whatever weapons or shields you need."

Cill nods. "My tribe take some weapons though we have own ways of fighting — but best be prepared."

I shout, "We're ready! Let's find Taffine!" knowing that's what so many want to hear.

They all cheer as they run into the building. But I can't cheer. I look back at Tom, but he's already loping across the clearing, heading for the side of the smithy. Is he going to watch us take off?

When the twenty pod riders arrive in the attic, Jowan and Gyro explain the mechanism using the pod I will pilot. It's very simple — the coordinates are set for Blackabrot's fortalice, but the pilots can change them to manual steering if they want. The engine is on top of the pod and controls the this-tledown filaments, which act as wings. When I sit in the pilot's seat, I'm amazed to find a window in front of me. From the outside it's the same bronze color as the rest of the pod. The interior is translu-cent, like amber. Jowan must be one of the Gobha smiths, capable of magick with metals — a good protector for the Wand of Fyre.

In a few minutes, the others run for their own pods, ready for action. When I pull a small lever, a section of the hull lifts open for easy boarding — and escape. There's a small metal seat for the pilot. The passengers sit on the floor. Dradia, Sarason and a Barroch called Jye climb in behind me. Sarason and Dradia are silent, but Jye clicks softly to him-self as he settles into the back of the pod. I close the opening in the hull.

My tongue is so dry it's stuck to the roof of my mouth. I check the buttons and the stick shift, then make my breathing calm and regular. Dradia touch-es my shoulder, and I realize that the other pilots are waiting for me to take off. My hand, shaking like one of Cill's leaves, pushes the stick shift forward. The pod slides down the ramp, slowly at first, then picks up speed. There's a loud buzzing sound above and the grinding of metal as we slide like a sled on a steep hill. Soon, sky fills my window. There's no sound but a faint hum overhead.

Suddenly, the pod drops. My heart goes into my throat — there are gasps from my passengers, but I pull back on the stick and we lift. Soon, all five pods are floating down the valley, the trees and bushes passing quickly beneath us.

No going back now.

54

Dradia's whistling voice says, "The sloop is leaving the dock."

I look over my shoulder. The little airship is small and camouflaged with leaves, moving just above the tree line.

We travel for maybe an hour. The trees thin out and rocky hills appear. I squint at something in the distance. A stone hill? No, it's ... I swallow hard. It's a domed fortalice surrounded by thick stone walls. Not high on a hill and spired like Fergus drew, but dug into the ground like a bunker. *Liar!*

As we draw closer, the pod begins to drop. Did Fergus lie about the coordinates too? It's clear the pods are set to land without allowing us a pass first! I need to contact my pilots. If I telepath, will they hear me? I imagine each pilot's face — Jowan, Cill, Pictree and Gyro — then send the message, *Go to manual. Fergus lied about the fortalice. Go to manual.*

One by one, the pods seem to stand still, then move forward again. They heard me! I change to manual and my pod reacts the same way.

"We've all gone to manual," I say to my riders. "We'll be over the fortalice in a few seconds. If we see fighting, we'll decide what —"

We are floating over the stronghold. Behind the wall is an octagonal 'circle' of flat ground around the metal dome. Other than that, there's nothing — no fighting, no guards, no beings.

Where *is* everybody? Did Mathus warn them somehow? Would Fergus do such a thing? Probably. But surely not with Tom's knowledge. No. Not Tom. Has Eefa destroyed Blackabrot and his Unseelies and taken the Wand? Is she waiting like a spider inside the domed building?

Past the fortalice, I turn the pod and put it in neutral. The others follow my example. Lined up alongside me, they wait. The sloop has also stopped, looking like a pile of bushes on an outcrop of rocks. Oh, how I wish Tom was here.

Okay, I telepath, *if you can hear me, move forward slightly*.

All four pods slide forward.

Good. One at a time, starting with Cill, then Jowan, Pictree and finally Gyro, I want you to speak to me. Just say, "Over and out." Open your minds to the others, too.

Over and out, comes Cill's squeaky voice, followed by Jowan and then the other two.

Can you hear one another?

The words come fast. *Yes! Yes! Yes! Yes!*

I guess you can see how quiet it is down there, I say. *Any ideas?*

Pictree says firmly, *Eafa's there. I sense her. And Arawn. The Duggs, too. They're moving cautiously — down — into the interior.*

Can you tell where Blackabrot and his Unseelies are?

I feel essences far below the dome. Eefa's trying to find them. Wait! They are on the move! The Unseelies are coming up from below!

We should land now. Be ready for them if and when they spill out, Jowan calls.

I agree, I say. *I'll go first, then Jowan, Cill, Pictree and Gyro. Once landed, leave one passenger in the pilot's seat to lift the pod. Stay alert in case we need you. Cill, whistle to the sloop to hover, drop Barrochs as needed and be ready to rescue the injured.*

I turn to my passengers and tell them our plans. "Jye, will you pilot the pod?"

His facial leaves flush rosy. "I be honored, Emma."

Okay, I telepath my pilots, *I'm going down!*

55

The pod lands with a crack of metal against stone. I expect it to roll on its side, but the thistledown whirs overhead and keeps us stable. With shaking hands, I pop the door, grab my sword and my shroud shield and get ready to jump out. Dradia hands me a small weapon. "It is a streak gun, with many lasers in it."

Sarason, Dradia and I run toward the door in the dome as Jye lifts the pod into the air. The fortalice's door has been pried open. Eefa has sneaked unnoticed into a highly trained Player's fortification and invaded deep into the interior.

I hope this means that Blackabrot has the lazy arrogance that no Gamer should give in to. Fergus would never be inside his castel without guards on alert.

The other pods land, drop off their Players and rise again, keeping above the stone wall. The sloop glides nearer. Caul waves and sends three Barrochs down, and the sloop glides out of streak-gun range.

"I thought we would come in on a battle," I say as we huddle around the door.

Badba stands apart, keeping watch, but listening to us.

"Should we pick them off as they come out?" I ask. "Or should we go in and sneak up on both teams at once?"

Gyro clears his throat. "It seems to me, Emma, that if we wait here, we may surprise them at first, but there is no refuge in this open yard, so to speak."

Jowan nods. "I think we have to go in."

Sarason says, "Weeas be here to findee Taffine, not fight."

I nod. "You're right, Sarason. *She's* our goal, she has the Wand. We'll face a fight if and when it comes. I'll go in alone and invisible first."

"No, Emma," Jowan says, "we need you to —"

Pictree cries, "They're coming up from below —"

He's cut off by a thunderous noise that roars out the door with a horde of green gargoyle creatures with streaming wings, followed by humanoids in black armor as shiny as beetles' wings, their beautiful faces a blur of dark blue.

Laser lights flare and swords ring. They haven't seen us yet.

I telepath, *Remember, they're all our enemy. Stay back as much as possible, but when you get a chance, pick them off one by one! Go!*

My comrades disperse around the edge of the melee, now and again dodging in and out. When the Faerseelies bring down some fighters right away using their stones, the Duggs and Unseelies realize that another set of Players has entered their Game.

"They see you!" I shout. "*Kill* them!"

What am I *saying*? I'm telling my troop to slaughter other beings. And many of my friends will also die. I'm no better than Fergus! I said I'd never play his Game, and here I am, ordering beings to *kill or be killed*.

I watch in horror as Cill attacks a shrieking Dugg. It's using one arm to hold her off and the other to jab at a spitting Unseelie. The Unseelie turns to run, becoming a thin empty shell. He vanishes, only to appear behind Cill, his streak gun aimed straight at her.

"NO!" I shout in panic and fury. A blue light falls and everything stops dead. The streak from the Unseelie's gun is an inch from Cill's face. The courtyard is quiet, all beings as still as statues. I gently move Cill to one side, out of danger.

The soft hum of the pods approaches. They float over the courtyard.

I've put everyone under a cunning, I telepath to the pilots. *I don't know how long it'll last. Tell Caul to get as many of our Players as he can on the sloop. The pods can collect the rest. Our Players should recover from the cunning once they're in the pods.*

Jye answers, *I hear, Emma. I talk to Caul. We take you with others.*

No. I'm going in to find Taffine. Just get our Players away from here. Then hide! I'll call if I need you.

His urgent voice tells me to wait. As I run to the doorway, the sounds of the pods and sloop grow louder. Relief washes through me when the first of my team, Dradia, her face a grimace of rage, is lifted up by a Barroch's vine hands. The pods land one by one and their pilots rush out and lead their friends to safety.

The full realization of what I've done hits me like a sword through the heart. If I hadn't gone to Histal, if I hadn't demanded to go through the border cave on Argadnel, none of this would have happened. Moraan set it up, but I could have refused to play the Game. I even agreed to Call friends to come and help me. How naive was I? Huw is dead because of me. I put myself and everyone I care about in danger. I called it a *Quest*. But it's just a sordid, ugly Game. I've even lost Tom. At least he knows where he stands with Fergus.

All my fault. And only I can fix it.

56

The light is hazy, the smell dank and harsh. The surface of the fortalice's dome is black, with dark gems embedded in it that give off a faint light. A long ebony pillar stops just short of the center of the dome. I'm on a metal walkway that runs around the wall of the sphere, which is studded with more gems. Straight ahead, a ramp tilts sharply down. I look over it. There's no floor, just a spiraling of the ramp around the pillar into darkness.

I no sooner start down the ramp than an Unseelie races up, hissing, his sword raised. I snap my shroud shield in place, but the weight of his sword knocks me off my feet. I lift the streak gun as he lunges again, but before I can fire, another streak light from behind him knocks him sideways and over the edge.

"Badba! How did you get here?"

"I've been hiding in a guard's alcove. I knew you'd attempt this alone," she says. "I've tried to go down the ramp a few times, but that center pole has sniper windows in it. My shroud shield has helped so far, but it's wearing down." She points to frazzled spots where she's been hit more than once. "I managed to hit a few and got three Duggs running up to the ramp to get outside."

I tell her what's happening. "Go with the others," I say. "I can do this on my own."

She shakes her topknot of feathers. "No. You need me. You even forgot to turn invisible. Come on, run! Fast!"

I transmute invisible and grab her hand. We head down the ramp at a gallop. Laser lights blast the walls at random. They know we're here by the clatter of our feet, but because I'm holding Badba's hand, they can't see either of us. Chunks of wall and pieces of gold and colored glass fly around us. As we run, I send a cunning to the pillar that holds the snipers, but it doesn't seem to stop them. Maybe I can't do it when I'm invisible. I transmute visible and send the cunning. A blue light skims around the pillar, but Badba falls with a shout.

She's hit in the leg and is wrapping it with one of the long feathers from her belt. "Keep going," she gasps. "I think you've stopped the snipers. But there's probably more down below. Keep your eyes and ears open!"

I order her up to the surface and she agrees, her yellow eyes full of pain. I telepath to the pilots, hoping one will hear me. There's a blurred response and I hear Benny's voice — he'll be on the lookout for her. He's loving every second of this. I cover Badba with my shroud shield in case someone gets past me on the ramp, then, transmuting invisible again, I keep going down, the ramp moving closer and closer to the center pole.

Finally, I reach the bottom. No Duggs. No Unseelies. I step down onto the floor. There's a muffled, dense quiet. Where are Eefa and Blackabrot? They *must* be down here. That shakes me. If Eefa realizes a cunning has fallen on her Players up above, she'll break it. My team, including Badba, could be dead in seconds.

I count four doors around the circular wall and one in the central pillar. I push open one and find a huge musty space with nothing but cavelike holes in the walls. Two of the other rooms are identical. The fourth has low tables covered with onyx dishes still steaming with food. The stench makes me gag. Clearly Eefa caught them off guard. But where is Taffine?

The last door is in the central pillar. Behind it, a collapsed sniper blocks my way up a flight of stairs. I step over the Unseelie's body and spot a lever in the wall three steps up. The floor under the Unseelie has spiral cracks in it, joining in the center. As I pull the lever, the floor opens — the staircase, the Unseelie and I drop into a long, narrow room with a clang that knocks my teeth together.

Along the walls are black cages. I can barely see anything. I transmute into Watcher mode staying invisible and adjust my vision. Something scrabbles in one of the cages. I expect to see a dying prisoner or an injured Taffine, but a blue mousel's sharp nose sniffs out at me, then retreats with a squeak.

"Taffine?" I call softly, transmuting visible.

No answer.

"Taffine?" I say in her language. "Sarason and Dradia sent me to find you." I change back into Emma and call her name again. The silence is broken by a fierce cry. A girl with pointed ears and dark eyes is sitting in one of the far cages. Her long bronze hair is gathered at the top of her head by a garland of huge smoky pearls. She's dressed in the rusty orange of her clann, but the fabric is filthy.

She grabs the bars of her cage and snarls, "Get me out of here!"

I check the complicated lock.

"Come on, you!" She rattles the bars. "I heard fighting. Shoot the lock off!"

I look at Taffine's small, ferocious face. Sarason will have his hands full with this one. I tell her to stand back, then wave a hand over the lock. It falls to the ground. For a moment, the fierce expression opens to one of surprise.

"Who are you?" she asks.

"A Watcher."

"You don't look like a Watcher. Give me your streak gun!" She reaches for it, and I step back. Her eyes glint with malice.

"Were you told to give something to Ena?" I ask. "I'll take it in trade for the weapon."

Taffine's eyes narrow. "Ena? Who is Ena?"

"I am Ena. I have three Wands in my pouch — Waeter, Erthe and Fyre. You were given the Wand of Aire. By a Druvid named Moraan."

"I was given no Wand!" she sneers. "What do you really want?"

"Look," I say, "Blackabrot's Players and a horrible Druvid called Eefa will be here soon — you must know —"

When she grabs for my gun, I flip my hand at her. The streak of light knocks her on her bottom. She scrambles to her feet, fists clenched.

"You're wasting time," I snap. "Dradia will be very angry with you."

"Dradia? You know her?" she asks suspiciously.

"Yes. She's waiting above for you."

Taffine searches my face, then nods, somehow satisfied. "I know of nothing I was given that I can give you, Ena. Dradia must be mistaken."

"Were you given an item by the Druvid Moraan?"

She becomes very still, then says, "A being in a yellow chiton, who was visiting Dradia before we went to the Faylinn camp, gave me something when he heard I was about to be wed. I did not know his name." She reaches up into her hair and untangles the pearl garland. "It was this."

When I take it from her, it becomes a clear tube with a round crystal on top. In the crystal is a yellow and blue sword surrounded by wavy blue lines. Taffine gasps with delight. A moment later, it becomes a small globe, filled with white smoke, lying cool in the palm of my hand.

"That is the Wand of Aire?" Taffine breathes. "It is so beautiful."

"And I can only hope I get to keep it," I say. "I think I'll need your help. Will you fight alongside me — to keep it safe?"

She grins. "I will!"

I am about to give her the weapon when her eyes open wide with alarm.

A familiar giggle echoes behind me. Eefa and Arawn are blocking our exit.

57

I go inside myself and create a cunning of protection for Taffine and myself. Eefa's hair bristles like sharp red feathers; her eyes shine with triumph and glee. Arawn is wearing a white mask with black eye slits.

"Do you always hide behind a mask?" I sneer at the boy who could be my brother. The pale eyes shift, then look down, but he remains silent.

Eefa points at me. "So here we are, Watcher. Give me the four Wands and I will give you back the people of Argadnel."

I gape at her. "You took them?"

"Ha! You thought Moraan took them?" she crows.

Arawn looks at Eefa, then back at me, a warning in his eyes.

"You're lying. You have MacIvor and his son, but no one else," I say.

She shrugs and grins, showing a flash of the silver tooth. "Then I'll kill MacIvor and his younger. Or, perhaps, I'll blast this little Faerseelie to bits."

"If you try, I'll destroy the Wands."

She leans forward, her face twisted.

"Don't pit your powers against mine," she snarls. "I've watched yours grow, but you are nowhere near my strength or *cunning*. I went back to Moraan's laborare after Erthe — and found all his notes. He'd burned them, but I used my magick to read them — the secrets to the portals. And other things you know *nothing* about!" She lets out a high-pitched giggle of satisfaction.

I try to snarl right back, but my voice spikes nervously. "You can't take the Wands — Moraan's cunning won't allow it."

"You will *give* them to me. Or I'll have you killed and take them that way."

Taffine shouts, "We'll fight *you* to the death!"

A searing jab of pain in my shoulder and leg takes my breath away. I drop Aire's sphere. Is that blood on my hand? A second later, a tall Unseelie with a ribbed helmet and shield runs through the door with a hiss. Shock makes my whole body stiffen. Why him! Why now! Oh no — my cunning protected us against Eefa, but not any other beings! I watch in horror as the sphere of Aire rolls across the stone floor.

"Blackabrot! Finally out of hiding, are you?" Eefa crows. "I have a proposition for you."

His answer is a growl and a laser round, which Eefa fends off easily.

I pull hard on all my resources to cast a wider cunning over Taffine and me. At that moment, Blackabrot shoots at me again, and it bounces off. Taffine shrieks with delight. I throw her the streak gun, telling her not to shoot until I tell her. She crouches, the gun aimed at Blackabrot.

Blackabrot dodges past Eefa, lunging for the sphere. Eefa tries to beat him to it, but his boot sends it skittering toward me. I lean over to grab it, but pain makes my eyes water and I fall to my knees. If my cunnings don't hold, Taffine and I are finished. My brain swims with pain. I'm going to black out. A hand wavers in front of me, holding the sphere.

I look up to find Arawn's mask close to my face. Our eyes lock. In his are a brightness, an awareness of something ... but then it's gone. I take the globe in my good hand. It grows warm in my fingers, and the pain recedes a bit. Quickly, I put it in my pouch and struggle to my feet, just as Blackabrot raises his streak gun and points it at Arawn. I fling my good arm in the air and the Unseelie leader is thrown into one of his own cages. The door swings closed and I fuse the lock shut. I try to blast Eefa with the same cunning, but she blocks it.

"You fool, Arawn," she shrieks. "You gave her the Wand. Clearly, you can go through her magick!" She thrusts a streak gun at him. "Shoot her. Kill both of them!"

Arawn drops the gun. "No."

She cries, "You mewling, useless creature. I've been doing this all for you — and now, when we're about to win, you *betray* me? That creature in the cage — he'll kill the Watcher — for a price, but *you* —"

She points at Arawn and his mask drops to expose the thin, intense face of a boy my own age, with uncertain eyes under straight black brows. He tries to turn to say something to me, but suddenly he can't budge. Only his eyes move, and in them isn't panic, but defeat and sorrow.

"You've paralyzed him!"

"Be glad I didn't kill him! He'll come round to my way of thinking again. He's never realized how much he needs Fadanys. When we can control the Tetrad, he won't have to do anything but play his harp and read his binnacles. I'll rule Fadanys for him."

Blackabrot is shaking the bars of his cage, glowering and hissing.

Eefa laughs at him. "If *that* is a strong Player, imagine how easy it will be for me to set and win Games!" She looks at me from under her brows, a cat curl on her lips. "Perhaps you would like to rule Fadanys with me."

"Never!"

"How foolish you are. You think I can't take those Wands? I have been in control from the beginning. And now —"

Suddenly it dawns on me. I laugh long and hard.

"Stop it!" she growls. "No one laughs at Eefa!"

"You're so full of yourself, you've missed it! You're not in control. None of this is *your* doing! It's all Moraan's. Like a board game of Fidchell. You're a pawn, like me! He left those clues in his laborare for you to find!"

She looks at me with such hatred I should fizzle into burned toast. As it is, I'm exhausted from the laughing and the loss of blood, and I'm having trouble keeping the cunning over Taffine and me. If I pass out, the cunning will break and Taffine and I will die.

Eefa crosses her arms. "I'll just wait here until you become too weak to hold the cunning. First, I'll kill the younger. Then I'll get that idiot in the cage to kill you!"

I whisper, "If the cunning fades, just kill me and take the Wands. Don't kill the girl."

She shrugs. "One less Faerseelie won't make much difference."

Emma, a deep voice says in my head. *Don't say a word. I'm right behind Eefa.*

Tom? Is it you? Are you really here?

Yes, Creirwy. I'm here.

My whole being, full of joy, suddenly floods with fear. *Where's Fergus? I won't give him the Wands, Tom. He can't have them!*

Emma, listen to me! Please! he shouts in my head. *Remember what the disk said, "All in hand the Phoenix* will fly fyre-winged / The Aire will feed the passion / Through the maze will Waeter flow / Into the Erthe's womb / Where She will find her homeland." I'm sure it means you must have all four Wands in your hand to get back to the maze and end the Quest.

Eefa is watching. A secret smile flickers across her face. She turns quickly. Even though Tom's invisible, I'm sure she sees him. Terror leaps into my heart so fast I break through my protective cunning and strike. With a scream, Eefa flies through the air, and lands in the cage next to Blackabrot. The door fuses shut. I wrap a blue Conjure around both cages.

Tom transmutes visible, grabs me and hugs me tight. He murmurs, his face in my hair, "Oh, Emma."

He strips off pieces of his jerkin and binds my shoulder and leg. I touch his hand, his shoulder, his face as he works frantically on the bandages.

"You've lost a lot of blood, Emma. I'll follow you to the maze," he says, tying the last knot.

Taffine pushes her way in. "I'll go with you, Ena."

"I think I have to do this bit alone," I say. "Does Fergus have an airship here?"

Tom nods. "Yes. Mathus broke your cunning. I *had* to make sure you were safe."

"I'm glad you brought them. Now you must take Taffine to safety. I can't break my promise to Sarason and Dradia. You can follow me later."

"But I won't know where to find you."

"I'll Call and you'll come to me." I lean my forehead against his shoulder, trying to draw strength from his warmth. "Now, take Taffine to Fergus's ship. Why isn't he here, trying to grab the Wands?"

"His Players are rounding up the Duggs and Unseelies, like good members of your team." He laughs. "See? He knows when he's been outplayed. He knows you're too powerful for him — for *now*, as he puts it."

"And my Players are safe?"

He nods. "All safe — even Badba."

Shrieks from Eefa's cage pierce the air. She's throwing bolts of energy. The cunning is breaking down.

"Go!" I cry. "She's going to break through!"

Tom picks up Taffine, leans over her and kisses me full on the lips. Then he whispers, "When you are a great Druvid — which you are clearly becoming — and I remain a Watcher, remember that I was always and forever ... *true*."

58

Blackabrot is grinning at Eefa with vicious delight as she burns apart my cunning.

Dizzy from loss of blood, I limp up to Arawn. "Don't be afraid." I touch his shoulder, and he drops to the floor with a squeak. A small black mousel with pink ears and pale eyes looks up at me. I put him in my pocket and hobble quickly to the stairs. I look up them to the spiral ramp winding to the top of the dome. I can't walk, but can I fly up there? And if I do, what then?

I have to get to the maze.

I take the spheres from my pouch. They instantly return to their original shapes. I keep Fyre and Aire in one hand and transfer Erthe and Waeter to my injured hand. It's hard to hold them because pain jabs from my shoulder down to my hand, but I grit my teeth and hang on.

There's a crash and a shriek of triumph from the cages. The mousel pokes his head out of my pocket, making high panicky squeals. *Take me to the maze,* I beg the Wands. *Take me to the maze!*

Eefa runs full tilt at me, reaching out with a bellow, just as wings of flame burst from my shoulders. A flood of air carries me straight through the dome into the night. Suddenly the skies open with a crash of thunder and rain pours down. My wings are extinguished and as I fall, a huge gust of wind takes my breath away, knocking me out.

I wake up to the pitchy smell of freshly cut wood. My hands are still wrapped around the Wands as if I'm fused to them. Waeter's fish are swimming at the top, Aire's smoky light shows Althane's sword turning slowly on its handle, Erthe hums with life — the faint buzz of bees, the sounds of animals and a tree waving its boughs in some private breeze — and the Wand of Fyre is burning like a torch, the bird inside it stretching its wings as if enjoying the warmth.

Fyre's light glints off wooden ribs and two low seats made of woven branches. More branches, thick with tiny leaves, grow out of the end of each rib. I'm in a living boat. A stiff breeze suddenly pushes the boat over the water. Where am I? Of course. Always the maze.

The little mousel pokes his head out of my pocket again. I whisper, "I can't change you back yet. You're better off as you are, so we won't get separated. When this is over, you and I need to talk."

He nods sadly and looks around. I try to move, but sharp pains scorch down my arm and leg. The bandages are shiny with fresh blood. I'm so weak I can barely sit up. I try to go inside myself and put a healing on my wounds, but nothing happens. Can't I do magick on myself — only on others? As the boat drifts, I wonder where Eefa is. She'll have a good laugh — she's probably watching me right now, gloating as I weaken — waiting for me to die.

I don't know if I pass out or fall asleep, but I dream of the bee farm, the sun bright on the clover fields. An owl swoops through the clear air. Mom and Dad are walking toward the place where Kera was found, Summer and Ailla running behind them.

I wake up with a jolt. I actually had my first real dream! How many times did I wish I could leave that farm? How many times did I wish I had conventional parents and a sister who wasn't sick all the time? How many times did I wish I didn't feel so responsible for them — that I didn't have to watch out for them all the time? *Now* all I want is to go back there, to be with my family in Bruide, to be a *human girl*.

The wind pushes the boat's bow onto solid ground. I drag myself out of the boat and limp toward a dark opening, my head spinning, the Wands held tightly in my hands. Behind the opening is a vast cold space. A circular wall of hedge sweeps up to an enormous curved ceiling. Fyre's Wand lights a floor of mosaic tiles laid out like a tree's roots, radiating from a pedestal that seems miles away.

I tremble all over, as if I have a bad case of the flu. My inner voice cheers me on. *Do it for Mom and Dad. Do it for Summer and Ailla, and Mr. MacIvor and Ryan and Cill and all the others. Do it for Tom.*

The pain in my leg makes me gasp each time my foot hits the floor. I trip on a broken tile and fall hard, biting through my bottom lip. The mousel runs out of my pocket, squeaking encouragement. A trickle of laughter drifts over us. *Eefa.* I try to get up, but blackness swirls past my eyes. When I come to, I hear footsteps running away from me, then silence. I struggle to my knees, and someone gasps. Why can't I see anyone? Arawn runs around my shoulders chattering. I get to my feet and keep going, the pedestal coming slowly closer. By the time I reach it, I'm sobbing like a little kid.

On the pedestal is a shallow black bowl. There are four holes in its rim — one for each Wand. I reach up and drop the Wand of Aire into the slot with its design beside it. It swirls like a small tornado, the tiny sword of Althane, now dark blue, spinning above it. I put the Wand of Fyre in its place. The shaft becomes a long flame with sparks bursting off it. The bird hovers above, wings fluttering. Pain makes it hard to reach the Wand of Waeter into place, but it slips down with a soft click. A shaft of water with droplets like glass dances around the silver flickering fish.

One more. Just one more. I have to pull myself around the pedestal. As I reach up to place the Wand of Erthe, a flock of blackbirds flies just over my head, wings slashing the air, croaking a warning. A shout from the entryway and Eefa runs toward me waving both arms. Her red hair is thick and flowing, her face smooth and almost beautiful.

I flinch, expecting a searing slash of electricity, but she stops and cries, "Don't do it, Ena. Moraan lied. If you place that Wand, Fadanys will be destroyed. The Tetrad will be consumed. Your family will die. You were right — he *was* controlling us!"

What is she saying?

One of her hands is palm up, as if offering me something. "Your family will die, Ena. Sima, the female younger of Aibell and Clust, was not taken by Aibell. Moraan *killed* her."

Aibell and Clust's daughter died? What does she mean? Aren't I that girl?

Eefa continues advancing. "Moraan wanted to kill Arawn, too, but I protected him. Moraan chose you — a young Watcher — to be his *dupe*. He thought a Watcher who grew up on Earth would never see through his trickery. If you place that final Wand, Moraan will live again. He will destroy you — and your family."

I stare, unable to move. My head is reeling with exhaustion and confusion. All I can say is, "But ... I am Arawn's doubler."

"No, you are merely Moraan's unwitting apprentice, Ena. Forgive me, my dear. I hunted you because I had to save Fadanys. Give me the final Wand. We'll rule Fadanys together. We'll make it a place of wonder, of beauty, of learning — the greatest world in *all* the worlds. Our powers joined —"

I stare at the Wand. If I'm merely a Watcher, how did I get my powers? *Will* my family die if I place this last Wand in its slot?

The little mousel chatters in my ear, then nips it hard. That startles me, and I twist my head just in time to see Eefa running at me, the old wild look in her eyes. She lifts her hand, and an arc of light slashes toward me.

A surge of energy raises my own hand, and I stave off her cunning with one of my own, but it knocks me off my feet. I crawl under the pedestal to come up on the other side and push the Wand into its slot. Bees fly off it like sparks from a fire, forming a massive swarm that heads straight for Eefa. The last I see of her, she's running, covered in bees. I still hear her screams in my sleep.

I expect to see all four Wands join somehow, but they turn into their sphere shapes and roll down into the bowl, where they melt together. A shaft of white light roars skyward, lighting the dry hedge roof with flames. It forms a massive cap of fire that slides down the walls, engulfing the entire hedge. The top of the roof opens and a mirror image of the maze lights up. There's no smoke or heat, but as the flames slide from the hedge along the roots in the floor toward me, I wonder if Eefa was right. Maybe I *am* going to die. Then, like good old human Benny, I faint dead away.

59

Histal is leaning over me, his green eyes full of concern.

"This was almost a disaster," he murmurs.

"But it worked," says a croaking little voice I recognize.

I turn my head. Two steps from me is a narrow waterway. Mennow is sitting on its edge, smiling.

Gernac's woolly head comes into view, his brown eyes gleaming. His body is whole and strong. Over his shoulders is a magnificent cape alive with plant and animal designs. Next to him is a tall, slender woman with a haze of blond hair, dressed in blue. Kera. So he *did* rescue her from her wax prison.

I sit up. My arm doesn't hurt anymore. I touch my leg. It's fine, too.

A rush of wind stirs my hair, and the long gray face of Nuit appears. "Are you Lilith?" I ask.

The voice is deep and tender. "Yes, Ena — in the shape you will recognize."

"And is Pillan here, too?" I ask, looking around. The hedge roof is covered now with dark green leaves and starred with flowers like an evening sky.

"Much to my amusement — *amazement,* really — you succeeded, Watcher," come the supercilious tones of Pillan as he pushes forward.

"Is my family here? Why are *you* here, Histal?"

"Your family is safe, Ena," Mennow says. "They will be brought soon. Moraan has kept them safe."

I nod, blinking back tears. "Thank you."

"You did well," Gernac says. "We're all proud of you."

I frown. "But, Histal ... how did you get ..." I leap up and face the Master Watcher. "Moraan? *He* kept my family safe? He's alive? Where is he?"

He smiles at me knowingly.

I gape at him. "No! You? You're Moraan?"

He bows and sweeps his cloak of light like a gallant knight.

I whisper, "You've been controlling my life since I was born? Made me the Watcher of the Sweeneys? Moved them to Argadnel? Kept my father prisoner?" Anger roars out of my mouth. "*You knew where my family has been all this time?*"

"Much of what has happened has been out of my control," Histal says calmly. "Eefa was very strong. She changed the pattern I'd laid out."

I can only stare at him in rage and shock.

"*Am* I the daughter of Aibell and Clust? Is Arawn my doubler?"

He shakes his head. "The female child Sima died soon after she was born."

"Then who am I?"

"*You* are the *merch* — the child of a female from Eorthe ... Earth, and a male, whose roots also come from Earth. He is the descendant of a powerful magician who once counseled a great Celtic king."

"Where is my ... uh ... Source-mother?" I ask.

"Gone from us. She came from Falach Bein — the Hidden Hills. She was a Uirsig — the offspring of a mortal king and a queen of the Siabhra ... in Earth terms ... Faeries. Her name was Caelia. So, you see, you have some human blood in you, after all."

"And my *father?*"

He smiles and turns aside, and when he turns back, he is no longer Histal. His white hair is shaved in a single wide swath from ear to ear, the smooth bangs lying flat on his forehead, the back gathered into a long ponytail — just like Huw used to wear his. His face is swirled with tattoos, his robe yellow silk — the yellow ghost that Mr. MacIvor talked to! When he moves, a wave of green light flutters around him.

"You're a Celtoi, like Huw!"

Histal smiles wider. "Yes. Huw and I did not know each other well. But, like a fine Celtoi knight, he died saving your life."

"But everyone said *you* — Moraan — were also dead."

"As you see, I am not. Welcome, daughter."

"Daughter?" I shake my head. "But you're …
Histal. How can you be my *father?*"

He laughs. "It is so, Emma."

I say firmly, "No. I already have a father."

He bows again. "Just so."

"Are you the also father of Arawn?"

"Aah, no, he *is* the child of Aibell and Clust.
When Sima died, Aibell kept it a secret. But then
she was afraid to take Arawn with her in case he
came to harm. So she left him in the care of Clust
— a useless creature. Clust decided he couldn't
live without his wife, so *he* left Arawn with Druvid
Eefa and went to find Aibell. No one has heard
from them since."

"Eefa decided Fadanys *would* be Arawn's — and
by controlling *him*, it would then be *hers*." Mennow
says. "Of course, she had no idea Sima was dead.
And we weren't about to tell her!"

Histal nods and adds, "I knew from the beginning that neither Aibell nor Clust would want to
stay in this new world when they saw the burden
of ruling it. But I was struck by its beauty, purity
and potential. I decided that *my* own child, whose
maithair had recently died, would become the
Sover-reign of this fresh, untouched place. I
approached the Tetrad with the idea and they will-
ingly agreed. But we hadn't counted on Eefa's
greed and arrogance — or her growing power."

I sneer, "Her goals weren't much different from your own, were they?"

He frowns at me, and I'm reminded that he is definitely Histal — I'd know that green glare anywhere. And that cold anger. "I would never use this world as a staging place for Games. Nor did I wish to become a destroyer of worlds."

That shuts me up.

"My goal," Histal continues, "is to *preserve* this world — keep it safe from Gamers. So, I decided to hide you until I could defeat Eefa's plans."

"But you set up a Game — something you claim to *despise*. And used me, your own daughter in it! Why didn't you just kill Eefa?"

"If I made a move against her, she would have destroyed Fadanys rather than let me have it. In fact, Eefa's power had grown to nearly equal my own. Then she made her first big move — to crown Arawn — before I could develop your deeper powers. But I knew with the Wands and your innate ability — stronger than either Eefa's or mine — we had a chance to save Fadanys."

"Even if I died," I murmur. Is he really my father? I can't *believe* it.

Histal nods in acknowledgment. "But I hoped you would be strong enough to win."

"Why did you set up those terrible portals? Threatening my dad's life, my memories of my happiest times?"

He shrugs. "I had to test your inner strengths. I had to show you how not to be *soft*. How to keep going no matter what."

"My dad would never do that to me!" I cry. "That's not what good fathers do!"

"Emma, whole worlds are being destroyed. It is my mission to stop it. You —"

I know what he's going to say, so I interrupt with the first thing that pops into my head. "What will happen to Arawn?"

He eyes me uncertainly and clears his throat. "He will be cared for. He has very few untapped abilities. But you, Emma — you will become a true Ollav — a Sover-reign *and* a Druvid. You've shocked us with your potential. Your gifts will soon exceed mine — once you learn to control them. It is your anger that worries me most. You must control your powers without ... such hostility. It's very human of you, I'm afraid. To be a true Ollav you must become a *thinker* — calm, cool, steady. Training you will be my main task before I return to the Watcher Campan." He changes back to his long white form.

"I — I don't understand. You'll return to the Campan? It wasn't created by you to have a place just to train me? "

He smiles. "No. There have always been the Pathfinder and the Watcher Kinn. I joined *them*, you see. They, like me, want one thing above all else —

the Games *must* end! Before I came to Fadanys with Aibell, I offered the Kinn ways of controlling the destruction of so many worlds."

"But you had a *child*," I say, " — a child you should have taken care of, not sent away and —" I stop. How can I complain about my life with Mom, Dad and Summer? I'm *glad* he sent me to them.

Histal sees it, too. "It was easy to put a cunning on my own younger to make you a Watcher and spirit you away to Earth."

I sneer. "And keep Eefa ignorant of my existence until the time was right."

"It took careful balancing. Especially since you insisted on getting so involved in the lives of your Earth family."

"They're all I care about. I don't want this world — *you* keep it. I want to see them — and Tom — and my friends."

"Emma, you will have plenty of time for that. But first —"

"No! *Now!*" A cyclone wind roars around the room. Did I do that?

Histal looks at each of the Tetrad, his smile indulgent. "I told you she was spirited — and terribly annoying. Never mind. We'll have plenty of time to teach her how to be a good Sover-reign."

"My *family?*" I demand.

"Your ... *family*, Ena." He waves his hand, and my mother, Leto, appears, blinking in the light.

Dad emerges next, followed by Summer and Ailla. Then Cill and her Barrochs, Pictree, Badba, Gyro, Dradia and her Faerseelies, Benny, the MacIvors, Taffine and Sarason and his Faylinns — and, finally, rows and rows of youngers, each looking more surprised than the other.

"You had both my family *and* the youngers all along?" I cry.

"They have been well cared for."

I run to my parents. Ailla and Summer are crying. So am I. When I get myself under control, my arms tightly around Mom and Dad, I ask Histal, "Where's Tom?"

He looks at me sadly. "You have feelings for Tamhas. But it cannot be allowed. You are no longer a human girl from Bruide. You are no longer a noviate Watcher. You are a Druvid Sover-reign — an Ollav. You are not only responsible for the welfare of *your* world, but you will one day take over my work as well. You wish to see the destruction of the Game, do you not?"

"Yes, but —"

"I have explained this to your ... *parents*."

Mom squeezes my hand. "No one can force you to be something you don't want to be."

Histal bows to her. "In *your* world, Madam. In our worlds, a Sover-reign who is against the Game, as Emma is, has a duty to the defenseless worlds being attacked. I know Emma won't let us down."

Dad says eagerly, "Leto, this could be exciting for Emma. And, Emma, Histal — uh — Moraan has promised we can visit you often — make sure you're safe and well. Think about it … how many people get the chance to *really* make a *difference?*"

I glare at Histal. "Will you allow the youngers to live in Fadanys? And the Barrochs? And any other group I choose that wishes to come?"

"All can make their homes here, safe from the threat of the Game."

Pictree steps forward. "Emma, I know this is hard for you. But I am the caretaker of my youngers — and we need you. Please think about it."

I look at my Earth family. If I become what Histal says is necessary, will I lose them — just as if I'd lost one of the Wand challenges? All my life I've wondered where I truly belonged. Twice now, I've discovered that beings I thought were my family *weren't* — the Sweeneys and then Aibell and Clust. And my real family turns out to be the Master Watcher, Histal.

No. He *isn't* my family. I know who my real family is! It's these four wonderful beings crowding around me, hugging me. These are the ones who truly love me and … nurture me.

Then my inner voice chides. *Will that be enough? You have been offered a life that could make a difference, Emma, even though you must do it alone. Histal lives in a logical universe. His idea of love is a benevolent place where beings can live in peace — not because he cares or doesn't care, but because it is the logical thing. Can you accept that?*

I don't know! I want the Games to end, but ... I look at my dad, Dennis Sweeney — whose adventure antennae are up and waving around like mad. Haven't I often wished I could be more like him? Why not take the risk? But do I really have to do it *alone*?

"Okay, Histal ... but only on my conditions."

He raises his eyebrows — and in that look, I *know* we understand each other.

I shout, "*Tom!*"

60

I lean back against Tom's chest. His arms wrap around me. Through the open barn door, the sun is setting across the bee field. We've been here for a month. I've thrown away the chair where Dad was held prisoner, and we've bought new furniture. Tom and I will stay here whenever we visit Eorthe ... Earth.

The farmhouse is ready for the new Keeper, Ryan MacIvor. He begged for the job — and when I said yes, asked if his father could help him. How could I refuse, after all they've been through?

I didn't use my powers to paint and clean the old place — it's much more fun to watch Tom learning from Mr. MacIvor how to use paintbrushes, power tools, scrapers. Once, his attempts at using a sander had me in stitches.

Negotiating a deal with Histal turned into a head-to-head shouting match that lasted three days — partly because one or the other of us kept slamming out in fury. But we always came back for more. I guess we *are* related. Will we ever be close? Probably not. But it'll be an *interesting* relationship.

Finally, a deal was hammered out with the help — or hindrance — of the Tetrad. And I won every point. Let's face it, when it involves my family, my friends and my life, *no one's going to make me do what I don't want to do.*

We agreed that for eight mooncrests every spancrest — about two months of every Earth year — Tom and I will come to Earth to … well … be together. And unless there is a dire emergency, we are to be left absolutely *alone*. We hope to spend some of that time traveling and we'll make a difference whenever we can. Histal has plans to change things on Earth, so I promised I wouldn't interfere in Earthly politics or Games, but …

Then, for ten mooncrests every spancrest, I will also travel, with Tom as my Watcher, to worlds under siege from Players such as Fergus — you didn't think he'd quit playing the Game, did you? Word came recently that Eefa had contacted Mathus, trying to convince him that together — as joint male and female Druvids — they would eventually gain unsurpassed powers in the Game. Mathus must have been tempted — he would love to see my powers weakened — but he is loyal to Fergus, who is, for *now*, still the Supreme Player. And curiously, Fergus let Tom know what had happened. I still don't know why Fergus has this odd loyalty to Tom — perhaps one day Tom will tell me. But it doesn't matter. I'll never doubt Tom's loyalty to *me* again.

Meanwhile, Tom and I will explore and report back to the Watcher Kinn, which has chosen Histal ... Moraan ... to be the new Pathfinder. The old and out-of-touch Pathfinder has agreed to go to Fadanys for a pleasant and well-earned retirement. But she's used to being in control, so we'll have to see how "retirement" suits her.

Don't worry about Fadanys. When I'm away, five very reliable, bright, conscientious High Administrators of Fadanys's Royal Court — Cill, Gyro, Pictree, Jowan and Ailla — will work with the Tetrad to keep our world stable and yet dynamic. We're building a citizenship based on ideas we've *all* contributed — including what to do with the youngers, many of whom need educating and health care. These young beings from so many different worlds are full of their own ideas and are eager to begin to build new lives. Not *all* will live up to Fadanys's standards, I know that, but we've made it clear that everyone must earn the right to live there.

I guess I want what Histal wants — a benevolent, peaceful world. But my reasons for wanting it are different, more than just *logic*. I want to create a nurturing place, where beings *care* about one another, where learning, curiosity, creativity and

... simple joy and love grow. I think a strong economy and general good health will follow. I know I'm naive, but hey, I'm also a powerful, influential Ollav. I'll make mistakes, but then I'm an old hand at that!

Cill's Barrochs have moved to our world and will be the Keepers of the Forests. The Muirgen Clann, with Varra as leader, has made their home in our oceans and Dradia and her tribe are a vital part of Fadanys, which is very exciting. I asked Finn of the Selkie Clann if he would like to leave Fomorii, but so far he won't give up his fight against Rhona. He and Varra are close — he often visits her — so perhaps one day she'll persuade him to live in our peaceful sanctuary for good.

Sarason and Taffine have gone back to Gray Sara and the oak forest. They know that anytime they are threatened by Gamers they have a safe place with us. Benny's decided to stay on as well and will visit Ryan in Bruide when he feels ready. I asked him how his parents would react, but he says they only noticed him to belt him, anyway. Ryan took a letter home from him saying he'd left to travel the world. If only they knew how *many* worlds! He and Whim are still very close.

Badba's yellow nose was out of joint when I didn't make her an Administrator. So, with some reluctance — and threats of dire repercussions if she messed up — I made her joint High Protector of

Fadanys with the Barroch Caul. He keeps her under control and she keeps him on his toes.

As for Fergus and Mathus? They *did* help us at Blackabrot's fortalice, I have to grudgingly admit. In fact, I guess, if I was pressed, I'd have to say they saved a lot of lives. Fergus has been *terribly* gracious about it all, but I know he's just biding his time. I have a feeling he's going to ask for pay-back at some point. I know both he and Mathus are nervous about the powers I now wield, so they'll be cautious for a while. But caution has never been one of Fergus's strong points, has it?

Meanwhile, for now, everything is peaceful, but I don't kid myself. The Game is still going strong and there is always the threat it will enter Argadnel or Fadanys — and maybe Fergus will be leading the pack.

Meanwhile, when I'm not traveling, I'm Supreme Sover-reign of Fadanys. Do I like this job? No. It's scary and weighty. I rely on the beings around me, especially my parents — and Histal — to keep me balanced. I can also share my concerns with the wonderful beings that make up this new mongrel Fadanyte Clann. I hope one day to be able to step down as Sover-reign so the clann can rule itself — but Dad says I must stay as benevolent leader for now — until I know the time is right.

Tom and I are strictly professional when I'm in Fadanys. He's the Most High Noble Watcher of the

Supreme Sover-reign of Fadanys — the highest-ranking noble — and my sounding board. He keeps *me* under control, and I like to think I keep *him* on his toes.

I may be his Sover-reign, but that doesn't stop him from arguing with me, pointing out my mistakes — and sharing with me a distant and intense … "faithfulness" when we are at court.

I put my head under his chin. His solid warmth makes me sigh happily. One more mooncrest and we must return to Fadanys and our official duties. But, for now, at this very moment, we're just Tom and Emma, and that's world enough.

Characters and Place Names

Ailla — Emma's parents' real child who was stolen from them at birth

Arawn — son of Aibell and Clust

Argadnel — the island of mists of which Summer is now the young queen

Badba — a member of the Ravan tribe

Baudwin — the Solitary of Moling

Bedeven — the emissary for the land of Fomorii in Argadnel

Benny — a boy from Bruide, Manitoba

Blackabrot — leader of the Unseelies

Bluemen of Mirch — the guards of Rhona, Queen of Fomorii's castel

Boggen Moors — the place where the Sifs are from

Branwen — Fergus's sister and emissary for the land of Cleave in Argadnel

Bruide — a small town in Manitoba, Canada

Cill — one of Fergus's slaves and a member of the Barroch tribe

Caul — a barroch who pilots the sloop

Dennis Sweeney — Emma's Earth father

Dradia — leader of the Faerseelies

Duggs — gargoyle-like beings

Eefa — A Druvid from Fadanys

Emma — the Watcher

Eorthe — Earth

Faylinn — a traveling group of beings that camps in oak forests

Fergus — the leader of the world of Cleave, Supreme Player of Cleave

Finn — leader of the Selkie clann

Gernac — Regent of Erthe

Grandpa (Ewan) MacFey — Emma's grandfather who allowed the Sweeneys' child to be taken and a changeling child to be put in its place

Gray Sara — the leader of the Clann Faylinn, the people of the great Oaks

Gyro — the Searcher who lives in the world of Hafflight

Histal — Emma's master at training camp for Watchers and one of the Watcher Campan's leaders, High Master, Master Watcher

Huw — Rhona's Druvid, a member of the Celtoi tribe originally from Earth

Jowan — a blacksmith in Cleave

Jye — the barroch who flies in Emma's pod

Keeper — the man who watches over Emma's father and also protects the circle gate on Earth. He works for Fergus

Kera — bee girl from Bruide

Leto Sweeney — Emma's Earth mother

Lilith — Regent of Aire

Lycias — Badba's giant drakon

Mathus — Fergus's Druvid

Mennow — Regent of Waeter

Mirkel — a world destroyed by a series of renegade gamers

Mirour — the mask maker

Mr. MacIvor — Ryan's dad

Nuit — Lilith's "helper" in Aire

Pictree Bragg — the boy who works for Mirour and a member of the Hobyah tribe

Pillan — Regent of Fyre

Rhona — the leader of the world of Fomorii

Sarason — Gray Sara's son

Summer — Emma's sister and Suzarain Elen of Argadnel

the Belldam — Emma's mother (Leto Sweeney)

the Pathfinder — the leader of the Watchers

Ryan MacIvor — a boy from Bruide, Manitoba

Sima — daughter of Aibell and Clust

Spriggan — leader of the Elfsig clan

Taffine — a member of the Faerseelie Clann

Tarn Rodach Burlam — a cove where Finn takes Huw and Emma

Tom — Tamhas, Emma's best friend and Watcher, the Owl

Watchers Campan — the secret place of the Watchers, including the training camp for novice Watchers

Varra — leader of the Muirgen Clann

Wefta — the rug maker

Yegg — the Taker

Glossary

Bakke — a bat-like creature

Bartizan — a tower in a castle or fort

Beelspear seeds — huge seed pods from trees in Cleave

Being — a general term for the inhabitants of all the different worlds

Belldam — the mother of a queen

Binnacles — books or reference materials such as maps, legends and historical tomes

Castel — a castle or fort

Chiton — a loose flowing robe of various fabrics and styles

Confiner — a jail cell

Conjure — a magickal place, event or spell created by a Druvid or Master Watcher

Cunning — a druvid's spell

Doubler — a twin

Drakon — a large flying creature with a dragon's body and a crocodile head, covered with fur, scales and feathers

Druvid — a Druid, a prophet or sorcerer capable of creating cunnings or magick

Freelooters — pirates

Gobha Smiths — Blacksmiths capable of changing metals by using magick

Gnomus — gnome-like creatures who guard underground treasures

Gromand — a large spotted cat with huge fangs

Heorots — giant white stags

Laborare — an alchemist's laboratory

Lightcrest — a word to describe the distance between the parallel worlds

Mooncrest — a measurement of time, approximately 8 Earth days

Mousel — a tiny rodent with long whiskers

Obligation — a job given to a Watcher

Ollav — a being who is both a Sover-reign and a Druvid

Risrac — a kind of flying rodent

Shape-change — to change from one form, nature, substance or state to another

Sifs — undead spirits (Boggys) from the Boggen Moors

Socle — an altar or table in the center of a henge circle

Solitary — a hermit

Spancrest — approximately one earth year

Star span — one night

Suzar — a king

Suzarain — a queen

Taithchuant — wanderlust

Telepath — to transfer thoughts through the mind, not through speaking

Transmute — to become invisible

Transport — to travel from one world to another through portals or circle gates

Youngers — the children of different world beings

Complete Your Collection of
The Watcher's Quest trilogy

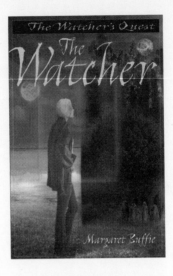

The Watcher

Emma has long suspected that something is not quite
right. With her long, pale face and white hair, she looks
nothing like her parents or her frail younger sister. She
acts nothing like them, either. While everyone happily
pursues their own interests, Emma watches anxiously
over the family day and night — why, she doesn't know.

When Emma takes a summer job looking after an
eccentric elderly neighbor, she is drawn into playing a
strange board game. Then the dreams begin. Strange,
frightening dreams that soon start invading her waking
hours. Emma suddenly finds herself hurtled into strange
worlds of intrigue and terror ... and running to save
her life.

The Seeker

Emma Sweeney has the potential to become an
exceptional Watcher, but her instructors are losing
patience with her. Raised by an Earth family, Emma
is prone to emotional human behavior that gets the
better of her logical Watcher instincts.

Emma's Earth mother, Leto, is dying in the island
world of Argadnel. Longing to be reunited with her
human daughter, Ailla, who was stolen at birth, she
has lost her will to live. Emma has pledged to find
the missing child and restore order to her adopted family's life. But the quest becomes a dangerous race when
Emma realizes she isn't the only one searching for Ailla.